Life Game

by
Emma Tallon

1

There she was again, that girl. She had moved in last week, renting a room in one of the buildings Freddie owned. He had watched her struggling along the path with her boxes, traipsing up and down on her own, from the back of the battered old Astra that was obviously hers. It annoyed him that no-one around had offered to help the girl. If he hadn't been in the middle of a business meeting in the café across the road, he would have helped her himself. That would soon have put the loitering bums surrounding her to shame and put a fire up their arses! It would be deep shame indeed for them to be seen by Freddie Tyler, doing nothing to help a young girl struggling on her own. Obviously they had no idea he was in the vicinity. But Freddie often preferred it like that anyway. It was a good way to suss out what people were really about.

She had disappeared by the time he'd finished his meeting that day, seemingly only having one car-full to unload. He had scanned the high rise building with a critical eye, wondering who exactly was sub-letting a room out. It wasn't her own flat she was moving into, not with such a pathetically meagre amount of belongings, and definitely not without Freddie knowing. There wasn't much Freddie missed in his various businesses. His intelligent head was full of all the details, large and small, and he had a good firm of people in his employ to remember anything that he forgot. The flats were one of his less nefarious businesses, the paperwork all above board. There were too many dwellings to know who lived there exactly, but he would have been made aware of any new tenancy contracts being drawn up.

She was walking up the road towards the same building again now, arms full of brown paper shopping bags, barely able to peek over the top. She wasn't paying much attention to where she was going, her eyes unfocused as if in a daydream. She most certainly wasn't aware of the man standing just across the road appraising her. As he watched, one of the bulging bags tore a little at the side and a net of oranges fell out, along with a bag of flour which promptly exploded on the pavement, covering her legs in a shock of white powder. Her eyes flew wide-open and her mouth formed a little O of surprise as she stopped and bent over the bags to check her legs. She looked at the oranges and then back at the bags, trying to figure out how to get them without everything else spilling all over the road. Freddie stifled a grin at the comical scene and quickly jogged across the road. He took some of the bags for her as she bent down to grab the runaway oranges. He squatted down with her and gathered some of them up into the bags that were still intact.

"I think you'll have to put some of these down to road kill, some of them are a bit past it on the bruising," Freddie said. The girl laughed, looked up and knocked Freddie Tyler for six. Her dark blue eyes sparkled as she laughed and were cloaked by a fringe of dark lashes. They fluttered against the creamiest skin he had ever seen. He felt himself hesitate, frozen for a second. It wasn't that he hadn't seen pretty girls before, he had. Lots of them. Of course he had. They were forever throwing themselves at him, desperate for the lifestyle and status that came with Freddie Tyler. But they all looked the same. The fake blonde hair, the fake orange skin, the fake plastic eyelashes and the fake plastic tits. This girl was pleasantly different to the crowd of women he was used to seeing. She was natural.

"Thank you." Her voice was quiet, melodic. She pushed a stray strand of thick, dark hair behind her ear and continued to pick up the oranges. The sparkle had gone from her face now, and though a smile remained, she looked sad. She looked vulnerable. Freddie searched for something to say to this girl, who had sparked such a bizarre reaction in him, but for once he really couldn't think of anything. Which was altogether a new sensation for Freddie. He was never lost for words, it was one of the things that kept him on top in sticky situations. He laughed at himself slightly. They stood up together as she dropped the last of the oranges in the bag and loitered for a minute, smiling, under an awkward silence.

"I'd... better..."

"Oh, yeah, of course! I'll carry these up for you." He motioned towards the bags in his hand, but she shook her head.

"Oh no, really, thank you for helping me though, I appreciate it. I've got it from here." She smiled up at him again, tentatively, and he realised she probably didn't want him to know where she lived. It was a sensible move really, he was a complete stranger after all. Single Girl Preservation Guide 101 – *'don't show strangers your home address'*. He decided he liked that about her. She seemed sensible, careful. The one and only thing he knew about her so far.

He smiled and handed over the bags, realising he had assumed she was single. Maybe she was the bird of one of the men living in the building. That would explain why he didn't know about her. Birds didn't really count. He really hoped that wasn't the case. Not that it mattered, but she had something about her that the rest of the girls around here didn't. She spoke differently too, more gently somehow, like she'd been brought up with a bit of class. His eyes flickered over his surroundings. She definitely didn't grow up around this gaff. It showed, even in the cut of her clothes. They were decent, well-made, fitted, skirt not too short, not showing too much cleavage. He realised that this was the biggest difference. She was so out of place. *'What is she doing in an area like this?'* He watched her walk away and raised his hand as she glanced round to smile before walking through the front door of the building. It wasn't that he didn't like it round here, he wasn't ashamed of it or anything, but this area was for a different cut of people. Harder people. People used to a certain way of life. The kind of life a girl like that certainly would never have been introduced to. He shrugged his shoulders and went back to the silver Mercedes parked across the road. It was parked on double yellows. That wasn't a problem. There wasn't a parking warden in the whole of east London who didn't know his car and who would have the bare-arsed stupidity to give him a ticket. He opened the door and slid down behind the wheel. Maybe he was wrong about the girl, maybe appearances were deceiving. Either way, she was gone now and he was more than a little annoyed at the effect that one tiny little bird was having on him. He firmly put her to the back of his mind and started off to one of his bigger clubs. He had a lot to do tonight.

Anna closed the front door of the tiny two-bed flat she now shared with a girl called Tanya and exhaled wearily. She called out to see if the other girl was home and went through to the kitchen when there was no answer. It was small up here but she had to admit, it was cosy. And that was all she needed at the moment. In a way she really didn't care where she was. Just as long as it was somewhere new, somewhere that she could start again and forget everything.

Just over a week ago she had been in her car driving blindly for hours down roads she didn't know, with no idea where she was going or what she was doing. Her heart had been pounding and her eyes sporadically filled up with tears of anguish. That she had even gotten as far as getting lost was an unexpected achievement. Half of her had expected to be dead already. The other half had at least expected to have been caught. Somehow, through the twists and turns of traffic and fate, she had ended up here. There had been nothing special about it, it looked grey and dreary to her, just like any other part of London, but after hours of driving aimlessly her petrol gauge had moved into the red, so she'd pulled into a petrol station to fill up before moving on.

She had paid for the petrol and was walking back to her car when she heard a row going on between a young couple in one of the other cars. As she unlocked her door she saw the woman, who seemed to be around about her own age, jump out of the car and slam the door. The driver screeched off, leaving her yelling colourful expletives at a pair of fading tail lights. Anna paused, anxious, and wondered if she should ask the girl if she was ok. The stranded girl stopped and felt her pockets, swearing again - to herself this time.

"Shit! My bag! Oh Christ…" Anna looked around worriedly, then deciding she couldn't ignore the situation, walked briskly over to the girl.

"Are you ok?" The girl glanced up at her, running her manicured hands through her long red hair, clearly agitated.

"Not really. That was my bloke, well, ex-bloke really. Stupid arse has buggered off with my handbag in his car, I ain't got my purse, phone, nothing!" she sighed heavily. "It's gonna' be a long bloody walk home!"

"Well…" Anna didn't know this girl from Adam, but she couldn't just leave her here, she could be attacked or anything. "Do you live far from here?"

"Not really, only about ten minutes away. Driving that is, walking is another matter." The girl's thick East End accent shone through her irritated tone.

"Well, I'm not in a hurry to get anywhere. I could drop you off if you need a lift."

The girl looked her up and down warily, as if trying to figure out if there was an ulterior motive.

"I'm not an axe murderer or anything," Anna laughed, her eyes crinkling at the corners "I just feel bad leaving you here and it's no skin off my nose driving an extra ten minutes."

"Well.. if you're sure you don't mind, that would be really helpful then, thanks mate." The girl smiled then, brightening up her face and showing small, white, even teeth behind the carefully applied lip gloss.

"I'm Tanya by the way."

And that was where it began. Tanya had invited her in for a cuppa to say thank you for the lift. At first Anna had thought it best to refuse and continue her journey, but the thought of a comfortable seat and a hot drink was too tempting after being in the car for so long. The pair got chatting easily and before long, Anna had explained that she was looking to relocate.

"Where to?"

"Um… actually, I don't really know yet." She stiffened up, worried that she had said too much. She didn't want to have to go into the whos and whys, she didn't want to share that with anyone, least of all a stranger. Tanya saw the panic run across her face and rushed to calm her.

"It's ok, you don't have to tell me anything. We all have our secrets." She smiled quietly and busied herself tidying the coffee table. Anna immediately felt bad. This girl had been nothing but kind to her and she must sound terribly rude.

"Sorry, it's not you, I just don't really like to talk about certain things. It's silly really."

"No it's not, mate. Seriously, don't fret about it." Anna relaxed a little and sipped at her tea.

"So, forgetting all the previous crap, you must have somewhere in mind that you wanna' go? Somewhere near family or friends?"

"No." Her voice a little too strong, she softened it, "No, I want to try somewhere new. Nowhere too special. Or expensive," she added. "Just somewhere I can be a little independent."

"And you have absolutely nowhere in mind? Not even short term?" Tanya's face looked comically appalled at the idea.

"No," she laughed. "Not exactly the best thought-out plan in history is it!"

"Where's all your stuff?"

"In my car. You're lucky, the passenger seat is the only one free to sit on, another bagful of stuff and you'd have been walking home!" They laughed together.

"Well, ok then," Tanya paused and pursed her lips. After a moment she nodded to herself. "I guess you're lucky too. My spare bedroom is, well, it's going spare. Can't let you sleep in your car. 'Specially not filled with all that junk." Anna stopped and put her cup down on the newly cleared coffee table.

"Are you serious?"

"Yeah, why not? It's empty. And I need to rent it out really. My previous flat mate only went and got herself engaged and moved out, leaving me on me Jack Jones, so why don't you stay tonight, have a think on it and if you want the room, you can move your stuff in tomorrow."

"Wow, Tanya, that's so generous of you—"

"—no, not generous mate, just sensible. You'll have to pay half the rent and bills - you are good for the money, aren't you?" she asked as it suddenly occurred to her.

"Yes, yes," Anna replied quickly, "I have a comfortable amount saved up, so I'm fine for a while, but I will need to find a job locally within the next month or two."

"Well that's not a problem" Tanya waved her hand dismissively, "I can find you one of those easy. How about we go week-on-week to begin with, make sure we rub down together ok and just see how it goes, yeah?"

Luckily for both of them, they had rubbed down together pretty well so far. Anna was the perfect housemate, and Tanya respected Anna's wish not to discuss *why* she had turned up in an unknown part of London, in the middle of the night, with nothing but a car full of clothes. Anna busied herself putting the shopping away and started on making a meal for the two of them, putting her pinny on as she checked the calendar on the kitchen wall. Yep, Tanya was working tonight, so it would just be her. She would leave a plate to warm in the oven for when she got home. Tanya was always ravenous when she got home and was the number one fan of Anna's cooking. She was constantly remarking that she had never eaten so well in her life. This Anna had to believe, as within just a few days of her cooking, Tanya's wan complexion became rosier and her face less drawn.

Anna looked out the window nervously at her car. It worried her that it was in full view while it was parked, though she had gone to painstaking lengths to ensure he wouldn't be able to track it to her. Having gone over and over her limited options of escape from her previous life – from him - she had finally plucked up the courage a few weeks ago and visited an old friend she knew from school. It had been years since she'd seen Ellen, so he didn't know she even existed.

"So what I'm asking El, is for you to keep this car under your name and put me down as a named driver. I'd take the car – and look after it, you wouldn't have to worry. And I'll give you ten grand to buy yourself a better one. No catch in it. I know it's been years and I can't tell you why, but I desperately need your help," Anna had asked her, shaking in hope and in fear that this would work. El put the coffee down and studied her.

"You don't need to tell me Ann. I'm still in touch with the others and I've heard the rumours...is...is it really bad?" she asked softly, touching Anna's knee, concern on her face. Tears began to run unbidden down Anna's face, but she held back the sobs. She held her voice in check.

"I need to get away El, and I need for nothing to be traceable to me. That's all I can tell you. And you can never, ever tell a soul that I was here. Ever."

Anna left the saucepans to bubble away as she turned the heat down in the pastel blue kitchen and poured herself a hot chocolate. She pushed the memories away and looked out the window. It was cold out tonight. Winter was coming in fast this year. She was considering pulling out her big overcoat and it was only early October.

Placing the slightly bruised oranges in the fruit bowl in the lounge, she sat down in the comfy armchair, musing over the man who'd helped her. He had swooped out of nowhere like a guardian angel, big, well-dressed, handsome and ready to rescue her when she had no hands. She knew she stuck out here. That's why she tried to keep herself to herself, not drawing any attention to herself. She knew she was probably an easy target for anyone looking to take advantage. A 'greeny', so to speak. But that man - yes, he talked just like everyone else around here, but he also looked 'different', like she did. He was wearing a sharply cut suit, his hair was styled nicely, his aftershave was expensive. Odd for this area. This area was not a wealthy or well-to-do one. It was an interesting mixture of things, this place: colourful people and businesses led it through the day and then it would thrive on its nightlife and the creatures that lurked only in the dark. Hmm. Well, whatever the story, it was nice of him to help her. She couldn't help but notice how his easy smile made little creases at the corner of those piercing, laughing eyes. It was a beautiful effect… She caught herself smiling and shook her head. She had no business thinking about men right now. She was definitely not in the right place in her own head for men of any kind. Especially after all she'd been through with the last one. It would be a long time before she could be convinced to trust anyone like that again. Anna picked up her book and slowly but surely lost herself in the world of another, forgetting about Freddie Tyler completely. The dreams she had that night reflected nothing of her encounters that day.

A few weeks later the two young women sat comfortably at the kitchen table, enjoying another of Anna's culinary creations. Anna wiped her hands on a dishcloth and picked up her fork. Tanya's voice took on a carefully casual tone. "I reckon we should go out. Hit the dance floor tonight. It's not often I get a night off at the weekend, what do you think?"

Tanya picked at the creamy carbonara in front of her, watching Anna through narrowed eyes. Anna didn't look convinced.

"Come on mate..." she wheedled. "You haven't been on a good night out, not once since you came here, and we would have a wicked time! I know the best clubs, we can dress up nice, find ourselves some more-than-willing dance partners…"

Anna sighed heavily. "Oh, ok. I'll come—" Tanya clapped her hands in delight, "—but no men. I just want a girls' night, alright? Oh, and another thing, if you think I'm wearing something as skimpy as you do on a night out, you have another thing coming. I'll go shopping this afternoon and find something – and yes, you can come – but you're NOT getting me into anything that short." She laughed, "some of us don't have the body for it anyway."

"Oh you do!" Tanya protested, "Come on, you'll look shit-hot in one of my dresses, you don't need to go shopping."

Anna threw the dishcloth at her. "You have no shame, missy!"

Freddie slipped into the kitchen silently, through the back door. He pulled off the bloodied shirt and tutted in annoyance. He hadn't expected company tonight. Vince had been a man short on the ground and had asked Freddie to collect a large amount of money from one of the bookies under their protection. And for once, Freddie Tyler had been met with the sort of resistance that actually gave him a challenge. He chuckled under his breath. It had almost been fun really, after the initial surprise. Only *'almost'* though. And it had been a surprise, too. Freddie was known as one of the hardest men in the East End. It wasn't often someone went up against him. The funny thing was, if Benny had just paid up there would have been no unpleasantness at all. If he couldn't pay due to financial stupidity, Freddie would have left him with a warning and 24 hours in which to raise the money. Freddie knew exactly what the business took and that their fee for all the protection they had given him over the years was more than affordable. Now though, with that stunt he'd pulled tonight, Benny had practically signed his own death warrant. The bookie was now safely tucked away in intensive care along with two of his men. Whether they had a chance at life or not, Freddie would decide later. Right now though, he had to clean up, get back to his club and sort the money out for Vince.

Freddie had gotten involved in this way of life when he was nothing but a kid. He was well-built and ripped with muscles from various labour jobs he had picked up around school, to bring in a few quid at home. He came from a big, loud and loving family, which rarely had two pennies to rub together. He had two younger brothers and a younger sister, all of whom hung onto every word he said back then. His father had died when he was just ten, leaving a gaping hole in all their hearts, but, as was the only way, his mum Mollie had carried on and done the best she could. It didn't matter how poor they were, she always made sure they had food in their bellies and a clean bed to sleep on. They moved into a dingy two-bedroom flat with no windows at the back and cockroaches crawling in the corners. Mollie had waged war on the insects and managed to keep them to a minimum, but they were never gone completely. It had pained him deeply to see his poor old Mum washing other people's clothes for a few measly quid each week, going out at the crack of dawn to scrub floors. It wasn't right. He knew it was his job to change things, to look after her like she had looked after them.

Big as he was, and hungry to better his family's way of life, at the age of 18 he had been the perfect candidate for Vince to mould. He'd started out breaking a few arms or legs here and there, when money owed wasn't paid, and in return *he* got paid very well. He blocked his conscience about what he did: it was survival. It was how it had to be. After a while he didn't have to even think about it anymore. It was business. Proving himself solid and dependable, everyone was happy. After a while, it became apparent that he not only had the strength and the mental capacity to do what he had to, he was very intelligent too. And he used that intelligence to the best of his abilities. Vince had watched him slowly crawl his way up through the ranks, never putting anyone's nose out of joint so much that he was put on any big shit lists, but working damn hard and making himself valuable. Over time he gave the boy different responsibilities, testing him out in different areas of the business. Each time, some way or another, the boy found a way to do it better, to make the work more lucrative. This pleased Vince no end and over time, Freddie had taken his place as Vince's right hand man.

Today, eleven years on, Freddie was one of the biggest East End barons in his own right. He had his own credentials, his own loyal group of men and his own businesses to run. These various businesses were all either created with the hard-earned money he'd made from Vince, or ones he had bought into alongside him, as equal partners. As soon as he'd started bringing in a regular wedge he had moved his family out of the dingy slums and into a detached house in one of the nicer estates. It wasn't too posh, his Mum wouldn't have liked that, but the houses were bigger, nicer and there was lots of space and greenery around. It was a much better environment for his siblings to grow up in. As time went on he had refitted every room for her, no expense spared, so that she had the best house in the street, and so that it was something she could be proud of. He knew this was important to her. He had paid for his brothers and sister to go to good schools and had made sure that his family never wanted for anything again.

He splashed water over his face and the back of his neck, then reached for the towel. Mollie came down the stairs quietly. He thought she couldn't hear his sneaking about when he came in late, but she could. She was a mother for God's sake, it was her job to hear these things. She stood staring at her eldest son leaning over the sink and a rush of affection washed over her. She loved each of her children with all her heart, but this one... this one had done so much for the family, so much for her that she could never repay him. She would always try though, every day, in all the little things she could find to do for him. Her smile faded a little as she saw the bloodied shirt and she quietly went to the linen cupboard and brought a fresh one out, ironed only a few hours before. She knew enough about what he did by the rumours and by the utmost respect she was given by everyone. She knew he was a face. She was grateful for everything he had done for her, so in return she didn't ask him about it, never tried to scold him about it. She knew he didn't want that. And she didn't want to know the details.

"Here you go son," she said quietly, passing him the shirt.

He smiled down at her.

"You don't miss much do you?"

She winked jovially and set about making some of the strong Italian coffee he liked so much. Whilst everybody else was settling down for the night, Freddie's night was only just beginning. They both knew that.

"Can I get you some cake, son? I made that fruitcake you like so much today, oh, or there's some angel cake too if you like. Thea made it earlier. She's getting to be alright at baking now."

"I'll have some of that then Mum, thanks. Though I do love you for it, I couldn't manage the fruitcake this late, it'll sit on me all night."

He sat quietly with his cake and coffee, watching as Mollie turned up the fire on the huge Aga he had fitted in the kitchen. She bent over and peered in, making sure the flames were high, then picked up the bloodied shirt with the end of a wooden spoon and tossed it in. She unearthed a bottle of bleach spray from underneath the sink and scrubbed where it had been sat on the side, though it hadn't really left any marks. That done, she checked there was nothing left of the shirt and turned the heat back down to low again.

"Another one bites the dust," Freddie joked and got a disapproving look from his Mother.

"I'll pick you up some more tomorrow. You're going through them like a baby does nappies!" she tutted and shook her head, "Where are you off to tonight anyway, one of the clubs?"

"Yeah, got to get some graft in, these shirts don't pay for themselves!"

"Oh, go on with you," she bustled him out the door with a kiss on his cheek as he shrugged his jacket back on.

"Thanks mum," he hugged her and flashed her a winning smile, "you're a diamond."

Mollie sighed as he disappeared into the darkness and the house was quiet again. She tidied up and lingered by the Aga, tracing her finger across the shining lead front. She worried about him, that son of hers. She sighed again and turned off the main light, leaving one on for when he got home. She pushed all the bad thoughts from her mind. There was no point worrying about things beyond your control.

Anna took a deep breath as she looked in the mirror. Her eyes looked dark in her small face with the little bit of makeup she had put on. She didn't plaster it on like Tanya did, all glitter and colour, but just enough to accent her features. She couldn't shake off her nerves. This was her first time properly out in public since… she didn't let herself finish that sentence in her head. She avoided going out to places where there were a lot of people. Where there was a chance that someone might recognise her. She had toyed with the idea of cutting and dying her hair, but she couldn't make herself do it. Besides, she would still look like herself. It would be a pointless exercise.

Tanya came in with a glass of something in each hand.

"Here, get some of this down you," she passed one to Anna, "It'll calm you down a bit. Honestly, anyone would think I was taking you to your own funeral!" she laughed and sat down at the mirror, adding more blush to her already pink cheeks. It was a stark contrast to her deep red hair, now wild with big curls and volumiser, but not an unattractive one. Anna laughed internally at the irony of Tanya's comment. *'Her own funeral'*. Tanya had no idea how true that would be if she was recognised. Anna gulped down the drink in her hand quickly, hoping - as Tanya had prophesied - that it would calm her nerves. Tanya looked at her strangely but said nothing. Anna could understand if Tanya thought she was a bit odd. She had been here nearly two months now and apart from going to the supermarket to get food, or to post the one letter she had sent, she hadn't left the house. She didn't need to get a job just yet. The rent and bills had been cheaper than she had thought they would be, and the money she had saved had stretched a long way. She could still go on comfortably for a while longer, though she knew she'd have to get back out there sometime.

Tonight was just a positive step in that direction.

The one letter she had sent had been to her mother. She missed her mother terribly and wished she could see her, or even speak to her on the phone, but she couldn't. The guilt of leaving her mother so in the dark, worrying, had made her write the letter in spite of her fears. She had sent it the day before yesterday, so it should have got there today. She hoped it had reached her without any issues.

Finished with her makeup, Tanya put Anna's coat and bag in her arms and propelled her towards the front door.

"Woops! Easy Tanya, you nearly had me over then!"

"Haha, you probably will be later if you keep drinking like that gal, come on, we are going to have a night to remember!"

Leslie Davis sat down in her lovely cornsilk-coloured lounge and stared at the letter in her hand. It was Anna's handwriting. She had to stop for a minute as relief hit her like a sledgehammer. She had been so scared. She was terrified he had killed her. She was terrified that if he had, they would never know. Her darling Anna, gone forever without a word. All these weeks, waiting. But she had known that she'd get in touch. She'd known that, if she was out there still, she'd find a way to contact them. Anna thought Leslie didn't know what went on behind closed doors, within closed meetings. But she did. Leslie always listened, never commented. Knowledge was power, and so she always sought it out. But the more she had found out, the more she had feared for her daughter. Then one day, she had disappeared. *He* had come round then, appearing grief stricken. Such an extraordinary actor if she ever saw one. She had played along, had comforted him even, outwardly keeping the peace while she waited to find out what was going on.

After agonising and thinking the worst for a few days, Leslie thought over the last few times Anna had visited. They had turned out to be special times, they did a few things that they had always said they would. Anna had been a bit more emotional than usual when she left. Like she'd known she wouldn't be back. Or maybe just not coming back for a while. Maybe she'd run away? Thinking logically, that might have been the only way out for her. The more Leslie thought about it, the more certain she had become. If he hadn't killed her, which - please God - he hadn't, then she must have run away. And she mustn't have said anything to keep everyone else safe too. They posed no threat to anyone if they knew nothing in the first place. He wouldn't stop looking for her though, Leslie knew that much. He just wasn't built that way.

Smoothing her golden, perfectly made-up hair, she took a deep breath, then stopped as she turned the envelope over. It had been opened and resealed, this much was obvious. She went cold. He had opened it before it got to her. It could only have been him, it wouldn't have been anyone else. Which meant he was watching the house. Waiting for Anna to make her move. The phones were probably being listened in on too, she was sure he would easily be able to fix that up. *Please God, Anna, don't have said anything in here that you don't want him to know!* She opened it up with trembling hands and began reading, scanning the lines quickly to make sure there was nothing he could have used.

Hi Mum,

I'm so sorry to have disappeared as I did. I can't explain why, though I think you know a lot more than you let on anyway. I have to go away for a while, but I will come home to you one day. Hopefully not too far in the future.

17

Please don't worry about me, I'm safe. I've got money and I'm renting a room in a nice flat with another girl. I'm ok.

I can't tell you where I am right now, I know that this must be so confusing for you and I beg you, please don't be hurt. I'll tell you everything one day. Just know that I love you and Daddy more than anything and that I really am safe and well and ok.

I will find a way to contact you again. Keep me in your heart. You're both in mine.

Your Anna xx

Her heart rate slowed down as she re-read it, more slowly this time. Squinting her eyes, she tried to make out the postmark. God must have been on Anna's side the day she posted this letter. It was smudged beyond recognition. There was nothing in there he could use to find her. She folded it neatly and put it back into the envelope. Sitting back in the chair and absentmindedly biting one perfectly polished burgundy nail, she pondered over what to do next. She had been right. That in itself was obvious. She *had* run away from him. And had left no tracks by the looks of it, or he wouldn't be rifling through her parents' post. Good girl. She let a ghost of a smile escape. The girl had a lot more strength than she gave herself credit for and now she was using it. *How to keep her safe though?* That was the more pressing question. She couldn't go to the police. If the gossip was anything to go by, he had more of those on his payroll than off, so that would do her no good. Maybe a private investigator, but then he would know she was doing that, and what's to say he wouldn't just buy him off too? Then again, she couldn't do nothing, because that would be suspicious… *What to do?*

The phone rang shrilly and made her jump. She hadn't realised how quiet it was. She picked up the receiver quickly, half hoping and half dreading it was Anna.

"Hello?"

"Mrs Davis, how are you?" It was him. She swallowed a lump in her throat and tried to hold her voice as steady as she could.

"Tony, hello. How good of you to call."

"Of course Mrs Davis, I'll call every day until we find our Ann. I worry about you two, sitting there fretting… I'd like to think my parents would have people who care about them if anything happened to me."

Oh, if only… she thought darkly.

"Really, we're both fine. Worried of course, but we're ok. Tougher than we look," she added. She heard him hesitate on the line.

"Have you heard anything from her, Mrs Davis?" he asked politely. Too politely.

Damn him. Of course he knows, he went through my post… She sighed with resignation. She could either play along or be seen as the enemy. And anyway, there wasn't anything in the letter he could use.

"Actually, yes, sort of….," she perked up her voice in an attempt to sound eager, "I was just about to call you actually, I've just finished reading a letter she's sent home!"

"Really? A letter?" his fake astonishment came down the line.

"Yes, isn't that good news, she's safe!"

"That's fantastic news Mrs Davis, so where is she, did she say?"

Leslie rolled her eyes.

"No, that's the sad part of it Tony, she says that she's safe, but it sounds like she doesn't want to be found right now."

"Oh right, I see. Well, I don't agree. I'm worried. I think it's too dangerous out there for a girl, all alone, with no family or friends around her. I worry about her mental state too, going off like that for no reason.

Anything could happen to her. It's not safe."

Safer than anywhere near you, she thought, but said nothing.

"If you don't mind, I'll send one of my boys to come and collect it, we have people working on finding her, perhaps it will help."

Leslie stayed quiet for a moment, wondering what to say, searching the letter over frantically for anything she might have missed.

"Not at all. That's fine. Anytime tomorrow morning before 11 is good for me."

"They'll be over around 10 then. Good day then Mrs Davis, have a good one." His silken voice made her want to tear his face off. But her own voice betrayed nothing.

"Goodbye."

Leslie hung up the phone and let the tears fall silently down her face. She walked wearily up the stairs and opened the door to her only daughter's childhood bedroom. Rocking back and forth in the chair, holding Anna's favourite teddy bear, she sat staring into the distance for the rest of the day, until her husband came home from work and led her away.

2

"...and then the idiot tells me he doesn't feel like paying anymore, that he's decided to *'go another way'*. Starts playing billy-big-balls because he's got his two mates in there with baseball bats."

"Baseball bats??"

"Yes, baseball bats."

"That stupid twat. He was on to a good thing there. We put a stop to all the skimming in his gaff, all the robberies, all the nit-picky stuff, we got him better security and this is how he repays us? He never had a better ally than us in there. He was taking home almost double what he was before we started."

"I know," Freddie said quietly. "He got greedy." He sat back in his chair and played absentmindedly with the tumbler of whisky in his hand.

"Where is he now?"

"Lying in a nice cosy hospital bed. Along with his mates."

"And the damage?"

"Nothing but the best. ICU."

"Hm." Vince nodded his agreement. They sat in companionable silence for a few minutes, enjoying the peace of Freddie's office. Freddie had many offices in his various places of business, but this was his favourite. He had decked it out with real class. The furniture was all dark oak, antique and expensive. The chairs were subtle and really comfortable, and there were four safes hidden away behind pictures and under vases which held assorted weaponry, money and fake papers, should he ever need them. Always better to be safe than sorry. It was also virtually sound proof, so even though it was only two doors away from the noise and hubbub of his largest club, you could only hear a soft droning, which was almost soothing.

"Perhaps we should buy him out. Take this, em, obviously very stressful place of work off his hands." Vince smiled a slow predatory smile, and Freddie laughed.

"Looks like he just nailed his own coffin shut, didn't he?"

"You'll get someone to take care of the paperwork, Freddie." Vince stood up and reached for his coat, "Get it valued, offer him half. If he's difficult, we'll cut that to a third, got it?" he started towards the door.

"Got it. Oh – and Vinnie?" The older man stopped and turned back. "Don't forget this." Freddie chucked a bundle of notes at him. "Got our brass out of them after all. Seems they had a change of heart once they saw James and Scotty behind them. And an even bigger change of heart once they were on the floor."

Vince paused and then chuckled. "You'll never stop surprising me Freddie."

Anna smoothed down the front of her new bright-blue dress. Tanya had chosen the colour, to go with her eyes, but Anna had been adamant about choosing the cut. It was a fitted, high-necked number, down to the knee. Figure-hugging enough to show off her curves, but modest enough to not look cheap. Finished off with matching heels and handbag, Anna felt like a new woman again. As she walked into the club she almost felt like her old confidence was beginning to creep in again. Although that was probably just the bubbles from the prosecco talking. Tanya strode confidently over to the bar with Anna in tow, all male eyes sticking to her as she passed by. She was incredibly impressive, Anna had to give her that. With her striking hair and plunging red dress to match, she was a walking sex bomb. Anna paled into the background beside her, but this she was happy about. The less attention she got, the better. Within moments two drinks had appeared, compliments of a man at the other end of the bar blinded by Tanya's curves. She waved her hand and rewarded him with a smile, before grasping Anna's arm and pulling her to a nearby table. Anna felt sorry for him as his face dropped, sorry to see his siren go.

"Right. Now. Let's enjoy these drinks, then head on out to the dance floor, shall we?"

Anna grinned at her and nodded. There were some good songs playing tonight, some of her favourites.

An hour later, Anna sat back down at the table with another drink. She needed to cool down. It had been years since she'd been out dancing. She happily sat there spectating for a while, watching Tanya enjoy herself, surrounded by all the best-looking men. She smiled. She liked it when Tanya was happy. She deserved to be, especially after everything the girl had done for her. She looked around, admiring the décor of the place. It was discreet and welcoming, mellow yet modern. Her eyes moved up to the gallery above the DJ booth. There were several doors up there, obviously offices or technical rooms. Staff rooms for people to leave their belongings in maybe. She barely glanced at the silhouette of the man who slipped back inside one of the doors as she looked up. She couldn't see much in the dark.

Just then, someone bumped into her from behind, causing some of her drink to spill down her dress.

"Oh!" she exclaimed, jumping up and brushing off as much as she could.

"So sorry, cor, didn't mean to do that darlin'... let me get you another one, yeah?"

"No, no, really, it's fine. I'm fine, no harm done."

The man tried to focus his eyes on her, obviously the worse for wear on his night out.

"Well, how about I buy you one anyway, gorgeous? You ain't bad looking! How about it, ey?" he pushed himself closer to her, so close she could smell the stale alcohol on his breath. She cringed as she was backed into a corner, the chair and table behind her and him in front. She put her hands flat against his chest and pushed him away with all her strength.

"I said, no thank you!"

The man toppled backwards and fell into a table full of people, knocking more drinks flying. Anna's hands flew to her mouth. He straightened up with some difficulty, then, face red with anger, he lunged towards her, swearing loudly at the same time.

"You cheeky fucking bitch, think you can get away wit–" but luckily at that moment, the bouncers, who had seen the whole episode unfold, stopped him in his tracks and dragged him outside, still shouting abuse.

Tanya ran over when she saw the commotion.

"God, are you alright?" she leant down, looking into her friends face and checking for any damage.

"Yes, sorry, I'm fine. He just scared me bit, but I'm fine now. I promise." She smiled reassuringly at Tanya, embarrassed at the spectacle she'd created and nervous at the attention it had drawn.

"Are you sure?" Tanya bit her lip, torn between staying with her friend and going back to the crowd of fans waiting for her on the dance floor.

"Yes, honestly, go dance Tan. I'm happy here." She urged her friend back to the floor, and after a moment's deliberation, Tanya traipsed back, a smile forming again on her pretty face.

Anna sat down awkwardly and forced herself to smile and sit still. Her heart was thumping inside her chest. She felt very exposed. The other club-goers kept looking at her, glancing over. Were they just gossiping about what had happened, or were they saying '*Look, that's her*'? People were getting up, moving. Was one of them on their way to make a phone call to Tony, to let him know where she was? Did he have people everywhere in the East End too, like he did in North London? Even if he didn't, she wasn't exactly a million miles away, there were bound to be people here who knew him. And if he had sent the word out, and maybe even her picture…She felt herself sweating, picturing Tony on his way here, thunder in his eyes. Her rushing blood began to roar loudly through her ears. She let out a small moan. She couldn't work out if she was being over paranoid or whether her fear was justified. She couldn't breathe though; she had to get away, get away from all these people. Get away from this place where she was boxed in, where there would be no escape if he walked in. There was only one way in and out. She needed to get outside, lose herself somewhere. Somewhere that no-one could see her. She picked up her bag and jacket and headed over to where Tanya was still dancing away, not a care in the world.

"Tan, I don't feel very well, I'm going to go home."

"What?" Tanya clasped her arm before she could slip away. "You're not upset about that guy, are you?"

"No, no, it's not that, I really don't feel very well. I just need some fresh air and to go home." Anna's throat began to feel like it was closing. She was on the verge of a full-on panic attack, she had to hurry.

"Ok, then I'll come with you." Tanya started guiding her back to the table, but Anna stopped her.

"No, Tan please stay. You're having a great time, you don't need me here, and I'll be fine. I don't feel like I'm good company right now, I just want to slip off quietly."

"But Ann, I can't just let you go on your own, it's late and dark!"

"So I'll get a cab! I promise. Just go back. I don't want to ruin your night, I'll see you in the morning." Her eyes darted desperately to the door.

"I'd rather you didn't go alone." Tanya looked at Anna's pale complexion and pushed the hair back from her face. "Ok. But you get a cab! I'll bring you breakfast in the morning, I'll play nurse for the day.

Well...depending on the size of my hangover," she winked. "Get home safe babe. Emergency numbers are by the phone."

Anna smiled fleetingly, then ran from the club as fast as she could. She got outside and it was still too crowded, so she turned towards the darkest route out and kept on running.

Halfway down the road, she stopped to catch her breath. Her sides were beginning to hurt. Then she heard the sound of running footsteps behind her. Soft, heavy thumps, like those of a man rather than the click-clack of a woman's heels. She heard herself draw in a high-pitched breath, almost a shriek, and silently cursed herself. Then the adrenaline hit her and she began to run for all she was worth. She couldn't believe it, she was right to be scared, all that time she had been in there… she'd probably only just made it out, he had probably seen her as she started running off. Paranoia and fear seeped into every pore. Of course someone recognised her. Tears began to sting her eyes. She should have stayed; why, oh why, would she run alone off into the darkness? She was done for. Whether he killed her or made her go back, her life was over. She began to sob as the footsteps caught up behind her and she cried out as two big hands grasped her shoulders.

"NO!" she tried to pull away as the man grabbed her closer.

"Stop, wait! It's ok! It's just me!" the man steadied her and she looked up in terror.

It was him, the man who had helped her pick up the oranges. She sobbed again, this time in pure relief.

"It's ok, calm down, nobody's after you." He looked in amazement at the wreck the girl in front of him had turned into. "Who did you think it was - that bloke from the club?"

Anna quickly processed this in her head as she tried to catch her breath. If he thought she was scared of the drunk guy from the club, he couldn't know who she was. He couldn't be working for Tony. She tried to be calm, suddenly aware of the spectacle she was making of herself.

"Yes. No. I don't know. I just, I heard someone chasing me and panicked."

Freddie took off his jacket and put it round her shoulders. She was shaking.

"You shouldn't run off like that on your own in the dark. It's bloody dangerous around here at night."

"I know, it was stupid." She cursed herself for getting into such a precarious position. Even if it wasn't one of Tony's henchmen, it still could have been someone else with bad intentions.

"Why did you run off anyway? Are you ok?" Freddie's voice was tinged with concern and Anna suddenly felt grateful that he was there.

"I'm sorry. I didn't feel well, I just needed to get away. Needed some fresh air. I was on my way home."

Freddie looked confused and glanced down the street. "What, this way?"

Anna suddenly realised she had no idea where she even was. She could have been running anywhere.

"Well, I…"

"You don't know where you are, do you? Your gaff is in the opposite direction." He stared at her for a few moments. "Come on, I'll walk you home. You do look like you need the air."

They started walking back the way they came and Anna, her fear subsiding, felt a fresh wave of embarrassment wash over her. How pathetic she must have looked. And she must have torn him away from all his friends. It was funny, she hadn't noticed him at the club, but he must have been there. She said as much and he grinned at her through the darkness.

"Nah, you didn't spoil my night. I wasn't out for pleasure. That club belongs to me, along with a couple of others."

"Really?" she asked. That would explain why he dressed so well:

he was a businessman.

"Yeah, get more work done here in the evenings. Plus, I like to keep an eye on the place, make sure things run smoothly. No hassle."

They passed the front of the club again and kept walking in the other direction. The bouncers nodded their respect to him and he nodded back with a slight incline of the head.

"Like tonight. I saw you earlier on in the evening. I saw that guy come up to you and was about to come down, but you seemed to be doing alright on your own," he chuckled to himself. "Right little spitfire you were in there."

Anna laughed. "Yes, well...I don't like people backing me into a corner. I get claustrophobic."

"Seems like you don't like people getting within ten feet of you."

Anna looked up, worried she had offended him. "It wasn't you, I just got scared."

"I know, I'm only messing." He put his arm around her, rubbing her shoulder, then dropped it, not wanting to scare her away. For a second there was a part of Anna that wanted him to keep his arm around her. Then she banished the thought. She had no place thinking about any man right now, let alone trusting one again.

"So that's twice you've saved me now. I'm beginning to think I have my own personal knight in shining armour," she joked.

"Here to protect and serve," he replied, flourishing a mock salute. He cringed internally at himself. What a stupid line. He was becoming soft. What was it about this girl that made him act so daft? He looked down at her out of the corner of his eye, as they walked in companionable silence. She looked so small, so fragile, and so...so haunted. That was the only word that could describe it. He'd presumed it was sadness, and maybe that was part of it. But it was more than that. She had looked utterly terrified when he finally caught up with her tonight. Like she hadn't just been running from a man, but from all of her own personal ghosts. Like she was afraid they had finally come to get her.

She was calm now. Her skin soft and clear in the moonlight, her eyes far away in thought. He wondered what it was she was thinking about. She really was a beauty. She had caught his attention before, but looking at her now, he realised just how stunning she was. For most of the men in his clubs, she would probably fade into the background amongst all the heaving bosoms, the cherry red lips and the platinum, glittery artworks that made up the bulk of his female customers. He had been interested in that once too. But unlike the other men, he'd grown tired of the fakeness. He'd grown tired of waking up in the morning to someone completely different from the bronzed, heavy-eyed woman he'd gone to bed with. None of it was real and therefore he could never conjure up any real feelings. Those girls fell in love - and into bed - more often than they had hot dinners, and typically the love they felt was for the credit cards, fast cars and status. He couldn't muster any respect for those girls. This one though, she seemed different. A mystery still, but even the way she looked tonight - she was stunning in the dress she had on. It wasn't a statement, it just fitted her right, suited her perfectly. It showed of her feminine figure without leaving her semi-naked, as seemed to be the fashion. Her hair was glossy and her face needed no help, it was perfect as it was. Freddie realised his thoughts were running away with him, like some school boy on a crush. He didn't know the first thing about her, for crying out loud! She was some bird who seemed not only accident prone, but a nightmare in the making, walking herself into danger everywhere she could. No, he definitely did not have time for this puzzle. It would have to solve itself.

"It's Anna by the way."

"Hm?" he brought his thoughts back to the present as she spoke.

"It's Anna. My name," she said a little awkwardly. He realised he must've seemed rude, dazing off like that.

"Sorry, world of my own. I'm Freddie."

"Well, Freddie. Thank you for walking me home tonight. I owe you one. Well, two actually," she smiled.

Freddie looked up and realised they were outside her building ,and felt a pang of regret at having to let her go.

"Oh. Right. No problem. Glad I could help."

"Goodnight then, Freddie." Anna headed up the steps to the front door.

She had the key in her hand when Freddie blurted out, "Tomorrow..."

"Sorry?"

"Tomorrow afternoon. Are you around?"

"Um, yes, I guess so. Why?"

"Well, you can start paying me back that one you owe me. Well, two."

Anna debated it for a minute, wondering if it was really wise. It couldn't hurt, she supposed. It wasn't like a date or anything. "Ok then. Come by when you want, I'm at number 22."

"Great, see you then." He turned and walked away quickly, cursing himself. What did he go and say that for? Now he would have to come up with ideas for tomorrow that made it look like he'd already had something in mind! *Pay him back the one she owed him? For God's sake Freddie...* he thought. *Smooth.*

Anna slept badly that night - locked in her own nightmares, replaying all the bad memories that she had been fighting to keep locked away at the back of her mind. Unable to wake herself up.

She was in the car trying her hardest to keep her face completely blank. It was futile, she knew. It didn't matter how compliant or quiet she was, he was in a black mood and she would be made to bear the brunt of it. Be made to feel that it was entirely her fault, whatever it was that had worked him up so much. She had no idea. She hadn't seen him since the night before, had thanked God for the short but sweet respite. He had come home like this. She shifted her weight and took a deeper breath, aware that she was hardly breathing. Wrong move.

"What's that sigh about? Ey? You're in that mood again, aren't you? Great. You're in that mood where you're going to start shit with me again, aren't you. Well, don't even think about it - not today."

She resisted the urge to roll her eyes and looked instead out of the window. It was useless trying to avoid becoming the one thing he took every piece of anger and frustration out on. If he couldn't find a good enough reason, he'd just do it anyway. It was unavoidable.

Tony started playing with his phone, texting a reply to one of his employees.

"Tony, lookout!" Anna shouted, natural instincts kicking in and making her cry out, alerting Tony to look up just in time to avoid hitting the parked car he was heading straight for. "Jesus!" she let out the breath she'd been holding.

"Oh shut up, I wasn't even close." He carried on texting away as he drove dangerously close to cars and objects. This driving was scaring her, it was dangerous and she knew it. Self-preservation battled with self-preservation and one of them ended up bubbling to the surface.

"Tony, please! Please can you put the phone down, it's not safe."

"What the fuck are you talking about? Just shut the fuck up Anna. I knew you'd be nothing but trouble today, I fucking knew it. Stupid bitch."

Anna bit her lip. She'd done it now, whatever she said, she would be in the shit for it. She glanced into the back of the car, where Tony's daughter from a previous relationship sat quietly. She had learnt from the word go to stay quiet and invisible. Tony, of course, blamed this on *everybody else but himself, not being able to conceive that he was a bad father. The car was veering into the middle of the road and she had to call out again.*

"Tony! I'm not trying to be difficult, please, but this is unsafe, you're all over the road, you have me and Alexis in the car –"

"I told you to SHUT – THE FUCK – UP." The thump to the side of her head came in hard and fast as he savagely yelled in her face. She froze. The pain was strong as she waited for the throbbing to get to a more reasonable level, and begged silently for the tears not to fall as she once more blanked her expression. Two and half days of abuse had followed that incident, two and a half days where she had to repeatedly apologise and grovel to him to forgive her for what she had done. For making him angry, for not shutting up, for making him hit her in front of his child. For everything she had not done, for everything she was not.

She hated herself for bowing so weakly to such a tyrannical, psychotic and delusional bully. But not half as much as she right now hated him for what he was doing to her. She had worshipped him when he'd first shown interest in her. She had been in such a vulnerable place and he, so strong and caring. She thought he had such a big heart, a good heart. She knew about him and what he did, and she accepted that. Not everything was perfect. But all the rumours about how evil-tempered and fucked-up he was, he had managed to convince her were untrue. That he was just seriously misunderstood. She had felt for him, wanted to be the one to understand him. But things had changed, and now she was bullied, abused and more than anything, already far too broken to stop it and help herself. She felt helpless, she felt like she was drowning.

He came at her again, the curses falling thick and fast, the vein in his temple throbbing as his anger built up inside him, ready to explode.

"You fucking cunt, you fucking dirty little fucking cunt, you think you can take me for a mug do ya? Ey?"

She just sat there. There was nothing she could do but take it.

Anna audibly gasped for air as she woke up, panting, crying, half with terror and half with relief that it had just been a dream. He wasn't here, he couldn't do it to her anymore.

Her bedclothes and linen were soaked through with sweat. She shivered. It was cold. Rubbing her tired eyes, she turned the light on and went to the closet to get a clean nightie. She shuffled to the bathroom and quickly jumped under the shower to wash away the last of her nightmare and rid herself of the cloying, sticky feeling. Anna hated feeling sticky now. Dirty in any way. It just reminded her of him, of how their relationship had been.

Feeling better, Anna looked at the bed, which was still damp. The clock on the bedside table was telling her it was 4.30 in the morning, far too early to be up. She was too tired to change her bedding now. She needed some proper sleep. Grabbing one of the warm blankets from under the bed and switching the heating on as she passed, she headed out to the couch and settled herself down, finally falling into a peaceful sleep.

It was the smell and the popping and sizzling of bacon that roused Anna from her slumber. Looking through half-asleep, half-open eyes at the sunlight shining in the window, she guessed it was probably late morning. She yawned and stretched then propped herself up against the pillows so she could see Tanya.

"Morning, sunshine!" Tanya chirped and handed her a glass of orange juice. "You haven't got a hangover have you? I didn't think you knocked back that much last night?"

Anna took the orange juice gratefully and sipped at it, recollecting the previous night's happenings. Her brain was so fuzzy from lack of proper sleep. The nightmares always took it out of her. She rubbed her eyes and ran her fingers through her long dark hair, massaging her head as if trying to clear it.

"No, not hungover. I was a bit tipsy, but not hammered. Did you have fun after I left?"

"Yeah, it was a good laugh. Didn't stay that long though, there wasn't much happening." Tanya flipped the bacon onto the plates and scraped the scrambled eggs out of the pan next to them. Chucking the ready-prepared bread and butter on top, she passed one of the plates over to Anna on a tray. She sat down next to her and tucked into her own breakfast. Both sat in companionable silence for a few moments, enjoying their food.

"Are you feeling ok today?" Tanya asked between mouthfuls.

"What? - Oh, yes," Anna added hastily, "much better this morning. Don't know what was wrong with me, maybe something I ate yesterday."

"Hardly likely, you cook nearly everything in this gaff and you're more anal than a Sunday School nun about your cooking," Tanya said skeptically, munching another mouthful of crispy bacon. "Though I have to say, you've been tossing and turning like you have ants in your pants all night and you were quite hot to the touch when I came in to check on you. Maybe it was a sort of fever or something."

Anna relaxed. Her nightmares had one positive to them: it didn't look like she had just been ducking out last night after all.

"When did you check on me? I didn't hear you come in."

"No, you were dead to the world. You were mumbling in your sleep, I thought you were talking to me, that's why I came in."

Anna started to feel a little coldness creeping in on her again.

"What was I saying?" she said calmly. Tanya laughed.

"Oh, I don't know mate. Just a load of old boot really." Tanya's smile faltered and she looked at Anna sideways, "I think you were having a bit of a bad dream though. You kept saying 'no' and 'please stop'… when

I put my hand to your forehead to check how hot you were, you pushed me away like you'd been burned." Tanya went quiet and waited for Anna to answer. It was silent for a moment.

"Well. Like you said. Sounds like a bad dream. It was probably the fever talking, I don't remember anything anyway." Anna picked up her knife and fork and carried on with her breakfast, the conversation obviously over.

Tanya slowly followed suit. "Yes, the fever." She said quietly. She hadn't told Anna everything she had heard. If truth be told, she had initially gone in to check that her friend and flatmate was alright, but what she'd heard had made her sit down in the dark and listen.

She had watched Anna struggle with her demons and heard her begging for the torture to stop. She heard Anna despair that the man she called Tony had found her, heard the utter terror in her voice as she begged him to leave her alone. She had recognised the defeat, and the submission elicited by the fear he instilled in her, even just in the dream. She had prayed that in reality, Anna's past had not been as horrific as the dreams that were being played out now, but looking at Anna's secrecy so far, along with her reaction to what she had just said, Tanya realised that it was probably all of that and more. Tanya respected Anna's privacy and evasiveness about her past. She was of the mind that everyone was entitled to their secrets and Tanya only judged people on what she saw with her own two eyes. And so far, everything she had seen of Anna had been positive. Well, almost everything.

She shrugged mentally and took her plate over to the sink. That puzzle could work itself out another day. She had too much on today to think about anything else. Trying to save up as much money as she could in order to open her own business someday, Tanya was pulling as many long or double shifts at the club as she could. She moved herself towards the bedroom to get ready for work.

"I'm on a double again today, so I won't be back till the early hours. Will you be ok?"

"Yes, I'll be fine. I actually have plans today." She smiled to herself. Tanya stopped in her tracks.

"You? Really? I thought you didn't like going out in the day?"

"Well, I've sort of made a friend. Just this guy I've bumped into a couple of times. Nice guy. He saw me home last night."

"Well, you sly dog!" Tanya exclaimed, a big grin stretching over her face. "What's he like?"

"It's not like that. Like, really, not like that, we only really talked last night and it was purely a friendly chat –"

" – ok, whatever," Tanya joked, "anyway, either way, you're going to have to tell me all about him later because I really do have to get ready now, but seriously – I want to know aaall the details." She winked saucily and swept out of the room. Anna rolled her eyes and smiled.

Tanya had had a turbulent upbringing. Being the only girl with three older brothers, she had been left to play by herself most of her younger life. Her mother, Rosie, had been an alcoholic who had despised her for her pretty face, being deeply jealous of anything that took her boys' or husband's attention away from her. Rosie's husband was a wastrel, who came home only when he wasn't living off whatever piece of skirt he had managed to shack himself up with. Rosie, loving him and wanting him still, always welcomed him back with open arms, convincing herself that he had changed. He, for his part, was a good actor, flashing his handsome smile and promising the world to her each time. But it never lasted. Sometimes he would stay a month, sometimes more, but he always went on his merry way once something better came along.

For all his fake promises and cupboard love for his gin-soaked wife though, he always had a true soft spot for his young daughter, displaying genuine interest and warmth for her whenever he was around. For this, Tanya suffered. Between beatings, verbal lashings and cruel punishments, Tanya lived only for the times when he would be home and bring some happiness into her dismal life again. When she was allowed outside of the house, which was not often aside from school and food shopping for her mother, Tanya would sit on the small bit of grass at the corner of the road, wishing, with each glimpse of a figure ambling towards her in the distance, that it was her Daddy coming home to save her from her dark existence. She would screw her eyes up, distorting the figures coming towards her into the shape of him, until the unsuspecting person was too close to pretend anymore.

As an added action of cruelty, Tanya's mother only ever dressed her in grey, shapeless garments; the cheapest, oldest items she could gather from the rag markets and pawn shops. She would tell her that she didn't deserve to have pretty clothes, that she had a bad streak in her. As she grew, suffering from cruel taunts at school about how she dressed, Tanya would ask her through tears why she tried to make her look so bad. Rosie would always tell her the same thing. That she didn't deserve to have pretty clothes. That her face was a blatant show of her personality - not that of a decent, pretty girl, but that of a shifty whore. It showed the whole world what a bad girl she was. She didn't need to be showing her figure off as well - she was already going to the devil.

With her brothers off married with families of their own to worry about, and her father returning less and less, no-one was there to see or intervene. Between her mother ensuring she had no friends at school due to the way she looked, and not ever being allowed out in the street to play and interact with the other children as her brothers once did, Tanya had no-one to turn to in her lonely life and nothing to do but comply with what she was told.

Once she was old enough to get a job, she had gone out and found one straight away, hoping to earn enough to buy her own clothes in future. Her mother had put paid to this immediately, collecting Tanya's wages herself. She had hissed viciously in Tanya's face when she'd asked her mother why she couldn't keep any of the money she earned. Rosie told her that she deserved none of it, seeing as it was her who'd put a roof over her head, clothes on her back and food in her mouth all these years. Tanya didn't fight her - she never did, knowing she could never win.

There was one good thing about the new job though. Her employer at the corner store said that if she was to work there, she would have to dress smartly and fashionably, so as to attract the right sort of customer. Although this had raged a fierce internal battle in Rosie's head, she had grudgingly allowed Tanya to buy one outfit, not wanting to part with the regular extra money coming in. Her gin supply had taken a boost since her wayward daughter had been working, and she had no plans to let her stock run low again. Tanya had gone running to the shops in glee, so excited to be able to buy something pretty, something to make her feel better about herself. Something she could finally feel entirely unashamed in. She had spent two hours trying on almost everything in the shop, looking at herself in wonder as the different styles gave her shape, while the colours transformed her. When she finally went home in a beige, high-waisted skirt and emerald green, fitted satin shirt, with pretty beige court shoes to match, she was so elated that for a second she thought her mother might look at her and realise how nice she looked. For the first time in her life she felt like she was floating down the street towards her home, walking on air. That feeling was short lived however, when she was dragged into the front room by her hair and told repeatedly that she was nothing but a whore, through and through. That people would look at her in that outfit and see her for what she really was. That the green of her shirt mirrored her jaded soul. Tanya had been crushed yet again.

When news came that her father had died, Tanya's heart finally died once and for all. He had been the one and only person she cared about in her life, the one piece of love and warmth, and now he was gone. She was grieving herself and her mother, seeing only her own grief, had dragged her by the hair down the stairs as revenge. Blaming her for every time he had gone away, blaming her for his death. Tanya had known then that although she had nowhere to go and no-one else in her life, there was nothing here for her either. Worse than nothing; here, was a place filled with hate and cruelty.

The next day, heading off to work as usual, Tanya hid the only other decent outfit she now had in her shopping bag. She had begged a second outfit after a year of working there so as to not wear the first one out completely. Working up the courage and trying not to shake, she explained to her employers that her father had died and that she needed to go away for a while. She asked politely if she could have her wages early and up-to-date, as if it was the most natural thing in the world. The man she worked for was a kindly old man, one who, privately, disliked Tanya's mother immensely for the suffering he could see she inflicted on her only daughter. He felt sickened by the way that poor girl was browbeaten and trodden down, but it was never his place to say. Tanya had been a good worker and proved to be a vibrant, friendly girl when she was let out of the cage of her mother's making. He'd be sad to see her go, but at the same time, he was elated that she had finally upped and done it. Sealing the envelope, he had grasped her into a big bear hug and wished her well.

"Now that lot in there is right, lovey. You earned every penny, alright? Go on out of it now, and maybe come back and visit sometime if you are back passing through."

Later, standing at the train station, not sure where to go, Tanya opened the envelope. Her eyes swam with tears as she counted more than double what she had earned. That small pay packet had set her on her way towards a new and better life, and for that she would never forget the kindness shown to her by the lovely old man.

Two months on, she'd found herself here. Having secured herself a job as a waitress, she could just about afford the flat, sharing with another girl. It was a complete eye-opener, finally being free of the restrictions she had lived with for so long. Her appearance became the most important thing to Tanya now, after the years of being dressed as an ugly duckling. She felt like the proverbial swan, blossoming gracefully into the colourful creature she now had the freedom to be. As long as she looked good - and she now knew that she could - she was happy.

There were two lessons Tanya had learnt in life. Firstly and most recently, that her looks gained her almost anything she wanted or needed, so she used that to her advantage.

Secondly, she never, ever wanted to end up like her mother. She hated her mother deeply, but in a way could almost see how life had turned her into the bitter lemon she was. Her mother had married for love and had ended up with nothing. Without the man she loved, without support and without money. Tanya would never allow herself to end up like that. If she ever decided to bite the bullet and marry, it would be with someone financially secure so that whatever happened, she would never be left to rot.

As time went on and Tanya settled into the delights of her new life, she became unhappy with the meagre amount of money she was bringing in. To be able to turn heads she needed money, but to get her lifestyle paid for and the attention she craved, she had to first turn those heads. Her flatmate, Karen, always seemed to have ample amounts of money, able to get whatever she wanted, but Tanya suspected that she carried out some dark deeds for it and despite her rebellious love for freedom, she wasn't up for going to that level just yet. Karen had laughed when Tanya voiced this.

"Love, what do you think it is we do? It's not like the horror stories you hear out on the street you know. We work in the club. Yeah, we wear our scanties, but we don't ever sleep with any of the punters. All we do is walk around showing off, spend a bit of time chatting them up and that, then dance for them. It's as simple as that. And we take home more in one night than you bring home in a week - including your tips!"

"I'm not so sure Kal…"

"Look, why don't you come along with me tonight and just have a look, see for yourself. I know the owner would be more than happy to take you on, you've got all the necessary bits and bobs."

Tanya went red. "And you don't do anything sexual with them?"

Karen had paused and lit a cigarette. "It's up to you, to be honest. No, you're not *expected* to, and no, it is not on the offer at the door. But if you want to and they're offering you a good price, there is somewhere you can go discreetly." Karen started moisturising her legs with shimmery lotion. "But you don't ever have to do that if you don't want to. Plenty of the girls don't, they're just there to dance."

Tanya had a think about it for a moment. It wouldn't hurt to go and just have a look. So she had gone. She had been quite surprised at how normal it all seemed, how relaxed and warm, and had spent the evening being charmed by the club's owner. Within a week she had given up her waitressing job. With her creamy skin, heavy breasts and vivid red hair, Tanya immediately became one of the main attractions in the busiest gentlemen's club in East London. An underworld starlet had been born.

Pulling the brush through her long sleek hair, Anna gave herself a little nod of approval. She had changed several times, not knowing what sort of outfit she should be wearing. Jeans, dresses, heels and flats were strewn across the usually tidy bedroom as she deliberated. In the end, she settled for a casual wrap dress with low heels that she thought would be a flexible compromise, whatever they ended up doing. She bit her thumb nail absentmindedly as she appraised herself. Yes, it would do. She looked at the clock and checked she had everything in her handbag one more time. It was coming up to 12:30. She had realised after Tanya had left for work that Freddie had not actually mentioned a time. Not wanting to be dithering around when he arrived, she had hurried to get ready. Now though, the excitement of getting ready was gone and she had nothing to do but wait. Not that she was excited, she reasoned with herself, this was just two people meeting up, making friends. It was about time she made new friends, that was what she needed right now. Feeling antsy, she set about cleaning the kitchen, scrubbing and polishing everything there and in the front room until they shone. It was as she was setting the duster down, gliding her eyes around the room trying to find any rogue specks of dust that there was a knock on the door. It made her jump.

She shook her head in annoyance at herself, *what a silly thing to jump at when you were expecting company*. As she opened the door, she realised it was because she had been expecting the downstairs buzzer to go first. She mentally shrugged, someone must have just been heading out or something as he arrived.

The first thing she saw when she opened the door was a huge bunch of flowers and she started back in surprise. Freddie's face peeped at her from around the side and registered the shock. "Sorry, didn't mean to startle you! Actually, to be honest, I thought this would have slightly better results as an approach than last night. Obviously got that one wrong…" he trailed off and gave her a large grin and a shrug. Anna laughed and apologised immediately, "So sorry, I don't know what's wrong with me these days, they're lovely." She took them from him and blushed, feeling a little shy. She hadn't been expecting that.

Freddie took this as embarrassment. "Well, you know, it's not a big deal, I just know you haven't been in here long, so, it's just a little housewarming gift...sort of thing..." *Oh Freddie, you bloody prat*, he kicked himself mentally. *What are you doing making excuses like some awkward little prick in the playground?* Before he could think of something better to say, or backtrack, she had thanked him and gone to the kitchen to put them in a water.

"Please, make yourself comfortable while I sort these out."

Anna filled the vase quickly and tried to compose herself. The flowers really were beautiful, soft pink roses mingled with other pastel-coloured blooms which she hadn't seen before. Her heart had jumped right up when he'd handed them to her, making her feel like a loved-up school girl. But she'd gotten it completely wrong, he was just being nice. Neighbourly really. A housewarming gift. She tried to smile. What was wrong with her? A perfectly nice guy had helped her out a couple of times and was offering her the hand of friendship, this was a good thing. She should grab the opportunity with both hands, so she resolved then and there that she would do exactly that.

The previous night when he'd left her, Freddie had gone straight back to find Vince. Finding himself with a dilemma outside of his areas of expertise, he was unsure how to proceed. He'd never had this problem before, never had to ask for advice on stuff like this before! With every girl he had dated, it had been pretty straightforward. Dinner somewhere expensive, champagne, VIP area in one of the clubs, then an expensive hotel room in the city. They all wanted the same thing. They were all impressed over the same unimaginative expenditure of a lot of money. But there were two problems where Anna was concerned. One, he didn't think that she would be particularly impressed by that and two, he had only gone and invited her out for an afternoon rather than an evening. What on earth was there to do in the afternoon? On top of this, he also realised he actually wanted to talk to her, find out more about the person she was. You couldn't do that in a crowded club. So he headed to Vince, his closest friend and the only father-figure he'd ever known, for advice.

Vince sprayed the brandy he had been drinking all over the long mahogany desk and choked as he tried to suppress the laughter that was already half out. He hadn't been expecting it. He tried to turn it into a cough to buy himself some time and so as to not embarrass Freddie any further. It had obviously taken him a lot and he must be truly stumped to come here for advice of this nature. Freddie rolled his eyes and clamped his lips together as he sat in silence, waiting for the older man to recover.

Vince mopped up the puddled brandy. It must be that he genuinely liked this girl to be so het up and to not give her the usual standard. This warmed Vince's heart, though he would never admit it. Neither would Freddie come to that, if questioned. Weaknesses weren't discussed in their world. And caring about someone was most definitely a weakness. So Freddie had asked nonchalantly as if it didn't matter and Vince would now answer as if in easy conversation. But he knew. He hoped he was right; it was hard to let yourself get close to anyone in their line of work, even a good woman.

"Sorry, went down the wrong way. Erm...I guess you could get out of London or something for the afternoon? Or you could act daft and do all that tourist shit in the centre, if that was more what you were looking for...getting stuck with a bird for an afternoon, couldn't think of anything worse mate!" he chuckled and looked at Freddie, giving him a platform to get back the street cred he felt he was losing.

"Yeah, tell me about it," he smiled and straightened his jacket. "but what can you do, ey?"

"Nothin' mate. They have a way of getting us into all sorts of situations, minxes - the lot of em!"

"Yeah..." he pictured Anna, her graceful elegance and her soft voice and thought to himself that Vince's comment couldn't be further from the truth in this case.

"Look," Vince said quietly, "if you really like her it don't matter what you do." He shrugged and lit a cigar, eyeing the smoke as it drifted upwards, "You could always just ask her what she wants to do? If it's a rubbish idea then take her to the country, find a little pub somewhere or something, if not, you have something else to do. Can't end up too badly."

Now, sat in her small but cosy lounge, Freddie was still deliberating. She came through and looked at him expectantly.

"So, what are we doing today?" she smiled.

"Well, that's what I wanted to ask you." He smiled back, "I was thinking we could maybe get out of the city for the afternoon, there are a couple of nice places I know. I like to get out now and then. Or if there's something you want to do, we could do that."

He cringed inside. It went completely against the grain for him to talk like this. Usually his women didn't get a choice. He would tell them

45

when he'd pick them up, where they were going, what they were doing and even sometimes what they should wear. Now he was sat here like a little boy, just trying to find something to please her. It was new and uncomfortable ground, even as he waited for her response.

She gazed off into the distance as though she was somewhere else. After a long moment, just as Freddie was beginning to think she wouldn't answer, she turned to look at him.

"Do you know what I'd like to do?" she asked softly.

"Tell me..."

"I'd like to get lost."

"Lost?!" Freddie asked, unsure if he heard her correctly.

"Yes, lost," she laughed, "let's get out of the city like you said, but let's just go somewhere we don't know. Go down roads we've never seen before and end up somewhere completely new." Her eyes shone as she tried to convince him. Freddie smiled. It was the first time he'd seen her animated since he had met her. No nervous smile or glances over her shoulder. If that was all it took to make her relax, then happy days!

"...don't you ever do that—" He tuned back into what she was saying. "—just go somewhere, disappear off the map?"

Disappearing off the map means something entirely different in my world, he wanted to say, but didn't. He doubted she had any clue that a world like his existed and he didn't want to spoil that. Not yet. She paused, waiting for him to answer her, suddenly not sure if she should have said anything. On impulse, Freddie suddenly grabbed her by the hand and twirled her round towards the door

"Come on then," he laughed, "let's get well and truly lost then!"

3

It was one of the best afternoons she could ever remember. She had quickly ran back in to get changed, pulling on a warmer outfit, then they'd run down the stairs together like children, past the gaping neighbours who watched their descent incredulously. This made Anna laugh even harder. What, had they never seen two people acting young and free before? They had looked at Freddie like he was some kind of ghost. Though she had to admit, their behaviour perhaps wasn't in keeping with his tailored dark blue suit and military-esque, neat appearance.

She slowed down when they got to the front door. As much as she wanted to feel carefree, in reality she wasn't, so she proceeded with caution towards the glistening silver Mercedes parked across the road, checking over everyone in sight for any old face she might recognise.

Freddie opened the passenger door and she slid in quietly. He said nothing, but noted the changes.

"Right, wait there a second while I get the top down…"

"No! I mean—" she softened her voice, "—why don't we save it for when we get out of London. Then we could pull over and put it down. Don't fancy the sooty air so much," she added with a smile.

"Ok." Freddie blanked his face, unsure what it was that was scaring her. Did she not want to be seen with him? He doubted it, she didn't know him well enough to want to keep him a secret yet, he smirked inwardly. It would still be doubtful then too though, women always wanted to show him off. A status symbol. Not her though, if anything she probably just wouldn't want to see him at all. Or would she? If he was honest with himself, he had no idea, all he could do was guess. Hopefully he would find a way to suss her out much better today.

"So where to then?" he looked at her expectantly as he slid into the cool leather driver's seat, "North, south, east or west?"

"South," she replied, "south east." He put the car into gear and swept out of the street.

As soon as they reached the smaller roads and quietness of the countryside, Anna relaxed once more. She pointed out little twists and turns, directing him right into the middle of nowhere. They sat comfortably with each other, Anna enjoying the feeling of complete escape and Freddie surprisingly taking immense pleasure in being part of an innocent adventure for once.

"Take that one! There! The road on your left."

Freddie turned as requested and carried on down the windy road.

"How far do you want to go today?" he smiled, watching her face taking in the countryside.

"I don't know really. We can stop if you want to... sorry, I didn't really think of you doing all this driving or whether you needed to get back. You probably do need to get back, don't you?" the worried look returned to her face and he quickly tried to banish it again.

"No, no, it's not that, I'm enjoying this as much as you are," he said, surprised at how truthful his words were, "we can go all day if you want."

"Really?" she asked, still a little worried.

"Honestly." He said seriously, looking into her face.

A little while later Anna turned in her seat to face him. "I suppose it wasn't entirely sensible to come out here with you, when I know nothing about you..." she began cautiously. Freddie didn't say anything, waiting for her to continue. "But, the only times I've seen you, you've helped me and been such a gentleman. So I guess I trust you, even if I don't yet really know you..." she trailed off, not knowing why she'd just voiced her thoughts so openly. He must think her an idiot. After a minute Freddie answered.

"What would you like to know about me? We have time on our hands, ask what you like." He hoped she wouldn't ask too many things that he didn't want to answer.

"Well..." she thought about it. Better to stick to things she didn't mind answering in return, as this opened her up for questioning too. "How about your family? Do you have a big family? Are you close?"

Freddie smiled, "Yeah, two brothers, one sister - all younger - and me mum. We're very close. No Dad, so it's just been me to look after them for the last few years. I guess that's what makes us so close." He turned the corner. "What about you?"

"Well..." it wouldn't hurt if she gave him no details. "It was just me, I have no brothers or sisters. My Mum and Dad and I were always a tight unit. We did a lot together. They really wanted kids and they tried for years without luck, then just as they gave up, I came along, so they tried to make the most of every second." She smiled, remembering. "We did everything and anything that we could, every weekend. I suppose some people think I was spoilt, but it wasn't like that. They just appreciated every moment we had as a family. Made the most of it." Anna compressed the pangs of homesickness that appeared with the memories.

"You're speaking about them in past tense, are they not around anymore?" Freddie asked. *Is that what you are running from?* he wanted to ask, but he didn't for fear of overstepping the mark.

"No, they...I just...haven't seen them in a while."

"Why don't you go visit?"

"Because I...well, just because." Anna shifted awkwardly in her seat and stared out the window again, red-faced at the corner she'd backed herself into. She crossed her arms and pointed out another turn for him to take. Her body language clearly demonstrated her reluctance to discuss it further. Freddie frowned. It was hard to get to know her when she clammed up every five minutes. But she still drew him in like some sort of magnet, so he reached inwards for the little patience he possessed, and let it go.

After some more ambling along country roads, periodically chatting or listening to the radio and relaxing with their own thoughts, Freddie came across a sign for the beach. He turned off and sped down the road towards it. As they approached the end of the road, Anna looked up and exclaimed in joy at the sight of the early evening turning pink on the water.

"Oh, it's beautiful! Let's go walk in the sand!"

Stiff from driving for so long and ready to stretch his legs and flex his muscles, Freddie parked up next to some seagulls and an old couple eating ice cream, watching the sea together. Immersed in their own thoughts, they both envied the old couple for a second. They looked so at peace, so uncomplicated. Anna, in her excitement, took Freddie's hand absentmindedly and led him eagerly down to the beach. Careful not to show his surprise, Freddie glanced down at his hand. It was the first time she had voluntarily touched him since they met. He had put his arm around her that night, spun her round her living room this morning, but she had so far kept a cautious distance. It came across as an unconscious habit. But now she grabbed his hand, and was still clasping it as they tripped down the sand dune towards the waves.

Anna kicked her shoes off and motioned for Freddie to do the same. She laughed and ran down the beach. She breathed in deeply and closed her eyes. Suddenly she felt so free, the chains she defended herself with flew off as she ran into the wind under the dying sunlight. The sand felt soft and pure under her feet, the air so clean, away from the smog and stress of London. There was nothing but the sound of the waves and the seagulls. She forgot everything. She forgot who she was, what had happened, where she was, Freddie. The muscles in her legs awakened joyfully from a long hibernation and she flexed them as she ran faster. Her dress whipped up around her legs exposing the lily-white skin to the sun and the air.

Freddie's breath caught in his throat as he watched her, spellbound. Her long dark hair glinted auburn in the light and danced around her playfully in the wind. She spun around, her arms in the air and her eyes closed in rapture. He had never seen such a beautiful sight. He walked towards her slowly, not wanting to break the spell she seemed to be under. She opened her eyes and he stopped in his tracks.

"Come and play with me..." Anna smiled, her eyes warm as she laughed a gentle, girlish laugh. There was nothing sexual behind the words, nothing suggestive like Freddie was used to hearing. Somehow though, this made him want her even more. He wondered if she had any idea of the effect she had on men, this unusual, understated, mesmerising woman.

Leaving his shoes and jacket on the ground beside hers, Freddie loosened the top of his shirt and rolled up the bottom of his trousers to give himself more freedom of movement. Anna was dancing around with her arms up, eyes closed again. He started running silently, trying to take her by surprise but she opened her eyes and saw him. He grinned and picked up speed heading straight for her.

"Haha!" Anna pushed off again, "You won't catch me!"

"I'll bet you my Grandmother I do!" he answered, laughing and pushing his hard muscles into action.

"You'd best get her packed then!" she shouted over her shoulder.

"Ha!" Her cheeky comment made him grin, fruitless as her attempt would be. She would never outrun him.

A few metres later though, Freddie started to get alarmed. Anna was incredibly fast and as much as he appreciated the view of her lithe figure streaking ahead of him, he couldn't believe she was actually giving him a run for his money! Or more technically, his Grandmother. He switched his head into competition mode and focused on getting closer, slowly but surely now, catching her up.

"No!" she squealed, as she checked behind her to see how far away he was. She put one final push into her game, but Freddie could see she was beginning to tire. He smiled. Now he had her. She was fast off the mark, but she was no endurance artist. And endurance was an area in which Freddie had trained himself religiously over the years. He was only just warming up.

Anna was out of breath, but she was determined to try to win. She hadn't had this much fun in ages, or exercise come to think of it. She turned to check just in time to see Freddie reach out to her. He wrapped his arms around her and tackled her to the ground, protecting her from the impact with his body.

He quickly looked up at her to see if she was hurt. He'd gotten carried away with winning, he shouldn't have tackled her. But Anna was laughing. She laughed so hard that tears came out of the corner of her eyes. He laughed with her, partly in relief and then looked at her lovely face as they lay, still touching in the sand. There was a wisp of hair coming out over her face that he ached to push back behind her ear, but he restrained himself, still scared she might retreat back to her wary state.

Anna wiped the tears from her eyes and looked up into the face looking down at hers. God he was beautiful. His eyes were mesmerising, with greens and warm golds running into each other, turning hazel right towards the middle. As he looked into her eyes, she felt like they were going through her, seeing right into her soul. Usually this would have sent her running, but somehow today, away from it all, it felt so good, so comforting. The early sunset behind him framed his head like a halo. Each was acutely aware of the warmth where the other's body touched their own. Anna thought to herself that if she could have stayed in this moment forever, she would have done. They lay unmoving for what seemed like both hours and just seconds, until a shiver through Anna's body from the cold damp sand below awoke them both from their trance.

"You're cold," Freddie tutted, annoyed at himself, "I shouldn't let you lie on wet sand in October, you'll catch your death. Come on, back to the car."

Anna hid her disappointment.

He helped her to her feet and she dusted off the sand, pulling her dress back into its proper position. They walked back to the car slowly, enjoying watching the sunset glinting on the waves. Freddie looked at his watch and frowned.

"It's getting late, I didn't realise the time." He glanced at Anna, "How would you feel about finding somewhere here to stay tonight?"

Anna blushed a little, unsure of how to answer. Her heart raced a little.

"Not like that," he rushed to assure her, taking her reaction as a negative one, "I'll get us separate rooms, you don't need to worry. I just mean it's late to be driving back, we could just make an evening of it then drive back in the morning...if you were up for that?" *And I just want to spend more time with you*, he added silently in his head.

Anna's heart dropped. Stupid girl, she thought to herself. Of course he doesn't look at you like that. He's incredibly good looking, obviously well-off, well-known for his clubs by the sound of it, he will have every pretty, single girl in the city after him. She thought of the girls in the club that night. They'd looked like bright lights next to her with their vivid colours and ample assets. She definitely didn't stand out in comparison. Even next to Tanya, whose vivacious air swept the room, leaving Anna in the shadows. And that was how she wanted it, she reasoned. She tried to quell her wish to stand out to Freddie, to be the type to turn his head. Anna still wasn't sure what it was that kept him in her company, whether it was pity for her obvious helplessness whenever he was around, or perhaps he saw her as someone to be a friend or a sister figure. Either way, it definitely wasn't for the same reason that *she* wanted to be around *him*.

"Um, yes, ok. That sounds nice," she answered, with a falsely bright smile. "The only thing is, I haven't bought anything with me, I can shove this back on tomorrow but I'll have nothing to sleep in."

"Nah, don't worry about that," he shook his head as he dusted off his jacket, "I have a couple of clean tracksuits in the back for when I go to the gym, you can borrow one of my t-shirts if you don't mind roughing it?" he grinned.

"I'm sure I can cope with that," Anna replied, and they set off to try and find somewhere nearby.

"I'm sorry Sir, but I'm afraid we have no single rooms available at all. There's a conference on this week, we only have two rooms left in the entire hotel." The balding clerk behind the front desk sniffed and looked bored as he waited to see what they wanted to do. He wasn't really fussed whether they stayed or not. It was extra work for him if they did, but given he was paid to accommodate that, he couldn't really complain. Not out loud anyway.

"Right." Freddie ran his hands through his hair agitatedly, worrying that Anna might be getting uncomfortable. He looked over at her. Her face betrayed nothing, but at least she didn't look worried.

"We do have one twin room Sir, a very nice suite overlooking the bay, one of our premium suites Sir, so slightly larger than normal."

"What do you reckon? We can check out some of the other gaffs around here if you'd prefer?" he looked at her expectantly.

"This one's fine with me, I don't mind."

"If you're sure...Alright then mate, we'll take it."

"Wonderful choice Sir, we shall be glad to have you here at the Birkham Royal. If you will just allow me to take some details, I'll book you in and take you through to your suite."

A couple of hours, a wonderful meal and several glasses of wine later, a very tipsy Anna was being led back to the suite by the arm. She giggled as she tripped up the last step and he strengthened his hold on her. They had talked and laughed animatedly all evening, though Anna had skillfully skirted around anything to do with her past or where she came from. Short of asking her outright why she wouldn't answer, there wasn't much more Freddie could have done to try and find out. She obviously had something to hide, he had surmised that much. Or something to hide *from*. Freddie could understand that better than anyone and he had done his fair share of topic dodging tonight as well. Unlike a lot of other people, Anna had not pushed, respecting his privacy. Which was the main reason he had extended her the same courtesy. It was frustrating though, having such feelings evoked by someone yet knowing next to nothing about them.

Freddie carefully manoeuvred her into the room, keeping hold of her while he found the key card and opened the door. Despite the cold outside it was nice and warm in the room, giving it a cosy feel under the dimmed lights.

Once they were in the room there was an awkward moment as they both looked towards the beds.

"Oh, here you go," Freddie rummaged in his big gym bag and pulled out a big, plain, white t-shirt. "This should fit you to sleep in. Might be a bit big, but..." he shrugged, unsure as to how to finish his sentence.

Anna thanked him and walked into the bathroom to get changed. She closed the door and leant on the marble top by the sink, looking into the mirror. Her face was flushed and her eyes bright. Probably all that wine, she smiled to herself. It had been an amazing night. And day too. She hadn't felt this happy and relaxed and carefree in such a long time. She unwrapped her dress and let it fall down to the floor. The soft lighting in the bathroom made her skin look even creamier than usual. She unhooked her bra and let that fall too. Slowly pulling back her hair, she exposed herself completely to the mirror and looked at the big fluffy robe on the back of the door. She could leave the t-shirt off and just put the robe on. Exit the bathroom and slowly walk up to him, wrap her arms around his neck and put her lips to his...undo the robe and let it melt away...

She snapped back and shook the thought out of her head. What was she thinking? Too much wine had given her silly ideas. He would likely push her away and then she would have ruined a perfectly lovely trip, not to mention causing herself untold embarrassment and, most probably, the loss of a friend.

In the next room, Freddie had got changed and was waiting for Anna to appear. Usually he slept naked or just in boxers, but he was in a very unusual situation, a novelty to be exact, and for the first time he could remember, he felt self-conscious so he'd thrown on his other gym t-shirt. He listened to make sure she was not being sick, he hadn't realised she was such a lightweight.

"Everything going ok in there?" he called tentatively.

Inside the bathroom Anna jumped at the sound, as it jogged an unpleasant memory. "I'm fine!" she called, "Just getting changed, won't be long." She sat down on the side of the bath and waited, unable to stop the wave of memories flooding her mind.

In a different bathroom in a different time, a different Anna looked at her drawn face in the mirror. She was in the en-suite of the master bedroom at their grand, sprawling house in Hadley Wood. She hated this room. It had no windows, made her feel trapped, suffocated. He liked to keep this house out here, just far enough out to feel like you were away from London, but near enough to quickly commute to wherever he needed to be. He kept her here most of the time. The house was built in a Tudor style; it was far too big, furnished with very expensive and exquisite things and protected by large, impregnable gates. It was her gilded cage. She had everything in it she needed but nothing that could bring her happiness.

Some days, when he was nice to her, she felt guilty for being unhappy. But that would always pass. He always started again, no matter what she did. He was home tonight which meant that her routine had to be adhered to. She had just finished putting Alexis to bed. Alexis lived with them full-time and was blissfully unaware that the way their family worked - or rather, was controlled - was not normal. It was all she had ever known. Anna had met the girl's poor mother once and her heart had leapt out to her. Tony had taken Alexis from her when she was just a baby. and had set about making sure she had no claim. He'd planted drugs and weapons in her house before reporting her, so that he, the doting father, would be given full custody. He had arranged for the mother's drink to be spiked the night before she was due to be drug tested and had paid a witness to say that she had hit Alexis repeatedly whilst drinking, and had left her crying alone in the house for hours. She had next to no chance of seeing her baby again by the time he was through with her. Now Alexis lived a barren life, only doing what her father thought was acceptable, never allowed to think for herself, play games with other children or read any books that weren't vetted by Tony, and as a result she was a withdrawn and lonely child. Anna had sought to build a closer bond with her, to ease both their suffering, but that had been cut short quickly.

"Don't even think about it. I don't want you putting any sort of impression on my child, I don't want her endin' up something like you. You'll look after her as per my instructions, but as for these games and acting like you're some kind of mate to her, no fucking way. I 'ave to protect her and that includes against you. Do not let me fucking 'ear about it again, do you understand me?" he yelled, as he held her up against a wall by the throat. She had understood this crystal clear, and from then on was too scared of the consequences to try to reach out to the sad little girl again. Later that day he had taken the two of them over to Hampstead Heath for some crepes and had cracked jokes and made them both laugh *and she had forgotten all about it. But now, staring into her own frightened eyes, she remembered with clarity. She pictured her unhappy family again but with another little person in it. Her own child. She started shaking uncontrollably. She was sure now. She hadn't been able to get a pregnancy test for fear he would find it, but now two months had gone with no sign of her period and she had started being sick. Feeling her flat stomach she shivered. It would show soon and then what? The minute he found out he had fathered another child that would be it. There wouldn't be a safe place on the entire planet for her. Not that there was at the moment, but she would have even fewer options then. The minute he found out, her child would no longer be allowed to be hers. He would take it away. Even under the same roof, she would never, ever be able to just be a mother to her baby. Anna bit down on her fist, stifling the sob. Tears streamed down her cheeks. She didn't know what to do. She would rather die than let her baby go through that. Suddenly she stopped and sat upright. Maybe that's what would have to happen. In a weird, detached way she couldn't believe she was watching herself consider this. But then, only she really knew how bad it was. To everyone else they were a perfect, happy unit.*

"What are you doing in there?" a low, calm tone floated through the door and she jumped in fright. Calm tones were always the most dangerous. Most of the time it meant that there was a calculated anger bubbling under the surface. He would watch her, waiting for her to give him any excuse and then he would pounce. She saw it coming a mile off every time, but there was nothing she could do. When his mind was made up to take out his frustrations on her, that was it.

"Nothing, sorry, I just...I felt a bit sick, that's all." She quickly splashed water over her face and then wrapped the see-through silk robe around her naked body. This was the only thing she was allowed to wear to bed. "I'm coming now."

"What's wrong with you?" he demanded as she walked out into the

bedroom. He looked her up and down and she tried valiantly to smile and walk towards him as if nothing was wrong.

"I don't know, perhaps something I ate, nothing serious."

"You look like shit." He curled his lip. "I work all day, hard graft to give you everything and I come home to this? What's the point?"

Then let me go, she pleaded silently, knowing there was no point voicing it. He would never let her go. She was his property, just like everything and everyone else.

"I'm sorry," she said lowering her eyes, knowing this was the only way to go now. "You're right, I should be pleasant to come home to."

"Pleasant," he mimicked her, "even your voice is pissing me off tonight, all plum in mouth at me, like I'm some sort of fucking mug who's underneath you."

Anna knew this was just an excuse to raise his anger at her. One of the things he liked best about her was that she spoke properly and came across as a better breed of woman. It made him feel like a better breed of man. That and this house.

"Sorry..." she whispered now, stroking his face and kneeling down, knowing this was her final attempt at peace. He would either allow her to grovel and make it up to him or he would rip her to shreds, dependent on his mood. He grabbed her jaw with his hand and forced her to look up at him.

"S'alright...you can make it up to me with that pretty little mouth of yours, can't you? Since you have one plum in there, let's see if we can fit two more, shall we?" he laughed quietly at his own joke. As he pulled her to him roughly, Anna closed her eyes, switched off and resigned herself to Tony's demands. It was pure survival.

Anna snapped back to reality. Her skin felt cold so she shrugged on the large t-shirt and wrapped the warm robe around her. Splashing her face with water again, she pinched her cheeks to get the colour back that had drained, then walked briskly back into the bedroom and away from her memories. Freddie was sat in the armchair with a brandy in his hand and his suit folded neatly over the back. She averted her eyes but not before she had clocked the tanned muscular skin on his arms and legs. She found her mind wandering to what he would look like topless. He was watching her as she walked. She probably looked about five years old in his oversized top. She shrugged mentally. Wouldn't change anything anyway. She lay the robe over the back of the sofa, warmer now in the bedroom.

Freddie sat watching her, swilling the brandy around in the glass. She didn't wear a lot of makeup anyway, that much he could already tell, but now, completely barefaced and in nothing but his top, she was just as beautiful. Naturally, quietly beautiful. He looked away as she slid onto the sofa, curling her legs beside her. His top rode up to the top of her thigh, exposing her smooth skin. He couldn't watch or his arousal would start to show. He looked out the window instead.

"Would you like a nightcap?" his voice was soft and relaxed as he unwound.

"No, thank you," Anna smiled warmly "I think I'm ready for bed, I'm tired out."

"Ok." Freddie put his glass down and slipped on the twin bathrobe to hers. "I just need to step out to make a couple of calls and I'll be back. I'll take the key, you settle down and I'll see you in the morning." He fished in his jacket pocket for his phone, which he'd switched off earlier in the day. He had wanted just one, completely uninterrupted day with Anna.

"Ok..." Anna walked to the bed, "Oh, and Freddie?"

"Yeah?"

"Thank you." Her eyes met his, "Thank you for everything today. It's been the best day I can remember in...a very long time. I won't forget it."

"Then you're welcome. But don't thank me, the pleasure's been all mine."

"Freddie!! Where the fuck have you been?!"

"Off Vince, just off-radar today."

"Off the radar or off the fucking planet Fred, haven't you heard??"

"Heard what? Vince what's happened? I switched my phone off, I'm not in London. You're my first call." Freddie's pulse quickened. It was extremely unusual for Vince to be anything other than cool and entirely in control, he must have missed something pretty big.

"Ahh, you got away with that pretty little bird you was on about then...S'pose an old man can't really blame you for turning your phone off for a few hours..."

Freddie cut him off, worried now. "Vince will you just fucking enlighten me, mate?"

There was a silence on the other end as Vince tried to decide how to proceed. Freddie waited impatiently.

"Big Dom's brown bread." There was another long silence as Freddie tried to take this in. Big Dom was one of the elite few faces that had been part of the East End underworld going back donkeys years, face royalty. He was older, like Vince. They had moved up the ranks together, since they were practically kids and were, up to this day, business partners in many ventures, as well as very loyal and close friends. Most of the East End and Soho massage parlours, the majority of which were a business front for prostitution, were owned by these two. They were run well and fairly, the girls worked through choice and in fair conditions. The pair of them had a big stake in the cocaine and cannabis that came into the country from the east. Half of the clubs they ran masked their various weapons' trades, and like the proper old-school faces that they were, they still had a big hand in the protection of other businesses. All of this, they did together.

Vince must be devastated. Not only would he have lost his best friend, but business partner too. This would leave the back gate ajar for trouble and everyone who was anyone would already know that.

"I'm so sorry mate...I don't know what to say..."

Vince cut him off, the last thing he wanted was pity, he couldn't stand it. "I don't need you to start spouting like me Mum's best bloody teapot, I need you to do something." Freddie bit his tongue and listened.

"It was a hit." Vince lit another cigar before continuing, "Who it was, I don't yet know. It won't have been any established firms, not around our gaff anyway. As much as they would like to get their hands on some of our assets, they definitely wouldn't want the fall out." He took a long puff as Freddie stood listening, silently. "Could have been someone we ticked off in the past, biding their time... but I doubt it. Our reputation proceeds us, always has. My guess would be that it's some young hot bloods betting on us being soft, betting on us being practically dead because we seem so old to them." His voice rose towards the end in anger. He inhaled deeply to calm himself before continuing. "Whoever it is, the fact they managed to get that close to Big Dom means they've got some sort of connection in the first place, which means that someone, somewhere, knows something."

Freddie took this in and ran his free hand through his hair in agitation. He thought before he spoke. "Right. So as of now we must assume that we and our joint firms are both on someone's hit list. We're all connected, all work together on the majority..." he paused, "give me the gories..."

"Shot. Close range. Looks like there was a struggle, he had two of his men posted in the vicinity. He was at his gaff in Soho, he'd been sorting something out at one of the clubs to do with a shipment. The other two are brown bread too. Paulie found them."

"Fuck." His younger brother Paulie was champing at the bit trying to follow in his footsteps. Freddie had fought against it for a while until he started acting out to get his brother's attention. Since then Freddie had been trying to give him work that involved him in his life - but not enough to land him in any real danger. Vince had humoured him on this, referring to it as a babysitting job. Freddie had been grateful for this, but knowing Paulie had discovered the stiffs worried him greatly. Now he'd be wanting to get more involved and that was the last thing Freddie wanted.

"I sent him on an errand. It was just to pick up a package," Vince started.

"Yeah, alright, it's just one of those things," Freddie answered. "Ok. Right." He stood up from where he had been leaning against the wall. "I'll get on it first thing tomorrow, start rounding up the usual suspects so to speak..." he tried to organise his thoughts, get back into work mode, "I won't miss anyone out - if there's information to be got, I'll get it."

"Good man. I'll be at Club 10 tomorrow night if you've got anything of interest."

"Gotcha, and Vince...? I'm sorry... He was a good man."

There was a pause before Vince spoke again in a hard voice. "He was one of the fucking best. And I'll unleash hell on the fucker that did this because of it."

Vince cut the phone off and Freddie stared at the blank wall for several minutes before picking up the phone again. It rang to voicemail.

"Paulie? Why the fuck do I not have any messages from you? You'd best be there, waiting for me at home tomorrow. Twelve sharp, ready to go." He snapped the phone shut and composed himself before walking back to the hotel room.

By the time he opened the door Anna was fast asleep, so he crept in and sat back down in the armchair. Picking up his brandy, he watched her, peaceful in her escape, a leg and an arm wrapped round the covers as if holding them close to her. He wondered what she was dreaming of. *Who* she was dreaming of. He watched her small chest rise and fall slowly with her breath. How nice it must be to sleep easy at night. He looked out the window at the sea, noting a vast change in its temperament from earlier in the day. The calm, still, glittering waters were now churning, deep and dark, as though unspeakable things lurked beneath the waves. If only he could see himself, he'd find the change mirrored in his face.

Freddie walked through the back door of the house into the kitchen. His Mother greeted him with a big smile and a hug. "Paulie said you'd be home, I 'ope you have time to eat, I've just taken a lovely joint of beef out of the oven, Yorkshires and all, just how you like em'!"

She bustled around the table and pushed him into a seat. "No arguments, a Mother has to feed her boys!"

He sat down and silently glared at Paulie, who was sat in a similar fashion at the other end. He shrugged and widened his eyes as if to say *'what?'* and Freddie just shook his head in frustration. Now was not the time for family dinners, now was the time for taking action. They had neither time nor the element of surprise on their side. Mollie, sharp as a pin, caught the interaction. "Now don't be getting mad at Paulie, he told me same as you probably want to, that you're busy today, but you can make time for food, the pair of you. You're growing boys. I won't be having you out eating trashy crap when you can have a decent meal here at home." She folded her arms across her generous bosom and shook a wooden spoon in their direction as she berated them. Freddie smiled. She was a good old girl, his Mum. The only living person within a hundred-mile radius that would dare try and have a go at him. The only one he would let.

"Just make it quick Mum, yeah? Things are looking a bit dark today, got to see a man about a dog pretty sharpish."

Mollie nodded and hurried to dish up. She wouldn't ask, he knew that. But she understood.

"Where were you off last night anyway? Thought I'd see a peep of you coming in to change or grab a bite." It wasn't a nosy question, Freddie knew, she just cared. She liked to know where her boys were, it made her feel more secure like when they were young. Old habits die hard.

"I went to the beach," he smiled through a mouthful of potatoes, waiting for her reaction to this random statement. Paulie laughed and choked on his food.

"The beach? What - in this weather?" Mollie's face was incredulous, "Are you 'aving me on, son? Why on earth would you do that?"

Paul, having recovered, chipped in. "Yeah, seriously, what made you go to the beach? A bird?" he winked, teasing.

Freddie put another mouthful in and didn't laugh. Yes, it was a bird, but the way Paulie said it got his back up. Not that Paulie was out of order exactly, that was the way they usually discussed women. Except Anna wasn't normal, she was...different.

"Is that it Fred?" Mollie prompted, interested, "Was it a girl?"

"Mum..." Freddie protested, wanting them to drop it. He felt like he was 15 again, under scrutiny.

"Well! I'm just asking! You've never once bought a nice girl back here yet, to meet me, and I'm your mother, it's natural that I'd take an interest."

"You met Sally, Mum." Paul put in wickedly, ducking as Freddie threw a piece of bread at his head.

"Yes, well…" Mollie pursed her lips, no longer smiling, "Like I said, you've never bought a *nice* girl back here. The least said about that dirty piece, the better," she sniffed.

Freddie rolled his eyes. Sally had been his high school girlfriend.

She'd come from the estate where they grew up and had seen Freddie as her ticket out of there. Sally had been pretty, and good fun at the time, all bright colours, hilarious ideas and infectious bubbliness, but eventually her roots took over. She had watched him rise through the ranks and spent her nights drunk as a skunk, dressed like a tart and clinging to Freddie like he was the last life jacket on the Titanic. When they were 18, she'd faked a pregnancy to try and manipulate him into marrying her. Taking his responsibility seriously, he had asked her to arrange an appointment so he could talk to the doctor about what to expect. She eventually broke down and told him. The moment he left her, she got herself pregnant elsewhere, got the run-down council flat next to her mother's and started sleeping with anyone for a bit of extra cash. The last he heard, most of that was being spent on having a good time down the pub flaunting her wares, and up her nose, while her little girl went without the most basic of things. After Sally, Freddie had developed a general disrespect for most women. All the girls whose eyes gleamed when they took in his smart suit and his nice car, they only wanted to use him. So *he* used *them* instead. The only women he had really respected and liked - up until now - were his Mother and sister. His Mother was a survivor and a true warrior in his eyes, the way she held it together and raised them. His sister was turning out well too: pretty, extremely quick and with an abnormally good head for numbers. She didn't miss a thing, which helped Freddie out no end with keeping tabs on his brothers.

Freddie finished his food quickly and in silence. His mother and brother had recognised that he wasn't in the mood and left well alone, discussing instead his youngest brother, who was currently away at a private boarding school. Michael was due home soon for half term and Mollie wanted to arrange a big, posh get-together with all their friends to welcome him back. The fact Freddie had paid for him to go away to such a prestigious school was Mollie's absolute crowning glory. On his first day, when Michael had first gone all shiny shoes and smart blazer, Mollie thought she would burst with happiness. She missed him terribly but saw this as a small price to pay compared to the value of such a good education and start in life for her little boy. Pushing his plate away, Freddie stood up and picked up his suit jacket.

"Thanks Mum, that was blindin'. Paulie, get moving."

Paul quickly shoveled in the last mouthful and gave his Mum a peck on the cheek before joining Freddie. They both waved goodbye with fixed smiles on their faces before turning to the car.

"Now, what the fuck happened?"

4

Tony paced the small office, listening to the youth sat in front of him with his oversized suit and high-pitched voice. Angelo had that look about him, like butter wouldn't melt, and appeared at least five years younger than he really was. He was known internally as 'Angel Face'. It was something he regularly used to his advantage. People talked in front of him, saw him as bit green and easily led. What they didn't know was that underneath his sweet and harmless exterior, there lurked a psychotic and truly dangerous young man with no moral compass and a hunger for money. Tony had him on the payroll for a good number of little jobs, most often the ones involving the dirty work. He had spotted him young and, realising his potential, had won over his loyalty, ensuring he was never without a good wedge. Dangerous little fuckers were always better onside. Right now though, he had him out scouting for Anna. The ungrateful little bitch was proving very hard to find. He fleetingly wondered if she'd ended up in a canal somewhere. His mouth flickered up into a ghost of a smile. *No*, he thought, *if she ends up in a canal, it'll be because* I *put her there*. And with pleasure at this point.

"So there's still no sign of her anywhere..." he said quietly, more to himself than to Angelo, who nodded slowly. "Nowhere." Tony's voice began to rise. "There has to be some fucking sign of her somewhere, what is she, a fucking ice cube? She didn't fucking melt, did she! Well? Did she?"

"No boss." Angelo didn't know how he was supposed to answer that, but Tony's face throbbed with thunder, glaring at him like he should have some miraculous answer. What was he supposed to say? *'No boss, she's just hiding under the kitchen sink, right near where you left her.'*? No. After a long moment, Tony exhaled loudly and went back to pacing the room again.

"No, of course she didn't. She's around here somewhere." He bit at his nails as he went over it all again, "She ain't abroad, I have someone watching for her passport to flag. She ain't working anywhere, 'cause she'd have money going into her bank and there's been nothing. She ain't even used her cards except for that once when she first left...and her car's here. She hasn't registered a new one, not taken any of the family's or friends', I've checked. So where is she?" He said this last bit to himself, looking out of the window onto the busy high street.

Angelo watched him from his chair. Tony was obsessed with this woman. He had always been possessive to a degree, liked to own things and people, but this...this was an obsession. He definitely wouldn't want to be in that bird's shoes when the boss finally caught up with her, Angelo thought to himself. And catch her he would, there was no doubt about it. Tony Christou always accomplished his goal, no matter what or who it was. He wouldn't rest or stop until he did. That was what made him so good at what he did. That was what made Tony such a successful face.

Tanya wrapped her coat more firmly around her waist. It was freezing out, her breath was lingering white on the air in front of her face. She couldn't wait to be home in front of the telly, with a huge mug of steaming tea warming her hands. It had been a long night in the club, she'd pulled a double shift again as it had been busy. Nights like these were very lucrative. She was being honest with Anna when she'd explained that it could just be dancing. You stripped off, give them a good eyeful, sat with them for the evening in your scanties. It was a technically respectable club to the outside world. There was, however, the underground option of offering more private services. Back in the old days this was up to the individual women to sort out, slinking off to seedy hotels late into the night with one of the punters, but that had resulted in too many beatings and mugging off of the girls. The manager of the club, Ellen, an older woman now way past her time as a dancer and hostess, decided to adapt the way they worked to avoid this. She lived in a spacious flat above the club, alongside the offices, one of the perks of her position. It made sense to the owners of clubs like these to have someone onsite. Rearranging her own living space, she turned two rooms into bedrooms where the girls could take the punters quietly and discreetly, and hired a minder to stand within earshot at the top of the stairs. This afforded the girls much more safety and in return, Ellen and the club took a cut of the money. It worked well for everyone.

Walking down the dark streets, Tanya felt the tight pull of her thigh muscles. She would run a bath, she decided, take away the ache. Not all of the girls went up into the back rooms with the punters, many choosing to work at this particular club because it was not an expected standard. Some nights, depending on who was working alongside her, Tanya would be one of only two or three on that sort of work. Tonight had been one of those nights. Having spent an hour with a large table of men on a stag do, eager to spend their money, Tanya had been quietly asked the golden question.

"Well..." she purred, "everything is available for the right price." She ran her long manicured nails down the top of the fat, sweaty man's thigh. He was short and round, ugly as sin, not to mention the incredibly bad breath that was assaulting her senses. But she would ignore all that. All she cared about was his money. She ran the price list off to him and awaited his response. He licked his podgy lips eagerly.

"Ok then. Me first though, then the others. I want a suck and fuck and no time restraints either."

Tanya swallowed but her smile remained, not portraying her surprise. "That price is for each 20 minutes." She gave a discreet hand signal to Ellen, who immediately sent one of the free girls to check the room was ready.

"No problem at all darlin', I've got money to burn and an appetite to feed!" he licked his lips again and then turned back to the table of equally fat and unattractive men. "Then, as a present to the stag and my fellow friends, one for each of them too." He grinned from ear to ear as they whistled and applauded him for his generosity. Tanya paled slightly but said nothing. This was what she did at the end of the day. Every second lying on her back was another second towards building a better life. So she would grin and bear it.

Five minutes later she was stripping off her already skimpy clothing in the dark red bedroom, trying not to curl her lip in disgust at the man in front of her. He was rubbing his hands together, his beady little eyes raking her body up and down.

"Oh yeah...you'll do," he grunted as he stood massaging his flaccid red penis in nothing but his socks. "I'll just get this nice and hard for you, wouldn't want to disappoint, ey?" he laughed, and motioned for her to sit on the bed. "Oh...yeah.." he grunted some more and closed his eyes. He was stood in front of her and at close range, she could smell his unwashed body and see how sticky with sweat he was underneath his boxers. She fought the urge to vomit. He opened his eyes and guided her head, forcing himself into her mouth and started grinding. After several minutes he pushed her back and pulled her legs apart.

"Pull them back," he ordered, "right back, as far as you can go. Go on, open that up for me." He ran his calloused fingers over her most sensitive parts, ogling away. Finally, he entered her and fucked her hard for just over an hour. When he was finally spent, Tanya sat there shocked at how much stamina he had for such an overweight man; her body was exhausted. Unfortunately though, this was only the beginning of a very long night and there were still seven more of them waiting for her. Each of them ensured they took full advantage of their friend's generosity, spending time and as much energy as they could muster pumping away at her in the large double bed.

Wincing, she had pulled her clothes back together and made her way slowly down the stairs. She nearly lost her balance at the top and Marvin, the minder, had grabbed her quickly and righted her gently. He caught her eye for a moment and she saw the quick flash of concern for her before he looked away. He had been aware of every second in that room and she knew he probably felt sorry for her. Nothing was said though. It just wasn't done in their world. She had to be hard to get through in this game. It was her own choice, there was nothing to be gained by going soft about it. He would never admit to feeling sorry for her either. She was just another tom.

As she walked through the cold, the pain started wearing off a bit. She wondered to herself whether Anna would be home yet. Tanya knew she had been going out for the day but Anna hadn't made it back last night. *Must have been a good night,* Tanya smiled to herself. She thought perhaps she ought to worry about her new friend and housemate, but Tanya wasn't the type to check in with anyone, so never expected anyone to check in with her. A conversation they'd had a few days before snuck unbidden into her mind.

"Have you ever been in love Tanya?" Anna had been curled up on the end of her bed as she got ready to go back out to work again. Tanya had thought about how to answer this, concentrating on applying the thick liquid eyeliner along the top of her eyelids.

"Yes. Once."

"When?"

Tanya coloured her lips a bright, blood red. Her war paint. Her daily mask. She touched her lips to some tissue, blotting off the excess colour.

"Recently."

"Was it the guy who left you in the petrol station?"

Tanya laughed, "Oh God no, not that worthless piece of shit! He was a bleedin' nightmare from start to finish. No, not him." She smiled at Anna, amused by her suggestion. Anna smiled back.

"Who then?"

"No-one you'd know. Just this guy I had a very short - but sweet - thing with." She looked at Anna, not wanting to look daft in front of her, "It was a couple of years back, way before you showed up all carpet-bag looking, with your house-car," she chuckled at the memory. "He was amazing..." her eyes glazed over as she continued, "he was something special. Had an air about him that not many men do. He was what we over this way call a face."

Anna paled visibly and sat back against the wall. Tanya stopped and turned to her.

"Mate, are you ok? You look all funny."

"No, I'm, it's fine, carry on, you were telling me what happened. What happened Tanya? Where is he now?"

Tanya frowned at this sudden intense interest. Anna certainly was an odd kettle of fish sometimes.

"He's around. The area anyway. I didn't mean anything to him." She looked down, the words hurt her as she said them, even though she tried to act nonchalant. "I was just another piece of skirt, not serious material to him. I still fell for him though, despite as much... I still loved him."

"Oh Tan, I'm so sorry..." Anna's face had regained its colour and she leant forward towards her friend.

"Nah, its ok." Tanya brushed her off, embarrassed by the heart to heart. "Anyway, I plan on showing him what's what, one day," she continued brightly. "He's the only man I ever loved and I wasn't good enough. Well, I'll show him one of these days that I can be. That he was *stupid not to see I had potential."*

"That's not true Tan, you are good enough."

"No An, I wasn't. And that's the God's honest truth. I'm an exotic dancer and that's putting it really politely—" Anna winced but Tanya continued, *"—no, I've got to* be *somebody, be able to offer someone something. It's the way the world works. That's why I'm pulling shifts night and day and saving every penny. I want to start up me own place. Become a real business woman. I'll show him. I'll show everyone."*

Snapping back to the present Tanya walked gingerly up the stairs and to her flat. Opening the door she saw the light on and happiness washed over her. Things had changed in the house since Anna had moved in. It felt like a home, like they were a family. She missed her presence when she was gone.

Anna popped her head round the bedroom door at the noise and took in her friend's weary and dishevelled demeanor. They never really talked about what Tanya did at work. Anna knew, and Tanya knew that she knew, but neither of them wanted to discuss it. Home was home. Home was peaceful.

Anna saw the bruises on Tanya's legs as she hung up her coat and averted her eyes as Tanya turned around.

"Come on, go get out of those clothes and I'll run you a bath. Your fluffy dressing gown's in the pile of clean washing on your bed."

Tanya squeezed Anna's arm gratefully and slid into the bedroom.

The next morning over breakfast, Anna looked over her cup of tea at Tanya and suddenly smiled from ear to ear like a Cheshire cat. After a minute or so, Tanya started laughing at her.

"What do you 'ave to be grinning about then ey? That bloke, I'll bet."

"Well yes, but no, not that," Anna dismissed her comment with a wave of her hand and sat forward animatedly, her eyes dancing. "I've had an idea. A brilliant one."

"O-kay... go on then," Tanya answered warily. She noted silently that for once Anna had not brushed the man comment under the rug like she was ashamed of something.

"You want to make something of yourself, right? Build up a business, get out of the club, etc, etc."

"Yeah, so what?" she shrugged, "I barely even have half of what I need to even begin thinking about starting something up."

Anna chewed on her toast slowly before answering.

"Well, what about if you had someone going into business with you? A partner, someone who'll also put up money for the venture... what would you think about that?"

"A partner? Who would do that though, who has that kind of money?" She pondered on this for a second, "You certainly don't, I've seen you being all careful and that lately, you ain't even working."

Tanya reached over and picked up another couple of bacon rashers from the serving plate Anna had laid in the middle of the table and stared at them glumly. Anna finished her corner of toast and wiped the crumbs off her hands.

"What if I said I *did*? What then?"

Anna had sat up for hours after Tanya had fallen asleep, contemplating the idea. She wanted to help her friend achieve the life she so desperately craved; each bruised and haunted look that passed across her friend's face broke her heart. It was also time to do something for herself and she had been mulling this issue over for a while.

Tanya looked at her with a frown but didn't say anything. Anna pressed further.

"I know roughly how much you have saved and I can match it. I can actually even put a little bit more if I needed to. So, I'm putting the offer to you. I'll go into business with you if that's something you're happy with. My only stipulation is that we don't open a club like the one you work in. We would have to work out something we're both happy with."

Tanya was stunned. It wasn't often she was knocked speechless but it looked like this was one of those rare times.

"An..I don't know what to say." Her mouth wavered open for a few seconds until she broke into a surprised smile, "Yes! That would be perfect, yes!" Tanya gave a little shriek and jumped up and the two of them laughed and danced round the living room.

"There's just one other small thing.."

"What?" answered Tanya, worriedly.

"Do you have a wig?"

Two days later Tony was sat watching the CCTV footage from a bank in Swindon. What on earth was she doing here, of all places? She didn't know anyone in Swindon...did she? The manager hovered nervously next to him, obviously uncomfortable with the situation. He was, however, being paid an awful lot of money just to let this man watch the cameras, and as the police weren't involved there didn't seem to be much that could go wrong.

"Do you remember her coming in?" Tony asked.

"There are a lot of people in and out of here all the time Sir, unless she's a regular client at this branch, we would have no reason to recognise her."

"Ok...so 2:34pm you say?"

"Yes sir, that's when the transaction took place - as you told me."

Tony had online access to all of Anna's accounts and checked them regularly, knowing she would have to access money at some point. She couldn't live on thin air forever. He had nearly jumped for joy on noticing she'd taken money out, and had gotten on the case quick-fast. She had withdrawn a large sum of money, so he knew this would be the only chance he would have in a long time - if she was careful. His heart had lit up then crashed into darkness once more when he thought back to what she had done. How dare she leave him? How dare she leave his home, his family? It was a disgrace, a dishonour and one he took very seriously. Tony was convinced that he loved Anna in the best way a man could. What he didn't and could never realise was that what he felt wasn't love, it was possession and a love of nothing more than control.

"Here we are, Sir." The manager leaned over and paused the image on the screen. Tony exhaled. Well, he thought, she certainly went to great lengths to change her appearance. Her hair was short and blonde and her face heavily made up. The clothes she wore were disgraceful, he shook his head in disgust. She looked like a common whore with her legs and cleavage out. Perhaps she'd been a whore-in-the-making all along. He would beat that out of her the second he had her back home.

"What's happenin' Sammy?" Freddie closed the door to the bookies behind him and turned the lock. Dressed in a dark grey suit and shirt, his face betrayed nothing under his cool and collected exterior.

"Freddie! Long time, no see mate, how've you been?" Sammy greeted him warmly. The two men walked through the back door into an office and Sammy immediately took out two tumblers from the cabinet underneath his desk. He fished out a bottle of whisky and motioned for Freddie to join him in the two comfortable chairs by the coffee table.

The bookies wasn't particularly big, looking at it from the outside. A few TVs, a couple of tables. Sammy's uncle had built it up and run it until a few years ago, when Sammy took over. Until then it had been a straight shooter, earning their family enough to be comfortable on but not much more. Sammy had seen the potential almost as soon as he started working there. The uncle and his family had lived in the same building, the flat above and the rooms out back serving as their cosy family home. As their children got older and spread their wings, moving on to university and homes of their own, Sammy's uncle and aunt grew increasingly tired and bored of London and the betting game. They had offered Sammy the chance to buy them out at a decent rate, considering he was family, and Sammy jumped at the opportunity. Having nowhere near the capital needed to fund such an investment, he'd approached Freddie with a business proposition. Freddie had put up the money for the venture, taking back part of it once Sammy was earning and becoming part-shareholder with the rest. Sammy had moved in upstairs and modified the back rooms into high-stake, illegal gambling dens, which was where most of their income now came from. He ruled his roost with an iron rod and stood for no nonsense. Freddie's input had been invaluable and word of his protection ensured that Sammy only received minimal trouble, usually from an upset client with empty pockets at the end of the night.

Over the years, the two men had built a solid friendship and although Freddie no longer spent much time there, he knew it was in safe and trustworthy hands and Sammy knew he only had to call if anything was needed. Now though, Sammy already knew why he was here. Word on the street travelled fast in their game. Sammy eased his large frame down into the chair opposite Freddie, and poured two generous helpings of whisky.

"Get that down you, mate, I reckon you need it."

"I certainly need something Sammy..." Freddie answered. "What've you heard?"

"Nothing of interest I'm sad to say...I liked Big Dom, he was a good old boy. It's a real shame. But I guess that's the occupational hazard, ain't it..." he shook his head. These things happened all the time in their line of business, but he'd always respected Big Dom. He had been one of the better gods of the underworld.

"I asked around and that, knew you'd be in, but no one knows anything. It's strange, there's been no whisper. It don't look like it's no-one we know."

This was roughly the same answer Freddie had been getting everywhere. Friend or foe, everyone he had visited was completely stumped. Stumped and worried. No-one knew this guy's motive or who was next on his list - and there *would* be a next. You didn't just gun down one of London's most prominent faces without a detailed plan and an end-goal.

"Have you been round the docks yet?"

"Yeah Sam, nothing there neither."

They both sat contemplating this. It was a weird situation, that was for sure. Freddie changed the subject, as there was obviously nothing left to discuss.

"How are things here, everything running ok?"

"Yeah, things are ticking over nicely since you last came. Willy Wanker's been trying to cause hag since we won't tick him anymore, but I gave him a little talking to a couple of days ago which seems to have shut his trap."

Freddie nodded. He had every faith that Sammy had efficiently dealt with it.

"Have a look over these, Sammy. Strictly between you and I. If you want in, you're in."

Sammy took the plain beige folder and took out the file. There were blueprints and schedules. It took his professional eye less than a minute to work out what Freddie was planning."

"Blindin' hell Freddie! Where did you get all this? You got someone inside?"

"Bent filth with a bad habit...do you get where I'm trying to go with

79

this?"

"Well, yeah." Sammy's eyes flicked over the pages as he took it in and worked it through in his head. It was a good set up as far as he could see, but he'd have to go over it in more detail before he was convinced.

"Can I keep these?"

"For tonight you can, I need them back tomorrow, that's the only copy."

Sammy nodded his understanding. You didn't want stuff like this all over the place. One copy was dangerous enough if it fell into the wrong hands. Especially when lily law came sniffing round.

Sammy pushed himself up from the chair and walked round to the back of his large pine desk. On the wall, he moved a small photo of his aunt and uncle when they were younger, and punched in a code on the security pad hidden behind. Across the room one of the cream, raised-wood panels made a soft clicking sound and popped out. Repositioning the photograph, Sammy walked across the room again, his gait unusually graceful for such a large man. He opened the door and slid the file into the steel reinforced safe and pushed the door closed, sealing it inside. From the outside, you would never guess it to be anything but a wall. Once the simply carved panel was shut, it sealed flush against the rest of the un-raised panelling, and even on close inspection you wouldn't be able to tell they were two separate pieces of wood. The room was decorated simply, in off-white and beige, with a minimalist look about it. There was no paperwork strewn across the desk, rather, stacked neatly in tidy trays to one side or tucked away in the small filing cabinets at the back of the room. Sammy liked to keep both his office and his life de-cluttered. With a clean fresh office, he found he had a clean fresh mind and so he lived by this in all areas of his life. His beige suit was elegantly cut, flattering the body he worked so hard to keep fit. Sammy also kept his offices at a temperature that would freeze most people into getting the flu. Whether that was due to the hardcore fitness regime he kept up or whether it was because he enjoyed the bite of the cold, no one knew, but they did know to wrap up while visiting him because the air conditioning was always on an Arctic setting. This was now beginning to set right into Freddie's bones, so he made to leave.

"I haven't put anyone else onto this yet. We've got time, a few months if necessary. If you want in, we'll figure out the right team together. We'll partner up on it." Rubbing his hands he headed towards the door.

"I've gotta go mate, it's cold enough to freeze the pope's bollocks off, this place. Don't know how you stand it!"

Sammy laughed, his teeth full and bright in his smile. "I'll come back up with this tomorrow after I've had a proper look. Where will you be?"

"At the club in Dean Street. I'll be there late though, come after 10." He walked out the door and the cold October air hit him like a sunny day in Spain.

5

Anna flicked through the post as she did every morning when she picked it up. This was more out of habit than anything else, no one knew she was there to send her anything. But she did glance over them to check there were no red bills coming through, or anything that looked too urgent. She hummed to herself quietly as she climbed the stairs, then stopped dead as she saw a handwritten envelope with her name on. There was no address or postmark on it, so it had definitely been dropped in by hand. She swung around and her eyes darted to the hall as if expecting Tony to materialise out of thin air. She tried to get control of her breathing as the familiar panic set in. *Come on Ann, just get up the stairs and into the flat!* Urging herself forward, she mounted the stairs shaking. She stopped. The door was open.

Did she leave it open? Yes, of course she did, she'd only run downstairs to get the post. But if whoever had posted that letter was still here, they might have slipped in whilst she was preoccupied downstairs. Her blood ran cold and her heart turned to ice. She bit her lip, trying to decide what to do. Cautiously, she retreated backwards down the stairs, being careful not to make any sound. At the bottom step she let out the breath she didn't know she had been holding in. Anna looked down at her feet and silently cursed. *Damn it, I haven't got any shoes on*. Wrapping her cardigan around her small frame, she took a seat on the top step just outside the front door, shuffling to the side so that her back was against the wall and she couldn't be seen from inside. Trembling slightly, she opened the letter, shutting her eyes for a moment before reading it.

A minute later, she burst out laughing, startling two children playing nearby. They looked at each other and shrugged. Who cared who the crazy lady was, it didn't matter as long as it didn't affect their game.

She put her hand to her chest as her heart finally slowed, and slumped back against the wall, rolling her eyes to the heavens. *Stupid girl...why on earth did I not think of Freddie?*

Pulling herself up, she tripped up the stairs and was careful to lock the door behind her. She sat on the side of her bed and read the short letter again.

Anna,

Had an amazing 24 hours with you. Are you free Saturday? I have a party to go to, would love to take you with me if you're around. You've got my number, let me know.

Freddie x

Smiling, she hugged the piece of paper to herself. Climbing up the stairs to grab the phone, she left a quick voicemail for Freddie confirming that yes, she would go, then filed the letter away in a shoebox under her bed. As she went to replace the lid, her eye caught the end of a pink satin ribbon poking out at the side. She trailed the end of her finger over it gently. She sat down and pulled it slowly out of the box and into her lap. A little girl had given it to her in hospital. That simple act of kindness had brought forth the realisation of what her life had become. What she had lost. She stroked the ribbon sadly and allowed the memories to overcome her once more.

Anna sat in the hospital wheelchair, shaking as Tony wheeled her out, roughly enough that she felt every bump and the wrath that radiated from him, but slowly enough to give the impression he was caring for her. He hissed at her as soon as there was no-one around to hear.

"You scheming little bitch. Three months pregnant and you had the fucking audacity to keep it to yourself? I bet you're blaming me for this mess, aren't you? I bet you have the fucking cheek to blame the loss of our child on me, well let me tell you this, you fucking whore – you weren't fit to carry, you murdered my child, you and your sick ways...You just wait till I get you home, you won't know what's fucking hit you."

Her body convulsed and her head swayed. She wasn't even supposed to be out yet, he had discharged her against the doctors orders. An icy chill descended on her heart. This was it. This was when she was going to die. Her body had been through too much already, she hadn't the strength to heal from this one. And this one would be bad.

The day before, Tony had lost a lot of money on a bad business decision. She knew she was in for it the second he'd walked through the door. She'd tried to stay out of his way, to get away, but that seemed to spur him on even more. Her mothering instinct had cut in and at the last minute, just as he went for her, she had bolted instead of taking it and waiting for it to stop. She might have made it the front door if she hadn't tripped, maybe even reached the gates before he caught her, but she never got that far. Falling over the edge of the rug, she had gone down and before she knew it, hard blows were raining down on her along with a torrent of abuse. She tried to curl up, to protect her baby, but he dragged her up by the wrist and delivered one last horrific kick to her stomach. She screamed out in agony as the miscarriage violently started. Blood seeped out onto the cream carpet from under her pale blue dress, and she writhed as he stood back, observing her with eyes wide.

"Ann?" he faltered, as if seeing her for the first time, "what's happening? I didn't mean it. I didn't mean it, babe." He ran his hands through his hair and tears filled his cold, dead eyes as he panicked.

His arms were almost gentle as he scooped her up from her bloody bed on the floor and ran out to the car. He put her in the back seat and strapped her in, wiping the tears of agony from her cheeks. "I didn't mean it, you know I didn't. I didn't mean it."

The concern hadn't lasted though. He turned back into his dark and vicious self as soon as he realised she had been pregnant. Rather than shoulder any of the blame, he went straight to his usual form of defence – attack.

Once he'd got her home, back behind the solid gates and big thick doors, he had beaten her to a bruised and bloody pulp, regardless of the fragile state she was in. He executed his punishment calmly and calculatedly and beat her within an inch of her life, only avoiding her stomach, to ensure she didn't actually bleed to death. Only once she passed out, her skin turned ashen, did he finally take her back to hospital with the explanation that an ex-boyfriend was responsible. In his version of events of course, he had stepped in and saved the day in the nick of time. The story was thorough and his lies silken. Within minutes, Tony was being comforted by the nurses and labeled a hero.

It was three days later, as she lay on the hospital bed, that a little girl had wandered into her room.

"Why are you so sad, lady?" her innocent voice had carried through the haze of shock that Anna was still in. She turned her head painfully and tried to talk through her swollen lips.

"I just am, princess." She tried to smile but couldn't quite make it reach her eyes. The little girl swung slowly from side to side, absentmindedly, and bit her bottom lip as her eyes swept over Anna's wounds.

"I think you're sad because you are hurt."

Anna blinked slowly. Out of the mouth of babes.

"I think you're right."

They stayed there in companionable silence for a moment, contemplating each other. Anna was surprised her appearance didn't scare the little girl, but then in the innocence of childhood it is often easier to look beyond certain things.

"I was poorly with chicken pox a little while ago. That made me sad."

She chewed her lip and looked around the room, still swaying from side to side.

"But my friends bought me some pretty things to look at which made me cheer up a bit. Don't you have any friends?" she turned her wide blue eyes back to the lady in the bed.

"Not around here, unfortunately. My friends are a long way away now..." she answered softly. The little girl didn't answer for a minute and then stepped forwards slowly, pulling one of the two pretty ribbons out of her hair.

"Well then I'll be your friend today and you can have this, because this is pretty. Maybe you could put it in your hair or maybe around your *wrist so you can see it."* She placed it in Anna's hand and closed it, her pink, chubby little hands warm around Anna's thin lifeless ones.

Tears sprang to Anna's eyes at the innocent gesture.

"Thank you," she whispered emotionally, *"I think that's made me feel a lot better already."*

A woman's voice wafted through into the room and the little girl turned.

"That's my Mummy," she whispered conspiratorially, *"I'm supposed to be sat in the hall and not bothering people. I'd better go."* She walked towards the door and then turned at the last minute, *"Sorry if I bothered you, I hope you feel better soon."*

"No—" but the girl had gone, *"—you didn't bother me at all,"* Anna whispered to herself. She fell asleep that night with tears wet on her cheeks, clutching the pale pink ribbon and yearning for a child that, twistedly, she knew was better off now in heaven.

Saturday came around surprisingly swiftly for Freddie. He had spent most of the week hitting his head against the proverbial brick wall and was still at a complete loss as to what was going on. It definitely wasn't anyone they had regular connections with, he would most definitely have routed that out by now with the thoroughness he was practising. It wasn't any of the Southend firms that they dealt with, he had gone through all the usual channels at that end. They certainly wouldn't want to upset the natural order of things anyway, they made a hefty wedge each week dealing with Freddie and Vince, and they wouldn't want to deal with any of the hag that came with taking on further ground.

He lit a cigarette and sat on the low brick wall surrounding his Mother's front garden. Paulie put the front door on the latch and joined him soon after. Freddie offered him a smoke and he lit up too, almost burning his hand with the match. They sat in silence for a few minutes, both turning over in their minds the strange lack of information they had gleaned so far. Paul exhaled slowly.

"So, let's go over what there is left then."

"That leaves the hundreds of small timers and the civilians Paul, we could spend a decade sifting through that shit pile and not get anywhere." He flicked his cigarette butt away in disgust.

"Yes. You're right. But it don't look like we have a lot of choice, does it really? So where do we start?"

Freddie smiled sadly to himself. Paul was getting more and more involved every day. In a way this was perfect, there was no one he could trust more than his own brother to be his number two, blood always came up on top. But it was also saddening to know that it was his fault alone that Paul was now only really fit for a life of heavy crime.

"I suppose we start looking at the firms that deal in other lines of work, first off. Maybe they know something. Though they've always stuck to their side of things before."

"Who like? What other lines of work are there?" Paul looked genuinely confused and Freddie rolled his eyes.

"Seriously Paul?" he shook his head. His brother never used his common sense. "Look around you. We supply the girls, the clubs, the spirits, the cocaine and the weed to various businesses and the general public. We import weapons, we supply protection. We own property for various purposes. We stick to the East and West Ends."

"Well, more than that Fred, there are the bookies, the yards—"

"Yes Paul, I could stand here all bleedin' day running off all the pies we have our fingers in. But what about all the rest of it?"

"The rest of what, Fred?"

"How about the other stuff on the street that we don't touch, like brown, crack, meth?"

"Oh.."

"What about loan sharking? What about the European girls that get shipped here and get tom'd unwillingly? What about protection outside of our area? There's loads of things going on Paul, I could be here all day naming them." He lit another cigarette and Paul followed suit. "Most of it is stuff we wouldn't touch with a barge pole, which is why we live in peace with the guys that do." He blew out his smoke, making an O shape with his mouth. "They don't piss on our cornflakes, we don't shit on theirs. Some of it, they had fair and square - before we wanted it, so—" he shrugged, "—we aren't unfair."

"Right...Ok..." Paul took this in and nodded to himself. He probably should have realised that without Freddie having to point it out. He felt a bit stupid now. He knew that he didn't have the same mental speed and thought-processes as Freddie. He always thought of everything, did Freddie. No detail was left unplanned, nothing slipped passed his acute awareness. It was what had helped get him to the revered position he was in now, what made him so good at his job. Ever since he could remember, Paul had tried to emulate his older brother, tried to walk like him, talk like him, dress like him. More than anything, he wanted to be as good as Freddie was in business and with people, but he knew that this was his failing point. Whereas Freddie always knew what to say and could read deeper into any situation, Paul could only ever see the black and white picture that was put in front of him. He wasn't as sharp as his older brother. Despite this, he ran around doing everything they asked of him, determined that one day he would at least become a valuable asset. One day he would make his brother proud to have him standing up there beside him.

"There are a fair few places and people to cover." Paul tuned back into the conversation, it wouldn't do to forget what Freddie was saying; he hated repeating himself.

"There are the yardies down south who run the hot dogs, ice creams and also act as one of our weed outlets."

Paul snorted, "Hot dogs and ice creams?" he asked incredulously.

"Yes." Freddie snapped, looking him in the eye, "Don't laugh at things you don't know nothing about. It might sound soft but the set-up is a bloody good one by all accounts. The turfs are controlled illegally and it's actually a good little earner. Let's just say you would think twice before attempting to turn that one over."

"Oh, ok." Paul mentally shrugged to himself. If Freddie said so...

"The Jews over in the West End – technically our ground, but we let them trade on it. Their game is some money laundering, scrap, blood diamonds and hot jewellery... Then there are the Turks, who deal mainly in heroin and crack. They have some toms lurking, but nothing major – that's more the scraggy end of the market. The Albanians... their business is the girls they bring over from Europe. They get pimped out, massage parlours and red light houses etc. Unfortunately it's not their choice. They have a few good hit men, but then all of us do really..." he trailed off, lost in thought for a moment. "Then you have the Greeks in the north, they hold the monopoly up there on gambling dens, laundering and loan sharking. They dabble in chemicals, but their preference is always set-ups to do with hard brass. A few bank jobs too... they bankroll a lot of the insiders, deal with a lot of large fraud set-ups."

They stopped talking as Thea tripped up to the front gate on her way home.

"What are you two brooding over, you look like a pair of slapped arse cheeks," she stooped and gave both her brothers a hug and a kiss on the cheek. She loved her brothers to death and they loved her right back.

"Nothing, you cheeky little mare." Freddie playfully slapped the back of her legs as she went up the path. "Go help Mum, she's preparing to feed the five thousand." Thea rolled her eyes and they both laughed. She gave Freddie a quick look before she went in. He nodded slightly. She smiled. He would tell her later then. Thea had privately been looking after the financial side of things for Freddie for a while now. She had been nosing around in his room once – which she had been strictly told never to do – and found his barely legible books. Thea was already well-aware of Freddie's profession, she was sharp like her brother and fast on the uptake. Open ears, closed mouth. That was how she grew up. By the time Freddie came home, she had sorted the books out into a basic and easier format and had written notes suggesting ways he can make them look more legit, should he ever need to prove anything. Freddie had been livid. He very rarely raised his voice, he never needed to, but his bellowing that night made her jump right out of her skin, and she ran and hid under her covers sobbing in shock. A few minutes later he had come into her room and she froze, wary, scared that he was going to go crazy again. Instead he sat down quietly, comforting her until her sobs subsided. He had given her a stern talking to, reminding her never to delve into his personal things again uninvited, but then he had asked her to go over her work with him in the confines of her room. Having seen sense in her advice, they worked together, creating a second set of accounts that showed most of his money going through his legitimate businesses, then hiding the rest where it could not be found. Over time, Thea had fully entered into his world on-paper, and was now more aware than anyone of the inside workings. He grudgingly respected her business sense and kept her up to date on everything that was happening. Up to now, this strange business alliance had been kept between the two of them; Freddie was sure that his Mother would not approve and he didn't want anyone else in his world made aware that she was not a pure civilian. Civilians were untouchable, out of bounds to anyone looking to take out any grievances. While Thea was seen as a civilian, she was relatively safe.

"There you are! Right, grab a pinny love, I've got so much going on in here I don't know where the food ends and I begin!" Mollie flustered around the kitchen, swinging her arms in the air, her round face reddened from the heat of the Aga. There were trays everywhere spread with baked goods, party food, various meats both cooked and uncooked. Mollie bent down and took another tray out, the golden tops of the cheese scones making Thea's stomach rumble in protest.

"Have you not eaten yet, young lady?"

"No Mum, I haven't had time today. They look amazing, I think perhaps I should try one, just to make sure they're ok..." Mollie swatted Thea's hand away and she grinned.

"Oh, go on Mum, just one..."

"Oh, go on with you! Just one. These are my Michael's favourite, I want there to be plenty left for him later on." Mollie's face lit up as she talked about her youngest son and Thea's heart filled with love for her mother. Mollie loved all her children with a passion. No matter what hardships they faced when they were younger, their mother's love was something they never lacked. Although she was fit to burst with pride at the fact her son was at such a prestigious school, Thea knew Mollie missed having him here at home with her. The last time they had seen him was in the summer holidays. He had started his first term at Easter and had come home in the summer, bursting with animated tales of his new life. At first he'd written a letter home every week, but for the last few months that had trailed off. Mollie had just shrugged it off and put on a brave face. "Well," she said, "he must be busy having fun and learning all these new things, you can't blame him for not finding time to write to his silly old Mum now. Young boys don't want to do that these days."

Personally, Thea thought it was out of order, that he was being ungrateful for the charmed life he had been handed. Though, she reasoned with herself, he hadn't really known how bad they used to have it. He had been blissfully unaware while he was an infant, and then Freddie had dragged them all out from the gutter way before he was old enough to understand. He didn't really realise what they had been through as a family. Hunger and desperation were a driving force. It was a darkness that, once touched, you ran from for the rest of your life.

"When is he getting here, Mum?" Thea asked through a mouthful of scone.

"In a few hours. Paulie's picking him up from the station. Everyone needs to be here for 6, he'll get here just after. Oooh, I hope he likes the spread, I've done all the things he likes." Mollie looked around at the food, excitement marred with anxiety on her face.

"Mum, he'll love it," Thea said gently, "don't worry yourself."

"I hope so, love. Really want it to be perfect for him."

Freddie and Paulie pulled up outside a block of grey, dingy flats. The desperation of this place seemed to seep out of every pore. They locked the car and walked up the stairs to a shabby front door. Freddie nodded and Paulie booted the door in easily, the wood rotten and brittle. The stagnant smell of bodily odor and chemicals hit them as they crossed the threshold. They walked into the lounge where a greasy young man with a twitch now cowered into a corner. He just stared at them, mouth gaping, revealing a set of yellowing teeth.

Freddie took an exaggerated look around the room.

"Lovely gaff you've got here David. Lovely. Love what you've done to the place."

The man seemed to find his voice as he stood up, warily eying the two well-dressed men in front of him.

"Well, I wasn't really expecting company..."

"Really David?" Freddie cut in, a cold smile on his face, "That surprises me. If I were you, I would have been expecting visitors, wouldn't you Paulie?" he turned to his brother.

"Oh yes," Paulie answered immediately, no emotion crossing his hardened features. "I would definitely have expected visitors, Fred."

"Hm." They looked at him expectantly, waiting.

"L-look guys, I can explain—"

"—explain what exactly David? Explain why you are treating Vince, therefore me, therefore my brother here, like cunts?" David flinched.

"It weren't like that Freddie, I'm getting it, I just need a bit of time—"

"—you've had time David. You've had time, you've had money and you've had trust. Three things that we expect to be respected and all three of which you have badly *dis*respected."

Freddie paced slowly across the room and studied the cheap, faded print hanging on the wall. The only picture in the sparse, depressing room.

"Do you like boats, David?"

"W-what?"

"The picture," he pointed at it. "Do you like boats?"

"Um, n-no, not really..."

"Oh, why's that then?"

"I d-don't like water. Can't swim."

Freddie turned and beamed at him, feigning interest.

"No, really?"

"Um, yeah, I never learnt." David leaned on the side of the armchair, not really sure where this was going.

"Would you say the thought of drowning scares you, David?"

David shrank back and started to hyperventilate.

"Oh David, I'm not going to drown you!" Freddie laughed. "Would you look at that Paulie, the geezer thinks I'm going to drown him!"

"I don't know why he would think that Fred, why would you want to drown him?"

"I don't know Paul, why would you think I want to drown you, David?" Freddie's laughter died and his eyes glinted like steel as he stared at the trembling man.

"I asked you a question David, why would you think I want to drown you?"

David tried to swallow the lump gathering in his throat as his eyes darted from one to the other.

"I-I know that I-I haven't delivered F-Freddie."

"No. You haven't. But you are going to, David. And I am going to tell you how. But first of all, I wanted to show you something new I learnt."

He pulled a pair of leather gloves out of his pocket and put them on, pressing them into the creases of his fingers with care. Paulie followed suit.

"Did you watch that film the other night, Paul? That one with the rogue FBI guy they had to sort out?"

Paul looked up to the ceiling as he considered.

"Nope, can't say I did Fred." He shook his head.

"Aw, you should have mate, it was blindin'. You learn all sorts of things from these films. For example," he moved one of the least broken, old wooden dining chairs into the middle of the room, "did you know you can make a man feel like he is drowning without actually doing it?" he looked expectantly at his brother as David started moaning in fear.

"Nope, didn't know that Fred. How's that then?"

"Well..." he walked into the kitchen and rummaged in the cupboards until he found a large bucket, then started filling it up from the grimy sink. "I'll show you. Tie him to the chair. Arms back."

David cried out and Paul silenced him with a resounding slap around the face.

"Shut it Dave. You give us shit and you'll come out worse, you got that?"

94

Paul pushed his face into that of his unwilling ward and David nodded, tears now making track marks down the dirt on his face. Paul grimaced.

Freddie came back into the room as Paul finished tightening the cable ties which now bound David's wrists and arms to the chair. He was lugging a bucket full of water and spilled some down the front of his trousers as he set it down.

"Aw shit...look what you made me do, David! Now I'm going to have to change before my brother's party tonight and I really like this suit and all..."

"That's a good point actually Fred," Paul pulled back his glove to steal a glance at his watch, a titanium contraption that had cost him an arm and a leg, but of which he was incredibly proud. "I haven't got long before I have to go get Mickey from the station."

Freddie frowned his annoyance at Paul, who immediately shut his trap.

"So!" Freddie clapped his hands together as if performing to an audience. "What we do now is this..." He dunked an old towel that had seen better days in the water a couple of times until it was sodden. David's eyes were agog, watching the slow, deliberate action.

"Hold the chair back so he can see the ceiling, Paul." Paul did as he was bidden and David tried to hold back the guttural moans that were coming from his throat. He was terrified. He knew that half of his fear was from not knowing what these two very cold, deadly serious men had in store for him. He'd fucked up big time. He kicked himself mentally as he tried to keep quiet. What on earth had he been thinking, messing around with the business of people like this? He hadn't been thinking, that was the problem. He had hidden his problem with cocaine and gambling pretty well, keeping his lines of access well away from his own doorstep. Obviously Vince and Freddie had been aware that he liked a flutter and a snort, but they had no reason to be worried, David had never been a big customer as far as they were concerned. There had been a large cocaine shipment in and once the usual outlets had been stocked, there was quite a lot left over. Needing to move the goods on, they offered David an in. Up until now they had used him to gain information, as he seemed to have his ear on many a rat-infested floor. He had been trying to get their attention for other employment for years. The instructions had been sent to him along with a large amount of the illicit product. All he had to do was cut it, sell some of it off, and keep the rest of it hidden until they sent someone round to get it, which would happen once one of their usual suppliers ran out. Instead, David had gotten high. Very fucking high indeed. After a week-long bender, he thought he could get away with cutting it more than usual to pad it out and hopefully smooth over what he had used himself. As if that wasn't bad enough, when he'd started selling it, he couldn't believe how much money he was making! As with all suppliers, he was told to keep a certain percentage and put the rest away, ready for collection. Somehow in a haze of chemicals, gambling dens and girls who suddenly found him incredibly attractive, David had spanked the lot. Waking up one morning sober, ill and cleaned out of every penny he had taken, he realised exactly what he had done. He was brown bread, of that he had been sure. When the brothers – incidentally, his worst nightmare - had walked through the living room door, he thought he was a goner. Now, however, he didn't know what to think. By the sounds of it, it didn't look like they were here to kill him. He was in for something, but what that was he didn't know. If he was honest with himself, he wasn't sure which was going to be worse.

Freddie put the wet towel over his head and held it taut at the neck. David couldn't breathe.

"And now Paul, put your hands where mine are—" David felt the change of pressure and squeezed his eyes closed. "—and we do this..."

Freddie poured the water over David's head and Paul shifted position to stop the chair from toppling over completely as their victim struggled.

After what seemed like an eternity, but which in reality was only fifteen seconds - counted carefully by Freddie, he stopped and whipped the towel off a now hysterical David.

"Sit him up." Paul pushed the chair up unceremoniously and David started crying like a baby.

"Shut up you cunt!" Freddie slapped him hard around the face and David struggled to contain his reactions.

"What did you think of that then, Paul?" he shifted his attention to his brother, appearing interested in his opinion. Paul however, did not look hugely impressed.

"Well, all you did was pour a bit of water over the fucker." He shrugged and shook his head, conveying his bewilderment. Freddie smiled.

"Nah, it's not just that. The towel see, apparently if you do that and then pour water, it tricks the body into thinking it's actually drowning. They use it as a torture method in the special forces."

"Oh.. ok.. is that right though, does it actually work like that?"

"I don't know, first time I've tried it, let's ask dick-head here. What did that feel like? Did you feel like you were drowning?"

All David could manage was a nod. The experience had been horrific.

"I don't think he's sure Paul, let's do it again."

"Please – no —'' they stifled his cries with the towel and repeated the process.

Six goes later, they appraised the quivering, barely conscious wreck in front of them. Freddie sighed loudly to himself and looked out the window.

"Best get on with the finale then Paulie. I'll meet you at the car."

"What?" Paulie frowned at him, annoyed to be asked to leave.

"Car please Paul. Get the engine started, I won't be long." Freddie commanded quietly and turned on the steely glare that made many a grown man's blood run cold. Paul nodded his acceptance and turned towards the door without another word. They all knew who was boss in this firm, blood relation or not.

David convulsed, still tied to the chair. Freddie set his mouth in a grim line and turned back towards him.

"You know, in most countries they kill traitors right off. They still do here, technically, though only if it's against the Queen..." he sauntered to the kitchen and rifled through the drawers until he came across a steak knife, blunt and dull from years of use.

"And we were all for killing you too David, we would be within our rights to. Street law of course. But you fucked off a nice little wedge of our hard-earned brass, not to mention our product and we want compensation. So here is what's going to happen." He sat back on his haunches and turned the chair towards him so that they were face to face.

"I'm leaving you with this lesson, along with a reminder that you never – *ever* – even begin to think about mugging us off like cunts again. Do you understand me?"

David nodded as hard as he could.

"Good. Now. You are going on a little trip. A little holiday let's say. You're smuggling a load of gear across one of the European borders I'm having a little trouble with. In fact, you are going to be going on several little holidays, doing the same thing."

David's face paled even more.

"You'll be watched, so you can't pull any fucked up stunts again – trust is not something you are being handed back. When you've completed what I want completing, you'll be bought back. You won't be paid and you won't be employed this side of London again." He looked him up and down in disgust, "but you won't be dead either. You can call it payback."

Picking up a tea towel from where he had left it on the sofa in anticipation, Freddie stuffed it into David's mouth.

"Now. The lesson you've had. The reminder is about to come. Vince didn't want you losing your memory any time soon." He looked at the knife before putting it against David's cheek. "We thought a 'T' on your ugly mug would perhaps remind you not to be such a treacherous little cunt in future."

The end of the knife bit into his skin, held taut by the gag in his now screaming mouth. Freddie cut deeply and quickly, before throwing the chair back against the sofa. Cutting the cable ties off David's hands, he pushed him onto the cushioned surface. He threw the knife into a corner and walked towards the door.

"You'll want to get that seen to mate. Your knife was rusty, God knows what infections you'll get from that. Oh, and don't bother running. You'll be off on your holidays next week, give that time to heal. We'll be in touch."

As he walked out of the building he took a minute to breathe in the cleaner air, and closed his eyes. It was all part of the life, he knew that, it had to be done. But he didn't have to like it. Mostly, he ruled his empire on respect and fear. He had established his reputation early on, stories still made the rounds through the pubs and clubs, and as such he didn't have to get his hands dirty too often. He found that threats and implied threats worked wonders if the need arose. But every so often someone took the piss. When this happened, everyone watched to see what they were going to do about it. If nothing was done, the firm would look soft and it would be an invitation for any Tom, Dick or Harry to have a go at taking over. They would be a running joke. That couldn't happen. Especially at the moment with a rogue hitman on the loose, who no one knew anything about and who was pointing his unfortunately effective efforts directly at them.

Squeezing the bridge of his nose, Freddie took a deep breath and headed for the car. As he closed the door, he turned to Paul.

"I'll drop you home; get changed and go get Mickey. I'll be round for six."

"Where you off?"

"Seeing a man about a dog. I'll be there for six," he repeated in a clipped tone. Paul mentally rolled his eyes. Freddie was a closed book, with friends and family alike. Although his worlds ran parallel, he disliked mixing them. This was often confusing to Paul, who was very much present in both Freddie's home and professional life. On a daily basis he ran with both the warm, humorous and family-orientated man and then the cold, efficient and dangerous businessman whose company he was keeping now. It was often hard to keep up with which personality was currently in play. He made a mental note to work on becoming better at switching game faces, just like Freddie.

6

Anna's jaw figuratively dropped when she saw Freddie walking up to the building. He had this effect on her now, she couldn't work out how to turn it off, how to go back to just being indifferent. It unsettled and excited her at the same time. His crisp white shirt was fitted perfectly to his sculpted body and the suit that accompanied it was obviously the finest money could buy. But it was more than that. Anyone could buy expensive things, money was available to anyone with half a brain cell if they used it. But Freddie always dressed with quiet class. And that was what Anna noted. Turning to the mirror, she quickly pinched her cheeks and then giggled at herself unexpectedly. She clamped a hand to her mouth. That was another thing, she found herself doing and saying things out of the ordinary around this guy. Pursing her lips, she scolded herself for the umpteenth time and smoothed the front of her pale pink wrap dress. It was a simple cut, as was her style, flattering her curves, cinching in at the waist. Reaching just to the knee, the dress made her look slightly taller than she was too, which she was secretly very pleased about. She would never be competing with the catwalk models, that was for sure. At 5'3'', nearly everyone dwarfed her. The material shimmered over the lines of her body as she walked away to open the door.

Freddie walked round to open the passenger door as they pulled up in front of his Mother's house. Though the street was now littered with cars - nobody having turned down the chance to be able to say they'd been to a party at the Tyler household - the space directly outside remained empty. No-one would ever take that spot whilst they could see his car was not yet here. This was a fact barely registered by Freddie now, though if someone did take it, it would certainly jump out at him. It was a mark of the general respect he was now afforded that this was an everyday occurrence.

How handy, Anna mused to herself. *Someone must have just left.*

Freddie had explained to her on the way over that it was a family event for his youngest brother, home from boarding school. It was also a belated birthday bash too, as the family had not been able to see him at the time, due to it being halfway through term. At first Anna was surprised that he'd invited her, surely this was far too intimate to invite a new friend, practically a stranger? He then, however, went on to explain that a lot of his friends and business associates would be there too, and she berated herself again for reading into things that weren't there.

Freddie got to the front door and frowned at his own nervousness. This was ridiculous! He automatically reached for Anna's hand, then pulled away at the last minute. He cursed to himself. He had to stop doing that. Apart from the one time at the beach, where all her defences and cautions blew away in the wind, she naturally shied away from him. He didn't take offence at this, it seemed she was like this with everyone. But the one thing he didn't want to do was scare her away. He didn't let himself dwell on the cause of these actions - that would just drive him crazy, and he didn't have time for crazy. He knew without having to be told that Anna had been damaged somehow. She hid it well for the most part. Most people would never guess it. But it screamed out of all the little unconscious gestures. And until such a time as she was willing to invite him in, he wouldn't push her. It was a case of the slowly-slowlys with this fascinating creature and, for once in his life, that didn't turn him off.

Anna, registering his gesture, raised up her hand to meet his, but just before her fingers reached his, he pulled them back. She looked up at the side of his face and saw him curse silently to himself. Her heart dropped through the bottom of her stomach. *Christ, why does that hurt so much?* she exclaimed inwardly to herself. Anna's natural reaction to any unbidden emotion was to blank her face. It was an action she wasn't conscious of, one which had started out as self-preservation. As it was, when Freddie turned to smile at her, no emotion marred her pretty face until she forced a smile to match his.

Mollie practically burst with excitement as her Freddie walked through the door with a beautiful young woman in tow. She had been privately praying to Jesus for Himself to find 'her Freddie' a nice girl to settle down with, and now look! She nodded to herself in agreement. Yes, the Lord was good to her. She had to be careful though, not push it and embarrass the poor boy, or her. If she was as nice on the inside as she looked on the outside, then it was just a matter of time. She nodded to herself again, this time in approval at the girl's attire. Yes, very nice. Pretty and fashionable, but not these awful gaudy fashions and not some tight, cheap piece of material barely covering her nipples and knickers, as seem to be the trend with young girls these days. The girl's hair was shiny and natural, falling in waves around her shoulders. The rich darkness of her hair made Mollie remember the days when her own hair used to be her crowning glory. Though white through and through now, it was still thick and she patted it into place now, absentmindedly. She waited patiently while Freddie was greeted respectfully by all the guests as he made his way through the throng towards her. Many of those invited were here to show respect to Freddie and his family, it was the way things were done. She didn't really mind what their reasons were, it was a fantastic turn out for her Michael. The young woman looked slightly puzzled at the attention Freddie was getting, but stayed one step behind him and kept her own counsel. That was a good thing, Mollie thought, the last thing Freddie needed was some loud-mouth Suzie drawing attention to herself. He stopped and introduced her to some people along the way and when that happened, she would smile widely and greet them politely. Good manners. Mollie mentally chalked another one up for her. By the time the pair actually got to her in the kitchen, she had already decided to like Anna, very much. Unless of course, she gave her good reason not to.

"Mum, this is Anna, a friend of mine...and Anna, this is my infamous Mother Mollie." He flashed a big roguish grin and put his arm around her. Mollie laughed and pushed him off.

"Oh, get on with yer! Infamous indeed..." But she blushed just the same, secretly pleased at the comment.

"Just don't get on the wrong side of her when she's got hold of a rolling pin – I'm telling you, she's scarier than Freddy Krueger on steroids!"

Anna burst out laughing with the rest of the room, as Mollie hit out at him with the tea towel she was carrying. Freddie backed away with his hands up in mock fear.

"Oh you!" Mollie narrowed her eyes, attempting a murderous glance and failing to hide her grin, before turning her attention back to Anna. Anna quickly composed herself and smiled politely.

"It's lovely to meet you, Mrs Tyler." She held her hand out, but Mollie batted it aside.

"None of that love, come here and give me a hug"

Anna's eyes widened in shock as Mollie pulled her into a hug. But the shock was pleasant and she hugged the lovely, motherly woman back. It felt so good just to hug someone. It had been so long since she'd had a cuddle with her own mother. She felt tears begin to prick her eyes and forced them back, not willing to make a spectacle of herself in front of all these people.

Mollie noticed the change. After a stiff start, Anna had gripped her tightly as if she were a lifeboat. She waited until Anna let go first. Bless the poor girl. That she would cling to such a small piece of affection! Mollie wondered why that was, but didn't say anything.

Across the small space, leaning against the table, Freddie had also noticed the exchange. He had watched as, after her initial surprise, Anna had melted into his Mother and hugged her back fiercely. She had her eyes closed and for a few split seconds she had accidently let go of her armour. Naked emotion played across her face, showing him all he needed to know. He saw her sadness, her loneliness. He guessed that she missed her own mother and that the heartfelt embrace with his had just accentuated that. Her eyes opened and she blinked rapidly. His eyebrows rose in shock. She was close to tears.

Suddenly she pulled back and smiled widely at Mollie.

"It's so lovely to meet you, thank you so much for having me here in your home," she said brightly.

"Don't be silly love, it's nice to have my Freddie bring someone over that isn't six foot, surly and dodgier than a jammy biscuit!"

The men within hearing distance of her just grinned at each other. They knew she loved them really. It was a case of the-more-the-merrier in this household, and Freddie's men were more than used to being told to wash their hands and sit down for dinner if they had to pop round to sort out a bit of business. She would never take no for an answer either. If they tried, she would shoot them down with a look and tell them that they weren't big enough that she couldn't call their mothers if they didn't do as they were told. They all humoured Mollie, because each and every one of them loved her like their own mums. Even if that wasn't the case, Freddie was fiercely protective of his Mother and none of them would so much as entertain the idea of disrespecting her.

Freddie did a quick shake of his head. The change in Anna was so swift that he wasn't sure for a minute if he hadn't just imagined it all. She smiled up at him now, perfectly happy and reserved as usual. Freddie's phone rang and he shouted over the mixture of conversations to get everyone's attention.

"He's coming into the road now guys, everyone quiet and get ready to scare the shit out of him." Everyone laughed and then quieted quickly as Mollie rushed to turn the light off.

Paulie racked his brains to find something to say to the young man sitting next to him in the car. He was like a stranger. At 16 years of age now, he had shot up and seemed like a completely different person than the young, pink-cheeked lad they had sent off less than a year ago. Paulie knew that conversation had never been his strong point, but had tried his hardest with his young brother, racking his brains for interesting things to ask him about. Before, when Mickey lived at home, he would ask a couple of questions and then listen to his boyish rambles for hours, just happy to let him talk. That was how it had always gone. Paulie always preferred to be listening than having to talk himself. Otherwise he got all awkward. But although he had asked how Mickey was doing and how school was, the answers he got seemed to be short and clipped, with no expansion. He was at a loss as to how to carry the awkward conversation forward. They pulled up in the road and started to walk towards the door. Paulie took Mickey's bag from the boot, as he seemed to have forgotten it. He saw his younger brother look around himself at the street, his expression unfathomable. He looked around too. It was probably nice to see it again after all this time. Mickey was probably taking it all in.

"I guess you probably missed all this, didn't you?" There was no answer. He wasn't sure Mickey had heard. Probably just lost in thought. "Well," he said awkwardly, "we all missed you. It's nice to have you home mate."

Mickey didn't answer him, but headed towards the door. Paulie was puzzled, but just shrugged. Kids.

Opening the door now, he gently pushed Mickey through it. The lights flicked on and there was a roar as everyone yelled *'surprise!'* in unison. Party poppers went off everywhere, covering Mickey and Paulie too in the process. The music came on from somewhere and everyone rushed forward towards the shocked young man, Mollie front and centre. Paulie shrugged off the streamers and quickly stowed the big bag in the coat cupboard under the stairs, before gravitating towards Freddie as usual. Mollie had her youngest son clasped to her bosom, tears in her eyes, telling him over and over how much she missed him and loved him and that she hoped he liked the surprise. Freddie eventually prised him away and ruffled his hair, happy to see him too.

"Come on Mum, share with the other kids! Hello mate, how have you been?!" He appraised the young man before him and grasped his shoulders, "Crikey you've grown, Mick! You're almost as tall as me! Dressing pretty sharply too – good man. No doubt you'll be breaking some hearts soon if you haven't started already!"

Mickey smiled tightly up at Freddie before turning towards the crowd of people and scanning their faces to see if he recognised anyone. There were a few he knew, family and that. He twisted gently out of Freddie's grasp and moved through the crowd slowly, stopping as people hugged and talked loudly at him, excited by his presence. Mollie bustled after him, staying right behind, talking at ten to the dozen the entire way through the front room. Freddie stayed where he was and observed their slow progression, his poker face back to its natural countenance. Something was wrong with Mickey, badly wrong. He hadn't uttered a word since he came through the door, didn't even hug his overjoyed Mum back. He hadn't answered Freddie either, which was not only rude, but secretly hurtful. He had genuinely missed his baby brother, thought about him all the time. He often indulged himself in wondering what innocent boyish pranks they would get up to in that school. It wouldn't be half as bad - or dangerous - as the things he himself used to get up to, because that school was for boys from a better background. The fun they would get up to would be things like pulling tricks on their teachers in the middle of the night, leaving itching powder in their beds, that sort of thing. The sort of light-hearted, fun things that Freddie had read about in books when he was young. Not that anyone knew about his passion for books, that little gem would have made him a laughing stock, but he had enjoyed them in secret, after-hours when the lights were off, with a cheap torch under the covers. But now Mickey was back, and in place of a boy full of laughter and chatter and tales of his adventures, there was a sullen, uptight stranger in their house. It was strange. Something was most definitely up. Freddie idly hoped that it wasn't a case of bullying. Mickey might be considered an oddity with his East End accent and loud personality next to the finesse and fine breeding that would encompass 99.9% of the rest of the school. But with his usual cheeriness and sharp wit, Freddie hadn't counted on it taking five minutes to win the other boys round and settled himself firmly into place. He would leave it for tonight and figure it out tomorrow, give the boy time to settle in. No good harassing the poor mite the minute he walked through the door. Paulie sidled up to Freddie and followed his eyes. He scratched his head and squinted, trying to figure out how to voice his own confusion. Freddie glanced across to him then back to the figures now in the kitchen.

"S'ok mate. Spotted."

"Ah, 'k." Paulie blew out a relieved breath. Freddie would figure it out. Freddie would deal with it.

Just a little too late, Freddie saw Thea swoop in on Anna. She had been standing to the side, watching everybody greeting Mickey. She didn't attempt to join in, just seemed to be enjoying the general hubbub around her. There was a relaxed smile on her face and a glass of bubbly that someone must have placed in her hand when Mickey arrived. Freddie loved it when she was like this. Unguarded. Thea started chatting animatedly to Anna and led her by the arm through to the back of the kitchen. Anna's face flashed with a quick flicker of surprise at being singled out, then the smooth shutters clamped down and a calculatedly polite, friendly mask took its place. She went along with Thea before Freddie was able to intervene. He cursed himself under his breath. He hadn't really thought things through with regards to the invite he had issued to Anna. He had meant to speak to his Mum and Thea, explain that she was a bit of a closed book and not to push her, but with one thing or another he'd forgotten he needed to mention it. It didn't need a mention the other way. No one in his family would willingly venture information about his life in the underworld to anyone without good reason. Even then, it had to be a bloody good reason. He started making his way towards them through the room, when Billy Banks motioned to him with a slight incline of the head. He warred with himself for a split second before heading out the front to talk to Billy. Some things just couldn't wait.

"Come and grab yourself a plate love, before the vultures descend!" Thea grinned and passed a plate to Anna. She moved close to Anna's ear and whispered conspiratorially, "Anything you don't like, just tell Mum you've already tried it and it was perfect, but that you're full and couldn't eat anything more. Otherwise she'll make you try it. Trust me."

Mollie bustled up to them just as Thea finished speaking, having loaded up Mickey's plate to maximum capacity. He was standing still, staring at it with eyes agape now, trying to figure out what he was going to do with it all.

"Ann, let's get you some food – can I call you Ann or do you prefer Anna?" she waited expectantly.

"Either is fine," Anna smiled warmly, and was rewarded with a gentle squeeze of Mollie's left arm.

"Right then love, what do you fancy? You just help yourself now, you look like you could do with a bit of feeding up, if you don't mind me saying, you ain't got an inch to pinch."

"Mum!" Thea protested, laughing. Everyone who knew Mollie

knew she was old-school in pretty much every topic of conversation you could think of and that included women. In Mollie's eyes a girl should have some solid meat on her and a pair of decent birthing hips. How else was she going to work through all the struggles women faced? That life had changed drastically for women since she was a young girl did not register in Mollie's mind.

Anna was self-consciously running her hand over her hips, blushing slightly. If anything, she struggled with keeping weight *off*, not putting it on.

"Just ignore her," Thea said, linking her arm, "You're fine as you are. Come on, dig in before she diagnoses you with anorexia too."

The two young women started filling their plates while Mollie moved on to accost the next person in line, an elderly neighbour who she had become good friends with over the years.

"Now Harold, have you tried some of that roast lamb yet?"

"I don't eat lamb Molls, never liked the stuff."

"But you haven't tried mine, have you! I slow-roasted that all morning with garlic and rosemary, it's absolutely pucker, as they say these days. Come on, let me put some on your plate, I won't take no until you've at least tried a bit…"

Thea threw a smirk at Anna and rolled her eyes. Anna couldn't help but laugh, though she stifled it enough that Mollie wouldn't hear. Thea was lovely, larger than life, as was all the family, each in their own ways. She had never seen so many colourful characters in one small place before. Watching from the sidelines before Thea abducted her, as was her preference, she had been drinking in the atmosphere around her. Although her own home and family were not quite as loud as this one, the obvious love and happy, carefree laughter reminded her of her parents and the life they used to have together at home. Before she had made the biggest mistake of her life...

"So, where are you from? You ain't from around here, that much is obvious." Thea bit into a mini beef wellington and smiled.

Anna froze. She had been so caught up in everything she hadn't realised how big a trap she was falling into by coming here. It was natural for people to ask questions, want to get to know her. Especially if she was some stranger their brother or son had bought into the midst. Especially when the people round here were a lot more forward than she was used to. Tanya had understood her need for privacy, as she led a shadowy life herself; Freddie hadn't pushed her even though he had every right to, and they were the only two people she had spent any time with since she left, up until now. She stumbled mentally for a moment. What should she say? She couldn't tell the truth, but she didn't want to tell an outright lie. Oh dear...just when everything was going so well.

Out the corner of his eye Freddie picked up on the change in Anna's face, just as he slipped back in through the front door. He watched her freeze, a very slight action that most people probably wouldn't notice, but one that he was now getting very familiar with. His eyes switched to Thea, who had a mouthful of food and an expectant expression on her face. He didn't have to have heard the conversation to understand the scenario that had just played out. *Well, that didn't take long...*He darted across the room, gracefully side-stepping around people, reaching her side within a few seconds.

"There you are! Was wondering where I'd left you. I'm stealing her Thee, you can have her back later on. Come on Ann, people to meet!"

He left Thea frowning fervently at his back, unable to answer without spraying her food out at him, and steered Anna off into the crowd. After several brief greetings later, Anna unsure she would remember any of them, Freddie led her out into the garden towards the wrought iron chairs surrounding a matching circular table. Despite being completely out of season, they had been a thoughtful and surprisingly insightful present from Paulie one Christmas to Mollie. She had instantly fallen in love with them and had insisted that they all have breakfast outside. Wrapped up in their winter warmers and breathing ice, they had all begrudgingly done so, to Mollie's intense delight. Paul had been the receiver of a sore ear later on that day though, as soon as Mollie was out of sight.

They sat down together, now slightly set back from everyone else and Freddie lit a cigarette.

"Are you ok?"

Anna smiled at him, a genuine one he reckoned.

"I'm perfect! You're family are absolutely lovely, so friendly and welcoming..." she trailed off, looking over at the warmth inside the patio doors. "Thank you for bringing me here."

Freddie watched her face, the light from the door bathing her face in a soft glow. Her skin was almost translucent. He fought the urge to stroke her cheeks and feel the softness of them. Her deep blue eyes were hypnotising and he shook his head to clear it. It was crazy, the feelings she evoked in him. They were entirely new, no other woman had affected him like this.

"Don't thank me, I wanted you to come."

Her eyes moved back to him and widened slightly. He continued, not wanting to scare her off.

"I mean, I know you don't know many people here, thought I'd introduce you around a bit." He finished lamely, kicking himself at his flimsy, cowardly excuse.

"Oh." The shutters closed on her face again, hiding whatever reaction she may have been having, "well, thank you, it's been nice to meet everyone. Your sister seems really nice, they all do."

"Fred—" they were interrupted, as Billie Banks approached the table. He nodded to Freddie and smiled politely at Anna.

"Bill, this is Anna, Anna, Bill - a work colleague." He didn't give her a title, which was usually expected, because he didn't know what she was exactly. She wasn't his bird, which is what people were now assuming, wide scale. He definitely did not want to introduce her as his friend, as that put him in grave danger of falling into the dreaded 'friend zone', which he mentally shied away from immediately. He saw Billie note this and knew he wouldn't question it. If personal information was not offered, then it was not requested. It was a rule of etiquette in their world. This was also the reason why he'd kept the introductions brief when leading her through the vast throng of people now adorning the front room and kitchen.

Bill paused a minute, before offering her his hand, "Nice to meet you, Anna."

"And you," she replied warmly.

Bill Hanlon was nearing 40, mostly bald and with a face any pug would have been proud of. He had carved himself out a solid career in bank robbery, having pulled and got away with some of the most outrageous robberies the country had ever seen. The first couple of big jobs he had pulled off had people calling him 'lucky', 'jammy', 'a cocky sod', but years down the line and with a past dotted with successful pulls, he had one of the most respected careers in criminal history. Like most people in their game, he had been unfortunate enough to get a tug by lily law a few years into his career and had spent a long stretch in a Category A prison, but instead of retiring from a life on the edge when he'd came out, he just learnt from his mistakes and improved his game. Each job that he either masterminded himself, or had a touch in, was intricately planned down to the last detail to such a degree that Einstein himself would have had a tough time matching it. Months of hard work and inside intelligence went into each one.

Despite his hardened shell and harsh appearance though, he was a warm-hearted man who lived his life to good old-fashioned morals, and nearly everyone who worked with him knew him also for his very large heart. This side of him shone out through his eyes, at odds with the rest of his appearance.

Anna noted the kindness she saw there and felt herself warming to the man in front of her. Almost immediately she drew herself back behind her defences. She didn't trust her instincts with people these days. She had been taken in before by a wolf in sheep's clothing. It wasn't a mistake she was about to repeat.

Bill turned back to Freddie.

"That phone call, all went as planned. I'll pop by the club later, twelvish, if you'll be in?"

Freddie looked at his watch, "Should be fine, I'll grab Sammy on my way in. He should be expecting me."

"Ok, see you later then mate." He glanced back at Anna, his gaze lingering on her face for a second before he continued. She didn't notice, having reached back to the table for her drink, "—Pleasure again, meeting you. See you again perhaps."

Anna smiled and sipped her drink. Freddie had noticed the hesitation and was surprised. Anna was a beauty, of that there was no doubt, but in all his years he had never so much as seen Bill glance in the general direction of another woman. His wife, '*his Amy*' as he referred to her often, was his whole world. Everything he had ever done had been for her. He worshipped the ground she stood on. At 5'2", she was tiny, with a tiny waist that Freddie was entirely convinced Bill could wrap his huge hands around and touch fingers at the back. Plain but with a warm smile and a generous, quiet nature, she worshipped him right back. They were almost sickeningly happy and would have run for Olympic gold of World's Most Perfect Couples had it not been for their sadness at never being able to have children. So it was out of the ordinary to see Billie study the pretty face of another woman, even for that split second.

Bill turned his attention back to Freddie, smiled briefly and then disappeared into the throng once again, heading towards the front door. Freddie shrugged to himself and turned his attention once more towards Anna and his family. Didn't matter. Maybe Bill was only human after all.

Bill made his way down to his car and leant against the bonnet while he took a deep drag on his cigarette. His eyes strayed to the lights of Freddie's house, listening to the clamour of activity still thronging. He hadn't realised who she was at first, but knew he'd seen her before. It was only as he was leaving that it dawned on him. It was her without doubt, she had a definitive air about her that he'd clocked the first time around, though it had been more subdued back then. She hadn't recognised him, that was for certain, though she wouldn't, because she used to be very careful never to lock eyes with someone in Tony's presence. Tony used to watch her like a hawk, jealousy and something darker marring his face when she was around. He had only seen her once when she was with Tony, it was well known that he guarded her with the determination of a Rottweiler. It had been by chance that he had caught that glimpse, an emergency meeting about a job that he had a touch in and he'd had to make a quick visit to Tony's home. Obviously trying to please and not knowing what the protocol was, she had interrupted them with a timid knock, entering the room with a tray laden with fresh coffee and a plate of biscuits. She'd put it down beside them, almost knocking over a crystal ornament in the process - her fright at this making her hand shake briefly as Tony tutted loudly in annoyance.

"S-sorry," she had stuttered, the refinement in her voice coming through clearly. Tony just sat staring at her until she smiled apologetically once more and made a hasty exit. He growled under his breath, narrowing his eyes as she closed the door, which had shocked Bill. Poor girl was just trying to be hospitable. His Amy did thoughtful little things like that all the time and he always showed his gratitude. This wasn't good form.

Tony had flapped his hand in the general direction of the doorway as if dismissing all thought of her, and returned the conversation to business, not mentioning Anna at all. Bill had filed it away though and noted that the quiet rumours about the girl he kept under lock and key probably had more than just a grain of truth to them.

Bill sporadically dealt with the Greeks in his line of work. Often they pooled their resources in together to pull off a particularly big job, and to their credit, they were very good at what they did. It hadn't been broadcast that Anna had gone on the missing list, and it wouldn't be either. It was seen as total disrespect for a woman to leave her man in the Greek culture and that man would then forever be seen as weak, unable to control his own family and therefore avoided in business by other Greeks. Tony would not want that gem of information reaching the general public. Even to the point that the information had been relayed only to close family and the small force that were now in charge of tracking her down. Bill only knew this because he had overheard a phone conversation between Angel Face and Tony, which he himself had stepped swiftly away from. It was not his business to know and it wouldn't be thought of kindly that he had private insight into Tony's warped and very dangerous personal life. Angelo had stepped out of a pub in Tottenham to take the call and Bill happened to walk out just after, having concluded some business there. Angelo's back was to him, so he walked silently off in the other direction.

And now it seemed, she was here. Half of London was being quietly turned upside down in Tony's ferocious search for her and she was sat quietly in Freddie Tyler's house in the East End. Well, good luck to her, Bill thought. She seemed a sweet little thing, not built to be torn apart by the sadistic, twisted bastard that was Tony Christou. The knowledge of where she was would go to the grave with him. He certainly wouldn't be the one responsible for leading that lamb back to the slaughter. *Hopefully she stays careful and doesn't get caught out.* She must have some nous about her though, to have got away and remained under the radar this long. Tony's reach was long, if nothing else. And his determination, although a credit in the workplace, was frightening. He never stopped until he got exactly what he wanted. Bill shuddered slightly, recalling her small frame, her cheeks pink, enjoying the simple pleasure of being at a child's party.

He wondered absently if Freddie knew who she was. He didn't think so. If he had done, he would've either left well alone or been much more guarded in who he introduced her to. He shrugged to himself. It wasn't his business. He would stay well out of it and see what happened. He pulled the sleeve of his suit jacket back and squinted at his watch in the darkness. If he left now, he could pop home and spent a couple of hours with his Amy before he had to head back out to meet Freddie and Sammy again. He got in his car and drove off, a smile on his face at the thought of his loving wife waiting at home.

7

It was Monday morning and Anna woke up to the cold winter sun shining in her window. She could hear Tanya pottering around in the kitchen. She showered and dressed quickly, pulling on a cornflower blue cashmere sweater and fitted jeans, before going through to the lounge kitchenette area to join her housemate. Today was an exciting day for both of them, they had plans to shop around for the right premises. The night before, Tanya having taken a rare night off from work, they had sat for hours discussing their plans. They'd gone through a few options together, some which Anna had instantly dismissed and some Tanya had not been keen on. Eventually they'd come up with an idea that they both liked and agreed would be a decent earner. Tanya had wanted to stay in the club scene, this being all she knew - and knew well. Anna had wanted to step away but had eventually conceded. After all, at least one of them needed to know what they were doing. Anna was under no illusion that although she was smart, she still had a lot to learn and currently didn't have expertise in any area that could become lucrative.

Tanya poured them both some coffee and turned the radio down until it was just a hum in the background.

"Morning sunshine, excited to get started?"

"God yes!" Anna grinned, "I was starting to go mad without something constructive to do, I'm champing at the bit!"

Tanya laughed.

"Ok. So we are sure on the theme?"

"Yep. Definitely. We need an edge, something different to offer. To be honest, at first it will be a novelty spot, if we market it right - then when people start to enjoy themselves I'm hoping we get a crowd of regulars." She paused a moment, sipping her coffee, then adding a couple of lumps of sugar from the bowl on the table. She stirred it and sipped it again, thoughtfully.

"I agree with you on the girls. That will be the main draw for the men. So, bar staff and table servers all in sexy military uniforms. Perhaps we could even divide the tables up into separate forces. Then on the stage, we have the performers. We can have different acts, all somehow relating back to the forces, have them in costume too. We need to make sure it has a bit of class about it. Not so much that people feel uncomfortable, but enough that it's a bit special, you know?"

"Mm." Tanya nodded her agreement, thinking about all the clubs she had worked in. Anna was right, it did need something different and a touch of class to succeed, to make it shine brighter than its rivals. And Tanya really needed this to succeed. It was her only hope of showing the man she had loved that he had been wrong. She was good enough for him - or anyone else she decided to turn her eye to. If she were honest, it was exactly what she needed, to prove to herself that she was good enough after all..

"I meant what I said last night, Tan," Anna warned, her voice cautious, "I know you do what you do through necessity and I don't judge you or anyone else that does it one bit. It's life. You have a commodity, you sell it. But this is different. I won't have it in our club. If we're running this together then *we* are running it, straight as a die. And the girls will be clean and classy."

Tanya fought back her natural defensiveness. She knew Anna wasn't having a dig, she was genuine when she said she didn't judge her. Anna could have judged her easily, Tanya knew that much. Her friend came from a completely different walk of life and although her past was never discussed, Tanya knew that she would never have encountered people like her before. She had probably been brought up to look down on people like her, as a lower class of woman. But she didn't. And that had been as surprising as it had been pleasing. She realised that she cared what Anna thought of her. Anna had been the first person she had ever encountered who actually cared about her and who thought more of her than she did of herself. She valued this more than her own weight in gold.

"That's fine with me. We can have a better group of girls anyway if we aren't hiring the ones who are flogging their clouts."

Anna saw her friend blush as she said this and realised she was referring to herself.

"It's nothing to do with class," she said quietly, "it's to do with survival. When it comes down to it, I imagine these women have little or no other choice. I doubt that it's always their fault. I certainly don't blame them."

She picked up their empty cups and left them in the sink to wash up later.

"Now...go and put on that killer black dress we bought and slap on your war paint. We're going to need a weapon of mass seduction to partner with a professional approach and that my dear, is all you!"

Tanya laughed and hopped up to get to work on her appearance, her favourite pastime. Perfect, Anna thought, the distraction ploy worked.

Tanya loved the way the new dress made her feel. Used to tight, bright and skimpy clothing, she had fought against Anna at first when she had dragged her out shopping for what she called 'more suitable attire'. Standing in the dressing room of several respectable shops that she had never bothered to enter before, she had been bad tempered and loud in her complaints. Anna ignored her, as she would a badly behaved child and had flitted to and from the changing room with layers upon layers of carefully chosen garments in her hand. Some of these things Tanya had immediately berated and refused to ever wear, at which point Anna would purse her lips and stubbornly hand her yet another load of full hangers. After a few attempts though, Tanya had to admit that in some of these things, she actually looked good. Really good. Standing in the changing rooms at Hobbs, she turned in the mirror, assessing herself from all angles. The dress she had on was a soft green, knee-length pencil dress. It was higher at the neck than she liked, but the tailored fit showed off each and every curve of her body to their best advantage. Even she had to admit that perhaps this was sexier than her usual choice of clothing. And classier too at the same time. It made her feel light suddenly. Like there had been a shift of power. In this get-up, she wouldn't be the sultry-but-cheap, fun-time girl. She was suddenly a sexy, independent woman with style. Perhaps, she admitted to herself grudgingly, Anna did know a thing or two after all. Anna smirked to herself at the other side of the curtain. The sudden silence inside the booth meant that Tanya had nothing she could possibly moan about. Finally she had stopped being so stubborn and could see how stunning she could be. It had taken long enough, but this was a small breakthrough at the very least. Silently, she handed the matching fitted jacket over the top and slid the matching stilettos underneath for maximum effect. After some shuffling, the outfit was complete and Tanya swept out, a vivid portrait of red and green, a huge smile on her face. The finished picture made Anna gasp. It was even better than she had hoped for. Tanya's figure and bone structure were made to be dressed up well. The expensive fabric clung to her every inch perfectly, accenting everything to the maximum advantage.

After that, Tanya quickly invested herself in the shopping trip and tried on everything Anna suggested without resistance. By the end of their long, exciting and very expensive day, Tanya had a wardrobe to die for and a smile that could have lit up a disused tube station.

It had never crossed Anna's mind not to open up her own business. Perhaps it came from spending too much time among the Greeks, in whose culture it was important to work for yourself and not others, or perhaps it was her hunger for creativity and freedom. Either way, she had never regarded working in a job for someone else's dream an attractive option. She hadn't been allowed to work when she'd been with Tony anyway, she was only allowed to stay at home and look after the house and him. That was a woman's place in life, Tony had said. She had given up trying to stand up for herself as a person after a short time, as the argument never landed in her favour. So instead, she had focused all her energies on running the house like she would have a military operation. To keep herself busy, she had a rota with all the things she needed to so do, and scrubbed and cleaned and shopped – online only, trips out beyond the front gate had to be authorised by Tony – until the place shone like a surgical palace. There had never been so much as a speck of dust allowed to land, not a tin out of place in the cupboard. She hadn't really cared about any of it, and was enjoying the relief of just living normally now, but at the time it had stopped her from going completely insane.

They tripped back up the stairs now, laughing hysterically.

"Did you see his face!" Tears streamed down Anna's face in laughter as they recalled the afternoon.

"Haha, oh God, I can't stop laughing!" Tanya doubled over clutching her stomach. After several minutes and several curious glances from neighbours walking down the stairs, they got a hold of themselves and made it, still giggling quietly, through the front door.

"Well..." Anna collapsed onto the sofa, "I think it's safe to say that those premises are ours if we want them. And for not too high a price either, oh Tan, you are funny!" she giggled again, pushing her forehead against Tanya's arm, who had collapsed beside her after grabbing a bottle of open wine from the fridge and two glasses.

"I know...here, take this," she poured them both a glass and set the wine down on the coffee table. "Either way, it worked. I can't believe he went so low when he thought I was going to walk out."

"Oh, his face was a picture!" Anna replayed the afternoon in her head. The poor guy hadn't stood a chance. The pair had walked into the estate agents, having seen details for a property that seemed like a good potential candidate, and asked to see it. The only person free had been a young twenty-something man in a suit that was obviously a size or two too big and thick glasses that he kept having to push back up his nose every two minutes. Tanya had worked her magic, practically purring at him as he nervously stuttered through the details. On their way to the property, Tanya had linked her arm through his, chatting away animatedly about how she hoped to achieve her dream and perhaps, if she was lucky enough, even find a nice, stable young man to share it all with one day. She asked him questions, apparently wanting to get to know him better. Red in the face and nearly bursting with pride at being seen with this glamorous vixen on his arm, who was seemingly fascinated at the details of his extremely grey life, his eyes gleamed at the possibility that she might actually be interested in him.

The first property had been a dud. It was ok, but wasn't as big as they had initially hoped and the place was just shy of being located on the edge of the buzzing West End nightlife.

By the third they were becoming disheartened, but eager to please the red-haired angel that had fallen into his life, Gerard, as his name was, practically begged them to go and see another property that had just come onto the books.

"It's not up on the boards yet, we've only just received instruction on it today," he pushed his glasses further up the bridge of his nose again and blushed as Tanya giggled and smiled adoringly at the action. "I was going to put it up this afternoon, but perhaps.. if you ladies..?"

"Ok, where is it?"

Gerard tore his eyes away from Tanya to answer Anna's question.

"It's just around the corner, on Greek street, so great location. Used to be a karaoke bar or something, but it got run down and the son raided the vaults and went on the trot. Old man couldn't get this place up and running properly again, up to his eyeballs in debt. Can't even sell it, needs to get it rented out pronto, get some money coming in to try and cover the mortgage. Gambling problem or something. Really stupid if you ask me..."

"Oh, I completely agree Ger, may I call you Ger? I'm sure your friends must call you that, it's smart and edgy, just like you."

"Oh, well, uh, yes. They don't, but, well, yes, they should, shouldn't they?" he preened under her praise.

Anna raised her eyebrows, though it was at the location rather than Tanya's role-playing. Greek Street. Of course it was. Sod's law it would probably end up being perfect too. Well, it was certainly ironic if nothing else.

She had of course, guessed correctly. The outside was shabby, but nothing some elbow grease wouldn't fix. The inside had been run down, there was a lot of work to be done. There were dangerous DIY fixes all around the place, it was a wonder health and safety hadn't shut it down sooner. Anna tutted to herself. What a waste of such a good size building in such a busy area. Hopefully it would bring the price of the rent down though. After walking round twice and mentally checking off everything they needed, Anna gave Tanya the nod. She nodded back in agreement and set about discussing the financial side of things. In fairness to the poor boy, for that's how she thought of him despite the fact they were probably not a million miles away in age, he did start off on a fair price, obviously being too bowled over by Tanya to be thinking about commission. But Tanya's face had fallen theatrically, all huge stricken eyes and colour-drained cheeks. Anna distractedly wondered how she was able to do that on cue, go pale like that. She really was a very good actress, she'd missed her calling in life.

"Oh dear...And I was so hoping we could get something agreed and then go to lunch together and celebrate. But never mind, we need to go, there are other agents we'll need to get around to today. Obviously wasn't meant to be..." big, sad eyes lowered themselves to the floor as she slowly turned to gather up her things from where she'd left them at the bar.

"No wait! Wait! Perhaps...perhaps I can talk to the owner, see if there's any wiggle room on that price."

Tanya, after a dramatic pause, asked hesitantly, "Really? You could?"

Anna rolled her eyes and fought the urge to laugh. It had taken less than an hour - and three obviously difficult phone calls - for Gerard to finally get them to a price that made the building an absolute steal. Anna would have been happy to stop after the first phone call, already content that they were getting a good deal, but Tanya wasn't having it. She wanted to go the whole hog, rinse it as far as she could. She manipulated, pouted and wheedled her way to almost half the amount they had initially started out at. The owner must have truly been in dire straits to have agreed to such a drop. Something was always better than nothing if you didn't have time to wait around. Anna was pleasantly surprised at Tanya's tenacity too. There was a steely business woman hiding under that pretty exterior, which was exactly what the venture needed.

They had handed over their deposit and signed a contract that day, not wanting to give the owner any reason to backtrack or any time to find a better offer, which in fairness couldn't be that hard.

Anna knew it was a risk putting her name to a business in London, or anywhere in England to be honest. It was a stumbling block that she had deliberated over for a while. She still hadn't told Tanya much about her past, but had confided in her enough to explain that she was trying to stay on the missing list. That she didn't want to be found, with good reason. In the end, after some fiddling around with the contract, the premises and the business were put under Tanya's name, with Anna down as a silent partner. If the paperwork was looked at closely, it was clear that she had a strong hand in the company, but if you didn't know what you were looking for you wouldn't notice her involvement. Anna was gambling on this being enough to keep her whereabouts under the radar. She doubted Tony would think to look for her name under a new bar opening in the West End. He would still be underestimating her, assume she was cowering away in submissive terror. Well, she wasn't. Sure, she was still mortally afraid of him, but her new life, and her confidence, was growing by the day. Like a phoenix, she would rise again from the ashes of her old self, and grow strong and bright. Anna Davies was going to leave her mark on the world somehow. She had once read somewhere that bravery was not the absence of fear, but to feel the fear and do it anyway. It had been filed away in the back of her mind as food for thought, and she'd been chanting it over and over in her head lately - like a mantra. It seemed very fitting for her situation. Now, sat at home in the small cosy lounge with her friend and business partner next to her, sharing a cheap bottle of plonk, Anna felt almost fully content. She felt warm and excited at the journey lying ahead of her. She felt safe in this house, slightly fuzzy as the wine kicked in, but still, there was a little ache in her heart. It never went completely, she doubted it ever would after the things she had gone through, but she guessed that mostly it was down to missing her family. It had been too long since she'd sent that one postcard. Her mother would be worrying and missing her terribly.

She had gone over a few scenarios in her head, trying to find a way to reach her or talk to her without being traced but, alone, it was virtually impossible to do so without getting either herself or her mother into trouble. There had been one plan that she had mused on, dismissed and mused over again a few times. It would have to involve Tanya. And to involve Tanya would mean confiding in her about what had happened, even if just to make her understand the importance of secrecy. But Anna still wasn't sure she was prepared to do that yet. In a perfect world, no one would ever know. It would just be erased, never to affect anything in her future. But she wasn't naïve. This would forever overshadow everything in her life going forward. She just held the hope that one day, the shadow was a small one in a life full of sun.

"We have *so* much work to do Tan," she mused, looking out the window thoughtfully, not really seeing the zigzag of brick buildings, lined up like soldiers opposite. "Why don't we get away next weekend? Or maybe the Monday and Tuesday if you'd rather not the weekend...You know, before we get the keys and the real work starts?"

"What, you mean like a little mini holiday type thing?" Tanya's face lit up at the thought. "Blimey Ann, I can't remember the last time I got out of the smoke! That would be well nice. Where were you thinking?"

Anna bit her lip. "I've got somewhere in mind. It's a lovely little town on the coast over in Norfolk. Very sleepy, really cute. I think you'd like it."

"Ooh, that sounds lovely mate! I've never really been anywhere like that, read about it and seen it on the telly and that, but city life seems to suck all the time away from you..." she shrugged, "Guess I never got round to it."

Anna turned and frowned. "Tan, have you ever been outside of London?"

"Nope." Tanya shrugged again as if apologising for her lack of geographical experience.

"But what about when you were a kid, did your parents never take you away?" As soon as the words came out of her mouth she regretted them. Tanya's face reddened and she pursed her lips. Anna kicked herself.

"Sorry, Tan, it's none of my business, I shouldn't have asked that." Anna jumped to a hurried apology, not wanting to damage the fragile and precious relationship they had.

"Nah, s'ok mate." Tanya smiled ruefully. "My dad was away a lot and me mum couldn't stand the sight of me." Her eyes pierced Anna's, "My upbringing wasn't quite as silver spoon as yours, babe."

It was a barb, but just a little one and tempered with a smile. No serious damage was done. As Tanya changed the subject to where to source their suppliers, Anna found her head wandering off in the direction of her mother again. She hadn't really meant to even suggest the trip out loud, but she had. Now it looked like they were really going. It had just been a thought and a potentially dangerous one at that, she hadn't fully believed that she could pull it off as an actual plan. But maybe she could after all. If everything went exactly as planned, if she was incredibly careful, and if Tanya was of course willing to help, then the idea that was forming in her mind might just work. She would have to work fast. It was just a question of whether or not she could brave telling Tanya.

Freddie walked up to the whitewashed mansion's large front porch. It looked more like a villa really, out of place in north London but Freddie decided he liked it. It had obviously been created lovingly, personal touches visible both in the architecture and in the gardens and driveway surrounding it. Bright flowerbeds and vines wove their way around the edges and a modest man-made brook ran through one side. There were voices raised in bubbling laughter and general chit chat coming over the wall that cordoned off the extensive garden and outbuildings. CCTV cameras followed their movements. Paul glanced behind him and pressed the central locking for the car, though there was no need. The gate they had already gained access through would have given the Krays a run for their money, let alone some petty car thief. Freddie shifted the large bunch of flowers to his other arm, as he pushed the bell and waited for the door to be opened. Sure enough, he soon heard the quick patter of light feet coming through the hallway. The door opened and a slim, olive-skinned woman opened the door. Her face broke into a smile as she saw who it was.

"Freddie! How lovely to see you!" She grasped his shoulder with a perfectly manicured hand, adorned with two banded rings encrusted with diamonds, and kissed him once on each cheek. The rings were both eternity rings which she joked were to make sure that if this eternity ran out, she could keep her husband for the next one too. She nodded to Paul.

"Haroula, you are looking as radiant as ever. These, of course, are for you."

"Freddie Tyler, I'm far too old for you and even if I weren't happily married, you're not my type, you're far too pale and skinny."

He laughed and followed her through the foyer of the house, their shoes clacking on the marble floor. Haroula always had a good joke and a warm welcome ready whenever he came over. With a fiery temper and a big mouth, she constantly either had her husband laughing his socks off or pulling his quite sparse hair out. But whichever it was, she looked after him better than anyone else in the world could, always understood the business and had a loyalty that burnt stronger than any fire. So for that, her husband loved her and gave her the best life that he possibly could.

Freddie had seen the other side of her once, at a meeting held in this house. She had made sure everyone had enough food and drink to feed the 500, all except for one man. Hiding their smiles at this blatant snub, for they all knew why and all knew that she was smouldering fiercely under the surface, they maintained their poker faces until the guy had piped up. The reason for this meeting in the first place was because the man in question had been uncovered as a snake. He had tucked them up badly, obliging them to put some serious damage control in place. He wasn't going to be leaving this meeting, but he didn't know that yet. It wasn't funny, not at all. But somehow, Haroula had taken the edge off and turned it into a story to be pissing themselves over for years to come. It had also earned Haroula some serious respect.

"You missed one Haroula, I'm gasping over here." The man smiled politely.

She turned and looked him up and down, turning up her nose. "Mmmm-no. Sorry." She set the last plate down. "I don't like waste and you won't be around long enough to even digest it. No point really, is there? Plus, I just think it would feel a bit strange clearing up after you when you're, you know... gone." She said it so innocently that the room erupted in a laughter that couldn't be contained any longer, at the look of sheer horror on the man's face, as it suddenly dawned on him why he was here. But then her mask slipped. She darted in front of him and grabbed his face, sinking her nails slowly and deliberately into his puffy cheeks. Her voice came across low and quiet: "And why the fuck would I pander to a two-faced little ponce, who had the fucking, bare-arsed cheek to cross my husband? You sick, twisted little pig." She let go and walked nonchalantly back towards the open door. She turned, "I hope they torture you." A smile played on her lips as she stared steadily for a moment before leaving the room. Freddie had shuddered, even through his smile. She was a fervently passionate woman and dangerous to anyone not on her husband's side. Cos threw in a little torture that day, purely on her say so. There was an old Greek saying he'd heard once, *'The man is the head of the family, the woman is the neck that turns it'*. He'd filed the information away in the back of his mind, not to be forgotten.

Freddie followed Haroula out into the sunshine of their equally bright and tended back garden. The patio was all in vanilla. with pots of flowers strewn at artistic angles. There were thirty or so people sat around tables and on benches, talking, laughing, enjoying their surroundings. A huge barbeque, with a grill two meters wide and staggered on three levels to work with different heats, was built into a large stone structure just to one side. Meats of all kinds were cooking away, big chunky cuts sizzling, smoke billowing up and travelling down the length of the garden. The smell was wonderful. Due to the time of year, outdoor heaters burned every few meters, keeping the chill away. Haroula led them towards the barbeque and the tall, overweight man proudly tending it. He had his back to them. The tight white linen trousers and floaty blue camisole made Haroula look younger than her years. Her olive skin was smooth and unblemished and the laughter lines around her big brown eyes only added to her attractiveness. Her arm extended forward now, towards her husband.

"Cos mou, Freddie's dropped in," she reached up and kissed him briefly on the cheek. He turned around and smiled, putting the spatula down on the side of the grill. He motioned slightly with his head and one of the younger men nearby immediately took over with the food. Freddie smiled inwardly. You certainly wouldn't find burnt burgers at a Greek barbeque. Or 'souvlan' as they called it. If there was something the Greeks knew how to do it was throw the best barbeques.

"I'm going to go and put these beautiful flowers in some water before they wither away. You boys have fun."

Paul had taken a seat near to the entrance of the house and quietly watched a game of cards taking place on the table next to him. He had barely been acknowledged, but took no offence. The Greeks only dealt with the people they ranked highest, the people of note. As Freddie's number two, he was treated politely but only included if he was to be of use. He accepted a cold drink from one of the young women and nodded his thanks.

Cos wiped his hands on his slacks and grabbed Freddie's outstretched hand with both of his own.

"Freddie, me old mate, how's things, what's 'appening?"

In his mid-forties he'd had a thick head of hair, now a mixture of white and black. Like his wife, instead of subtracting from his swarthy handsomeness, it added an air of sophistication. His dark eyes twinkled with a mischievous grin. He was overweight, but content enough in himself not to be particularly bothered by this. Even if he could've been bothered, trying to slim down would've been fighting a losing battle, Haroula being a natural-born feeder. Their fridge was always full to the brim of mouth-watering concoctions.

"It's good to see you Nic, just sorry that I seem to have crashed your party." He gestured to the crowd of people in the vast garden.

"No, no, not at all," Cos gestured wildly with his hand, trying to dispel Freddie's embarrassment, "the more the merrier, it's always good to catch up with an old friend." He smiled warmly and Freddie relaxed. He felt bad, barging in like this. He'd stopped off at the yard where he knew Cos spent most of his time, but had only found Nicky, Cos' nephew, who'd told him to go on up to the house, that he would call and let them know they were on the way. Nicky knew Freddie was a welcome visitor. But Freddie hadn't expected to gatecrash a gathering.

"Can I get you a drink Fred?" he gestured to the same young woman who'd taken Paul a drink, and she raised her eyebrows at Freddie expectantly.

"Erm, just a lemonade would do lovely, thanks." She nipped away and came back ten seconds later with a glass of lemonade, ice chinking away at the side. "Thanks." He smiled at her and she went back off to join her group of chatty young friends at a nearby table.

Cos scanned his eyes absentmindedly over the garden to make sure everything was as it should be.

"Shall we go through to the study? I take it this isn't purely a social call."

"I wish it were mate." Freddie smiled ruefully. "Sadly though, there's no rest for the wicked."

"Ain't that the truth!" Cos grinned back and the pair slipped off into the house.

They seated themselves in the comfortable back room Cos used as his study. There was a large collection of books, though Freddie doubted the man ever had the spare time to devote to reading them. It was funny, he hadn't noticed that about this room before. Obviously he'd been too wrapped up in the jobs at hand to notice anything else. He glanced over some of the titles and was impressed. It seems Cos had a hobby of collecting classics from around the world, some looked very old, perhaps even first editions. Perhaps this was a chunk of his legitimate retirement. It always did to have one, as his old Mum would say.

"So...what can I do you for?" Cos opened a glass cabinet on the far wall and poured two brandies into crystal tumblers. He passed one to Freddie then sank into the comfortable leather chair opposite. Freddie swirled the amber liquid around in the glass.

"Got a couple of things I wanted to mull over with you, so to speak. Firstly..." he hesitated, "You must have heard about Big Dom." Cos nodded and waited for Freddie to continue. "Obviously this has hurt us personally. It is not something we're prepared to allow to hurt us professionally, however, it is obvious that this is exactly what whoever is responsible is aiming for." He paused and breathed out loudly. "To be honest with you Cos, as embarrassing as it is at this point...we haven't heard a dickey bird on the grapevine. There's no gossip, no speculation, no leads whatsoever on our side of things. It's just weird." He took a sip of brandy and placed it in on the table. "It can't be anyone over my way - we'd hear something, anything, to lead us. So, it must be someone further afield. Perhaps someone not on our immediate radar. So, right now, we're putting the feelers out where we don't usually meddle. I need to know if you've heard anything or have any way of finding anything out, from a friend to a friend." Freddie stopped there. It was a delicate task, feeling out people beyond your own goalposts. The last thing he wanted to do was offend a good friend and business contact. He didn't want to tread on toes or sound accusing in any way, shape or form.

Cos nodded, a serious expression on his face. "I don't know anything more than you do at this point. If you're asking if there's been any involvement on my side, then no. But I'm pretty sure that's not what you are hinting at, you know me better than that." He shifted his weight in the chair. "If you are asking if I've heard anyone else in my neck of the woods having involvement, well..." he shrugged. "I haven't as yet, but that's not to say I could give you my word that it wouldn't have happened. I keep on top of my business and my people. I work with a lot of separate people, mainly family, but like me most of them have their own agendas. I have 34 cousins, half of who - as you know - work in various underhand businesses. As closely as we work sometimes, I'm not up-to-date with their every movement..." He raised his hands up in a surrendering shrug. "What can I say. It's plausible. You could be barking up just the right tree - I mean, it's green, it's made of wood, but let's face it, you're in a fucking

133

forest Freddie. It could be practically anyone. If someone wants to be king of your fucking castle, they have a lot to gain by taking out Big Dom. That's an attractive prospect for a lot of cunts."

They both sat in silence for a moment, each lost in his own thoughts.

"I'm just surprised he didn't see it coming, you know," Cos said quietly to himself, "I mean, he was one of the originals. Grew up in the old school. He never took his eye off the ball, never left himself open. *'Occupational hazards'* was one of his favourite bloody sayings for crying out loud. He was always telling the young ones to take more care..."

"I know," Freddie answered. Cos's eyes flicked over Freddie and lingered on his face.

"Whoever did it son, is looking for the biggest trouble he can get his hands on. And this geezer has currently got the upper hand." He fiddled with the arm of the chair and gazed out the window. "You know I can't get involved in this. But for the sake of me friendship with Big Dom and you, if I hear something I don't like - I'll drop you a visit."

Freddie nodded to himself. He didn't take offence to Cos not getting involved, it was part and parcel of the game. It didn't directly concern him, therefore he wasn't expected to take sides. And he wouldn't either. That was just good business sense. But Freddie appreciated Cos' last comment. It meant that as long as it wasn't close enough to home to have any effect on him, then he would tip him the wink.

"Now!" Cos slapped his hands on the chair and pulled himself up swiftly, replacing the serious look on his face with a smile. "Haroula will have my balls for earrings if I don't get back out there, and she'll have yours and all if you and your brother don't stay for some food, so cheer up, look lively and let's go enjoy ourselves, eh?" his tone brooked no argument and Freddie resigned himself to joining in for the next hour or so. It would be bad manners to leave and it would insult both Cos and his larger-than-life wife.

"Well, lead the way then, maestro."

8

Three days later Leslie Davis walked down stairs slowly, unrested from yet another sleepless night. She paused as she caught herself in the hall mirror. She ran her fingers over her face, feeling the deep hollows under her eyes and the sharpness of her cheekbones. It was funny really, she had wanted to get the definition on her face back for years, age having put a little weight on and making her skin softer and plumper. But not like this. She didn't want them back like this. They were now too sharp, a contrast to her general softness. It made her look older. She sighed quietly to herself and continued to the kitchen, wrapping her soft, fluffy white dressing gown around her to keep out the chill. She didn't bother turning the light on. She quite liked it like this, this time in the morning. The world wasn't up yet, all was quiet. It was still dark but with the light breaking gently over the horizon, starting to outline dormant objects and flowers. The early morning mist was beginning to curl away, retreating until the next dawn, and the tiny flakes of ice making intricate patterns in the window corners began to disappear as fingers of light reached them. She made a coffee, moving around the kitchen silently, trying not to wake her husband. She loved her husband deeply. He was a kind, thoughtful and loving man. They'd had many happy years together now. He had always been her rock, but right now even he couldn't help her. She realised he was going through the same as her, could see the hurt and the helplessness underneath his solid exterior. But nothing he did or said made her feel any better. All it did was make her feel guilty that she was pushing him away and that she was unable to help him as she should have been. Nothing helped any more. She got through her days as best she could, went through the motions, kept it all together, but her worry and heartache never went away. For some reason it seemed easier at this time in the morning - when the world was quiet. She sat alone at this time every day. Perhaps it was just that she was so tired she'd run out of feeling, but at this time in the morning she just felt calm. Not happy, but not so sad either. It was a small relief to help carry her through the day.

She heard the soft thump of the post hitting the thick beige carpet and raised her eyebrow. They thought she didn't know about the man posted outside the house each morning, rifling through the post before it was put through their door. Obviously she knew it was happening, but she hadn't realise they were doing it in full view of the house until she saw the man in the car one morning by chance. It was a joke. Sometimes when she was particularly restless, she would watch them from behind the net curtains, rifling through their mail like pigs in a trough. They couldn't see her, it was too dark and she kept the lights off, but she saw. She watched. And every time they found nothing she rebelliously rejoiced. Good girl Anna. As long as they were there and as long as they found nothing, Anna was still safe.

After a few minutes Leslie shuffled slowly to the post and took it through to the kitchen. She glanced at it uninterestedly. Bills, bills...a postcard?

Her heart skipped a beat as she looked over the picture on the front. It was a silhouette of a woman holding a little girl's hand on the beach. She dropped the rest of the post and turned it over, frantically reading the carefully penned lines before her. She squinted. The writing was tiny, the writer cramming as much as possible into the small space.

Dear Leslie,

It's your old friend Marge! How are you? As usual it has been far too long since we last saw each other – 15 years in this case! Do you remember dear, the last time we had a good catch up over a weekend away? We stayed at that little hotel right on the beach front, you remember, that big old place in that sweet little seaside town in Norfolk? Well, it turns out I'm here again, not in the same hotel, but staying right nearby. I realise it's last minute and you're probably far too busy, but I wondered if you were free and fancied coming down for the weekend to visit me and my niece, Tanya? You remember her, the one with all that red hair. You should bring your daughter too, if she's around. Would be fun.

Anyway, let me know. You have my number. If you do decide to come you'll find me along the promenade most days, braving the weather as always. Do you remember that spot where we used to sit to eat our fish and chips?

I do so hope you will come if you can.
All my love,
Marge xx

Leslie's eyes filled up and she choked back the sobs. There were too many emotions running wild within her to cope with all at once. Relief, terror, pure happiness, excitement, more terror, caution. After a few minutes she wiped her eyes and read over the postcard again, her eyes bright. It was definitely her. When Anna was little, they had gone on a few girly weekends away. They'd started when she was about two and carried on until she hit her teens and was no longer interested in the small town with its beach and shells and ice creams. The little town she spoke of was popular with elderly holiday-makers and the two of them had created a long standing joke about a little old lady called Marge who would holiday there come wind or high weather, each in turn pretending to be their fictional character, resulting in peals of laughter between them.

Leslie bit her lip as she processed the situation. The man posted outside would probably be on the lookout for anything coded, so could easily have photographed the card before putting it back through the door. Tony would no doubt let her walk right into it, create a trap. She pondered on what best to do. Anna would probably realise this, hence why it was sent in code in the first place. Perhaps she would find another creative way of contacting her once she was there, so as to not give anything away. Yes, that had to be it. She was sure that after all this time, all the care Anna must have taken to stay concealed, that she would not be so silly as to give herself away.

For the first time since Anna had gone, she found some energy inside herself and bounced up, popping her coffee mug down on the side and running upstairs to wake her husband. She would get ready and go down there as soon as she could. She would go alone, as to not raise suspicion, but would keep in touch with Arthur every step of the way. Perhaps he could come most of the way down but stay elsewhere. If it was an "old girlfriend" she was seeing, it would look a bit odd to take him along. But then if he wanted to come she wouldn't stop him, after all, Anna was his daughter too. Oh, she didn't know, she just wanted to get going!

"Arthur! Arthur, wake up! I have news, I have some real news..." her voice went from loud excitement to conspiratorial whisper as she shook him awake.

"Get up, we need to pack."

"Erm...what?" Arthur groaned as he dragged himself into an upright position, squinting his eyes painfully as his wife flicked on the light.

"Darling, it's Friday morning, we need to move now if we're going to get there tonight." Leslie tutted excitedly, pulling out a suitcase from under the bed.

"Leslie... Les. Leslie!" Arthur raised his voice to get her attention. She stopped what she was doing and he laid a hand on her arm.

"Ok, calm down and tell me what's happened. From the beginning."

Tony awoke to the sound of the phone ringing next to his ear. He sat up groggily and stared down at the screen bleary eyed, trying to make out who was calling him at such an ungodly hour. The phone rang off and he closed his eyes for a second before it started up with its annoying tinkle again. It really was an annoying ring tone, he thought absentmindedly. He should change it. This time he was awake enough to answer.

"What?" he accused, curtly.

"It's Angelo. Sorry about the time, but you said to call you if I got any sniff of her. Well, I think I might have one. A sniff I mean. It might be nothing, but better safe than sorry, right?"

Tony sat up and shook his head to clear it.

"Yeah. Yeah, you're right in calling. Get over here and show me, I'm getting up now. Bring coffee."

Half an hour later Tony was showered and dressed and in a thoroughly bad mood having realised just how early he had been woken. It had been a long night the night before, with a lot of brandy and a lot of good looking girls, who were the type that made themselves available to anyone with a large wallet. He saw nothing wrong with overindulging in either of these pleasures.

Angelo passed him a large takeaway coffee and brought the picture up on his camera. He enlarged the image, which made it clear enough to read.

Minutes went past with only the sound of Tony sipping his coffee to fill the silence.

"It could be." He said slowly, trying to rack his brains for anything she could have mentioned about Norfolk. To be honest, he knew very little of her life before him. When they first started dating, he had feigned interest to try and gain her trust, to get her under the thumb. Romance, care, attention, he had lavished them all despite his complete irritation at having to do so. But he hadn't really listened to all her prattle and nonsense. He just smiled and nodded at the appropriate times like a good boy. Once he had her where he wanted her, he put paid to her chatter whenever he grew bored by telling her to shut up. Or by making her, if she wasn't quite getting the hint that her female opinions and feelings were unimportant in the grand scheme of things. Now though, it would have been helpful if he could remember if anything was ever mentioned about this.

"I don't know. She's never mentioned anything about her mum's mate down there. It could be her, in which case we'll get her there. On the other hand it could genuinely be her mum's mate and niece, in which case we don't want to blow it all open and scare the old lady off. She could still be useful, still thinks we're all on the same side."

Angelo wasn't convinced. He had seen her once or twice looking at him with pure hatred blazing in her eyes, while he'd been tailing her on various trips out of the house.

"Mmm...I don't know boss...I think she's more savvy than you give her credit for, over there."

"Are you joking?" Tony snapped, then laughed. "She's an old bat who saw all the riches I gave her daughter and who sees nothing but the full force of my concern about the situation. She's a woman for Christ's sake. As far as she's concerned, I'm the incredible and heartbroken boyfriend who just wants her lovely daughter back safe."

He glanced up at Angelo, whose face betrayed nothing.

"Which I *am* of course,." he added swiftly.

"Of course."

Tony rubbed his face up and down roughly with his hands - a sign of agitation. "I can't do this today. I have to see a man about a baseball bat, amongst other things on my very busy schedule. I want you to go, take Dodge with you. Tail the old woman, follow her wherever she goes. You see any sign of her, you grab her and you bring her back here."

He slurped again at his coffee. "If you do see her, use whatever you need, it don't matter what the mother thinks of me then. But unless that's the case, don't let her know you're there if you can help it. Who's out there now?" he was referring to the post he kept stationed in view of Leslie and Arthur's house.

"Dodge, conveniently. I'll call him and let him know the plan."

"Good. Keep me updated."

Just at that moment Angelo's phone rang shrilly. He looked to see who it was then answered.

"Dodge."

"Angel, think you were right about that card, she's woken her old man up, all the lights are on and they're rushing from room to room like no-one's business. Hang on...He's just driven a little two-door sportster out of the garage. Didn't know they had that..."

"Fuck." Angelo moved into the next room and swore quietly so Tony wouldn't hear. "Are they heading out already?"

"Don't think so, she's not even dressed yet. But they're definitely getting in gear, so better get over here quick-smart."

"Right, on my way." Angelo snapped the phone shut and said a hasty goodbye to Tony, who was already absorbed in another task and wasn't really paying attention.

Leslie glanced in the side mirror of the car and sighed inwardly. Arthur looked in the rear view and tutted. They were still there. The black nondescript estate car that was keeping a respectable distance, but following them all the same.

"Did she say the name of the town on the postcard?" Arthur asked thoughtfully.

"No, of course she didn't," Leslie tutted impatiently as if correcting a small child, "she only put what she had to, gave us just enough to find her without saying too much."

Arthur rolled his eyes, silently. He had just been checking to see if it was worth trying to lose them and it appeared it was.

"Right, hold onto your hat then Les, I'm going to open this baby up!" The little sportster roared to life as it jumped forward out of its leisurely stroll.

"Oh!" Leslie squealed. She turned round and watched the black car disappear as they turned a bend. "You genius, Arthur!" she hissed, her face beaming in excitement.

"That's why I bought this car, just incase I got the chance. Luckily, they don't know these country roads like we do and if they don't know the destination..." he trailed off meaningfully.

"Perfect." They grinned at each other and Leslie settled into position to watch their pursuers. They shot round the bend and back into sight.

"Damn. Come on Art, you can do better than that. Take them round the houses." Arthur glanced at her animated face out of the corner of his eye and smiled to himself. They hadn't had fun like this in ages.

An hour and a bloody good attempt later, the car was still managing to keep up. They had lost it once or twice, but only for a few minutes, it had always managed to catch them. The problem they had was, in such open country, they couldn't just turn off the road and hide behind something. All the turn-offs were either locked gates, led on to muddy fields that the car would not be able to handle, or just little lay-bys with nothing to hide behind. The land around them was broad and flat and they could see for miles. So they had to keep moving. The car was sporty and nippy, but their pursuers car was powerful. It was a pretty even match. Leslie scowled and cursed as she threw herself back into the passenger seat. Arthur slowed the car down to a safer pace and they continued in silence for a while, the earlier excitement having moved over to a feeling of frustration.

"Well, we tried," Arthur said.

"Yes, we did."

"I'm sure like you said, she'll be careful. She isn't stupid our Anna, you know that."

"Yes, I know you're right, it just would've been a bonus, wouldn't it?"

Arthur smiled sadly. He was desperate to see his daughter but he knew with the men in the car behind, it wouldn't be safe. The most he could do would be to try and distract them while Leslie met her. *If* Leslie met her. But he would be content enough just to know she was ok. That would always be enough for him.

Tanya sat motionless on one of the comfy twin beds in their cosy little room at the B+B. It was a small place, out of the way and barely even noticeable, which Tanya had complained about at the start. Why couldn't they go to one of the big, bright hotels on the front? But Anna had been insistent, so she moodily agreed.

Now though, she understood why.

Anna bit her lip, her nerves jangling away like Christmas bells inside her body. It went against the grain of her whole new life to bring someone into her confidence. To tell her story to someone. Tanya's silence was panicking her. Hot, frightened tears began to well up behind her eyes and she tried to quell them before they spilled over.

Tanya just stared at her blankly and one of the tears toppled over and down her cheek. She wiped it angrily, hating to cry in front of anyone. This action seemed to break the spell Tanya was under and she moved forward with a start.

"No, oh no mate, don't cry. Sorry, I'm just...I don't

know...shocked? Surprised?" she walked quickly to the bathroom and grabbed a wad of tissues, handing them to Anna to wipe her face. "I mean, I knew you was hiding from something, we all have our secrets and that, but I hadn't realised it was so..I don't know...serious."

They both sat silently for a moment. Tanya stroked Anna's back gently as she got her emotions back under control.

Anna hadn't gone into any further detail than she felt she needed to with Tanya. She had told her that her life was unhappy, violent and controlled but had not elaborated. That Tony was now hunting her down and wanted to punish her, this she had to confide, to explain the total secrecy and general nervousness. She told Tanya how he would be staking out her parents and would bug any possible means of her contacting them. She explained her plan, hoping against hope that Tanya would agree, but at the same time understanding if it was too dangerous for her to consider. In the same situation she wasn't sure she would have the confidence to go through with it, knowing the kind of vindictive snake Tony was.

"Of course I will help you with your Mum, An. We're mates, roomies and business partners. We may as well be married!" she laughed, "So yes, of course I will. You just have to tell me where I need to be, what to say, what you want me to do and all that. Believe me, gal, when I say I'm a good actress." The lights went out of her smile at the last few words, but she held it in place, squeezing Anna's arm to let her know she could count on her. Anna took in a large breath and sighed in relief.

"Ok, if you're really sure...?" she looked at her friend gingerly and Tanya nodded vehemently. "Well, let's start with wardrobe. You might be out there some time, I don't know when she will get there, I had to be pretty vague." Anna pulled out a woolly jumper from her bag and a pair of binoculars fell to the floor. Tanya raised her eyebrows. "Well, we are going very Tin-Tin and Snowy aren't we! Bags not Snowy." She wiggled her face and both girls laughed out loud together.

Less than an hour later, Tanya walked down to the promenade, having taken the long route shown to her by Anna. It wouldn't do to let anyone know where she was staying. She shoved her hands deeper into the pockets of her beige overcoat. It was incredibly warm, something Anna had bought her as a present when they were shopping. Tanya had gone pink when she'd handed it to her back at home, all wrapped up neatly in silver tissue paper. It was the nicest present she'd ever received. In fact it was the *only* proper present she had ever been given. It fitted perfectly too, tailored in at the waist and with cashmere in it, making it warm without being overly thick. She nodded and smiled in response to the polite greetings she received from other people walking about. It was all new to Tanya, being treated like a respectable person by respectable people. It was a feeling she found she liked very much and one she was determined to hold on to. She pulled the hat down over her ears, tucking stray strands of her hair up into it. The fur of the hat was beige with white tips to match her coat. As she walked past all the little shops, lights twinkling in the windows and colourful displays reminding her that Christmas was not far off, breathed in the sea air and smiled. This village was truly enchanting, each house and shop made of thick stone and the streets cobbled as if a hundred years old. It reminded her of something out of one of the fairy tales she'd read at school when she was young. She smiled happily, glad they had come away to such a magical place for the weekend. She stopped off at a little coffee shop on her way down to the promenade, stooping to get through the low doorway, and grabbed a hot takeaway coffee to warm her hands with while she waited.

"Do you want cream with that my love?" the plump, rosy-cheeked woman asked her in a soft lilting accent which Tanya quickly decided she adored. She smiled.

"Um, alright then, just a dash."

The woman nodded, pleased. "Fresh this morning this little lot is, my love. Come straight from my Tom's dairy – that's my husband. I only ever use local produce you know. You're not from around here are you?"

The woman's interest was innocent but Tanya answered cautiously.

"No...I'm visiting an Aunt of mine. She isn't from this neck of the woods either, just fancied getting away from the city."

"Ahh, that sounds nice dear. Well, you be sure to come again now and bring your Auntie with you."

"I will, thanks."

Tanya smiled her goodbye as she stepped back out into the bracing cold and walked down to the bench Anna had described, to commence her potentially long wait for Leslie.

In the end, she didn't have to wait too much; Tanya spotted Leslie's hesitant figure walking towards her about an hour later. Her coffee gone, she had just about become acclimatised to the bracing wind coming in off the sea and was now enjoying the calm around her. It had been a peaceful hour, just sitting there watching the waves roll in and back out again. There had been none of the unnatural white noise she was used to back home, traffic, thousands of busy people, music, the general hubbub of London. She felt as though she was finally relaxing and letting the breath out that she had been holding in since childhood. There was no need to brace herself against the unknown here.

Leslie made her way up the beach, studying every figure she passed. As she began to scrutinise Tanya, Tanya got up and waved at her energetically, calling her over. Tanya's shrewd eyes had already spotted the two men following behind her at a distance and rightly placed them in her mind as Tony's men. Leslie glanced anxiously behind her and as she did, one of the men melted out of sight and the other lifted a camera in front of his face, pointing at the grey-blue sea. Tanya pursed her lips. She studied the other woman quickly and noticed that she had two big, open pockets on the front of her large navy overcoat. Perfect.

"Leslie! How lovely to see you after all this time! I bet you don't even recognise me now." Tanya flashed a bright smile and drew the older woman into a full bear hug. Leslie hid her surprise and played along, realising at once that this must be part of Anna's plan. Tanya's grin was infectious and she found that she was genuinely smiling back at the girl.

"I'm so sorry, but Aunt Marge can't make it now. She took ill all of a sudden, but felt awful after inviting you up so I thought I'd come anyway." Tanya let her forehead crease in concern as she talked, shaking her head solemnly. Leslie fought the urge to smile at the girl's theatrics.

"Oh, that's terrible...I do hope she gets better soon." She bit her lip and looked around, searching for a sign of her daughter. She lowered her voice. "Tanya—"

"Not here," she cut her off, quietly, "you've got two bleedin' followers, those bastards. Let's go shopping."

She made a point of looking at the men curiously before taking Leslie's arm and steering her towards the quaint little shopping arcade across the road. They didn't talk about it further, just wandered slowly, looking through windows and commenting on the pretty things on view. Leslie kept the smile plastered to her face and a calm exterior, but inside she was bursting with impatience and longing. It had been so long and she had come so far that this last leg of the race was impossibly hard. Twice more, Tanya turned and stared pointedly at the men, as if confused as to what they were doing there. Each time they quickly moved as if to look elsewhere. The last time she did this she adopted an air of annoyance, hand on hip, frowning at them.

This time Angelo backed off properly. All these birds had done so far was chit chat and shop, it was a waste of time. It could have been a ruse, so he would stick the weekend out, but they didn't need to be followed everywhere, that was just ridiculous. He kicked a stone in anger. The whole thing was ridiculous, he was one of London's hard men for Pete's sake, not some fucking babysitter. He blew out a long, slow breath and signaled Dodge to follow him away. The last thing he needed was for the local police to be alerted by some little bird. They walked down the road to grab some food.

Tanya watched them leave in the reflection of the shop window opposite. When she was satisfied they were out of earshot and no longer watching them like a hawk, she breathed out a sigh of relief and looked around for a suitable place to sit and chat. Her eye caught a tiny little shop window and door with an advertisement outside for afternoon tea. That would do. One way in and out, no surprises. As she opened the door she spotted a table at the back which was half tucked away and she headed straight for it, leading Leslie with her. Leslie looked around her as she took her gloves off. She hadn't seen this little place before, though it was years since she'd been in the village. It was cosy and warm with low ceilings and Tudor beams issuing from the lily-white background. The tables were laid with red and white gingham and a small fire was lit in the corner, by a couple of overstuffed armchairs. Anna would have loved it. She swallowed the lump in her throat and blinked rapidly before turning back to Tanya. The girl was ordering them both afternoon tea in her blunt East London accent, trying to talk softly so as to seem less out of place. Leslie grasped her hand as the waitress ambled away.

"Please, where is she?" the hope and agony was clear in her soft voice, her greeny grey eyes pleading. Tanya felt a pang of envy course through her, at the love this woman irradiated for her daughter. She was a real mother.

"She's here, Leslie, in Sheringham."

"Oh, where?" she made to rise, but Tanya stopped her.

"Leslie...you can't go to her." She was firm, though her heart went out to the poor woman in front of her. "It was dangerous enough for her to come here, and I have a message for you and something else to talk to you about, but as for seeing her...you just...can't. I'm sorry."

Leslie mutely dropped her head into her hands. She didn't move for several minutes. Tanya let her be. The whole thing had to be hugely draining. The tea arrived and she poured it, thanking the waitress who tactfully ignored the distressed companion of the flame-haired beauty. When she finally lifted her head she looked as though she had aged ten years. Tanya said nothing and handed her a cup of tea. Whereas vodka was her go-to drink, tea was usually the answer to problems where the older generation were concerned.

Leslie took a deep breath and shook off her disappointment. She reminded herself that the most important thing here was Anna's safety and that she was lucky to even have this meeting with Tanya. She turned to the younger girl and smiled, bravely. She grasped her hand.

"Tell me about my girl," she said, simply. "I take it you're a friend of hers?"

Tanya smiled back at the older women, warmly. She couldn't help but like her immensely already. She wished again that she could have known the love of a mother, instead of the hatred and bitterness that was all she had received from her own progenitor. It must be nice to have someone who loves you so completely. She placed her longing aside and began to tell Leslie everything that had happened since Anna had left. She told her of their chance meeting and how they became flatmates, about how sensible and careful Anna had been which seemed to soothe Leslie immensely, and of their plans to open up the club together. She left out the details of what sort of club, under Anna's firm instruction. Leslie and Arthur did not need to know that. They would neither understand nor approve.

When Tanya had finished telling her everything she could, she sat back and took a deep drink from her cup. Leslies eyes were shining, her face full of hope and radiance again. She looked pretty good for her age now that she wasn't so stressed, Tanya noted.

"I'm so glad that she's ok and so happy. Thank you Tanya." Leslie squeezed Tanya's arm. "Thank you so much for being such a good friend to her. She needs someone like you." Tanya felt her cheeks grow warm at the unexpected compliment. She looked down awkwardly, not used to it. "She lost all of her friends, you know. When Tony got his claws into her." Leslie's eyes clouded back over as she looked back in her mind's eye. "He is an evil man. He tried to destroy her, to break her. We thought..." she faltered, "we thought maybe we had lost her towards the end. That he'd won and finally broken her." She stared through the wall, swallowing the hard lump in her throat. "But then she disappeared. We don't know what happened to finally make her snap back; I doubt we ever will. She hid the worst from us. Or at least she thought she did." The flicker of a sad smile played on Leslie's lips for a second. "But whatever it was, I'm glad she finally did it. I'm glad that no matter what he did to her, he never truly put out the spark in her that finally made her leave and start again. She has such a strong spirit you know, underneath her quietness. It's often the calmest waters that run the deepest." Leslie's voice was full of pride for her daughter. Tanya nodded.

"Oh, I know. She has some serious determination, that's for sure. I'm glad to have her as my business partner. And my friend," she added. She wondered if Anna knew just how lucky she was, to have parents like these. "Anyway," she cleared her throat, "there is something else I have to tell you." She looked around, wary of anyone she may have missed. "Don't touch it now, just in case. But I slipped a phone into your pocket earlier, on the pier." Leslie gasped, her eyes widening. Her hand automatically moved, but then she stopped it and placed it carefully back on the table.

"Ok. It is a pay as you go phone, totally non-traceable," she continued as quietly as she could. "It has a number programmed in the contacts, just under the word 'Phone'. That number is for another non-traceable phone, which Anna has. Now, this is important. You must *not* take it out of your pocket until you're in your house and then *only* in the on-suite bathroom. Hide it under that sink. That is the only place in the house that Anna is absolutely sure no one can see or hear into."

"Ok, ok I will." Leslie could barely contain her excitement. She was going to be able to talk to her little girl! She felt like bouncing for joy.

"Great. The other thing is, Anna got this one specifically because she used to have the same model. There's a charger for it in the bottom drawer of the small chest of drawers in her old room." Tanya recited the very specific information Anna had given her earlier that day. "Don't go out and buy one - or anything else to do with this phone."

"No, no, I won't," Leslie said hurriedly.

"If it gets discovered by Tony, then Anna will have to dispose of hers to avoid him being able to get to her. So please, be careful," Tanya stressed. "Oh, and whenever you speak on the phone, say the word *'lemonade'* first, to let Anna know that it's safe to talk. If you speak without using the word *'lemonade'*, Anna will assume it's because Tony or one of his men is there listening, ok? That's your secret code word."

"Got it." Leslie nodded strongly to show her understanding of the situation. *Gosh*, she thought, *this was like some sort of spy movie.* If it wasn't that her only child was in such danger and if it wasn't so serious, she might have found this all quite fun. She played with her perfectly manicured nails, absentmindedly. She was suddenly desperate to get back to Arthur and make their way home, so that she could turn on the phone.

"Anna will wait for you to call her, when you're back. No hurry, she'll keep hers on her. Then you guys can arrange your next call and what not." Tanya gathered her coat and stood up. "I'll let you get on then. It was really nice meeting you, Leslie."

"It was very nice to meet you too, Tanya. And thank you again. I really am so happy to see that Anna has such a good friend." Leslie smiled. She meant what she said. It was obvious that Tanya came from a very different walk of life than she was used to, but Leslie could see that she had a heart of gold and cared greatly for Anna. That, above anything else, made her an absolute treasure in Leslie's eyes.

"Yeah, well..." Tanya shrugged and awkwardly pulled Leslie in for a swift, one armed hug. "See ya, mate. Get home safe, yeah?" She moved towards the exit.

"And you both. Give her our love, Tanya."

"Will do."

Tanya stepped outside into the crisp fresh air and breathed it in deeply. The wind blew across her exposed neck and she pulled the collar of her thick coat around her, more tightly. Pushing her hands deep into the pockets, she set off at a brisk pace, back towards the hotel. She kept a sharp eye out for the men she had seen earlier, but didn't see any sign of them. Satisfied after a few minutes that she truly was alone, she took herself off of the long route back to the hotel and headed straight for it. It was too cold to be staying out for no good reason.

Anna was pacing the room, wringing her hands when Tanya opened the door. She jumped forward and grasped Tanya, her eyes bright, the second she saw her.

"How did it go? Was she ok? Was it just my Mum, or was Dad there too? Were you followed? Did you get the phone to her?"

"Jesus gal, slow down yeah?" Tanya laughed, holding her hands up in mock surrender.

"Sorry," Anna stepped back and made an effort to compose herself. She waited for Tanya to take off her coat and hat quietly, but her impatience and fearful excitement sat bubbling away, just under the surface of her now calm exterior. Tanya sat on the end of her stiff, single bed and rubbed her hands in an attempt to warm them up.

"Ok, so it was just your Mum, she's fine; your Dad's fine too. Slipped the phone into her pocket, told her everything you asked me to and parted ways happy. Ok?" Tanya raised her eyebrows in question. Anna nodded, digesting. "She's nice, your Mum." Tanya said, wistfully. "Must have been nice at yours."

"Yes, it was." Anna studied Tanya's face. She never opened up about her past and Anna never pushed her. Mostly because she had never wanted to be pushed herself. But Anna had noticed how Tanya never discussed her family and it was obvious that she was not in touch with any of them. In the few months that Anna had lived with her friend, she had never had any family over to visit or even had a phone call. Perhaps she didn't have any family, Anna considered.

"So, now you just need to wait for your call then mate. Mission accomplished."

"Yes, mission accomplished," Anna nodded and looked out the window at the windy beach front. "Now for the wait."

9

Freddie and Sammy sat together in one of Freddie's offices, a portakabin on a small junkyard near the docks. Freddie had acquired the junkyard early in his career, buying it from a tired old man who wanted to sell up and move to a quiet retirement in Spain. It had proved to be a shrewd move, working well as one of his legitimate businesses in which to hide a fair amount of his illegitimate money. It also provided a well-protected and very private office, due to the location and the large, none-too-friendly guard dogs watching out for any uninvited guests.

Sammy pursed his lips as he studied the plans in front of him for the umpteenth time.

"Is it really worth it Fred?" he asked. "How much went in there?"

"Just over half a mil."

"Ah." Sammy nodded and continued looking at the plans. Freddie sat back in the battered leather armchair and waited. He knew Sammy's methods. He was a very logical man. He was working the process over in his mind and going through all the possibilities before he would give his answer. He didn't rush into anything without weighing up every single angle first. Freddie respected Sammy for this. Hot-headedness was not an asset in their game. As Vince was fond of saying: 'only fools rush in'. Sammy sighed heavily.

"It's ballsy Fred. One wrong foot and that's it for all of us. There won't be no plan B here. It's risky. Even for half a mil."

"I partly agree with you Sam," Freddie conceded, his face serious, "But we have several bent filth on the payroll working that night, running this from the inside. Once we're by that fire exit—" Freddie leant forward and pointed it out on the blueprint, "—then that's it. Five minutes whilst the stuff gets loaded and then we're gone. Done."

The blueprints were the plans for the local police station. One of Freddie's men had been collared by the law a few months previously whilst transporting nearly half a million pounds of freshly laundered money. It had been confiscated of course, and since then, had sat in the evidence room of this particular station. Freddie's man, a Scottish bloke called George, had kept his mouth shut and done his time with his head held high, as Freddie would expect from any of his trusted men. They knew the score. In return, Freddie had put a large wedge aside to go to him upon release, as reward for his loyalty. He also made sure to keep sending George's wages to his family each and every month. Family were always looked after in situations like these.

Now though, Freddie wanted his money back. He would have ignored it if it had been a lesser amount, but this was worth over five hundred grand and even Freddie couldn't ignore that.

He had several police officers on the payroll, men who couldn't help but be romanced by the extra money coming in each month. What Freddie gave them pretty much doubled their wages, allowing them luxuries that otherwise they would never be able to afford. Freddie couldn't stand them. A straight policeman he respected. They may be on different sides of the law, but he respected that they stood up for what they believed and worked hard doing what they said they were going to do. A bent copper, however, in Freddie's eyes was scum. A bent copper betrayed his own and no matter what side of the coin you sit on, that just made you a spineless scumbag who shouldn't be trusted.

That being said, having them in your pocket came in useful at times like this. They had happily sat there raking money in all this time, now they could actually do some work for it. So he'd called them in and told them what needed to be done. They had to work it so that several of them were on shift at the same time. That was crucial. The security cameras would be taken offline for maintenance for a ten minute window. Once they were down, the gate would be opened and Freddie and his men would be able to drive into the back of the compound. Someone would need to keep watch by the gate, in case of any unexpected activity. They would drive around the back of the building to a small fire exit. One of the bent filth would be waiting there to let them in. One man would have to be stationed there to open the door each time they came in and out, as an alarm would be triggered if the door was left open for more than a minute. The same copper who met them would then lead them through another two locked doors, into the evidence cage. There were nine large, heavy bags full of money, which would have to be run back to the car quickly. Freddie had calculated for three men to do this, including himself and Sammy. They would have to get the bags in the car and get out of the compound, within the ten minutes that the cameras were down. No one would stop them, not when he owned most of the men on that graveyard shift. But it was extremely time sensitive, that he couldn't deny. Once the money was discovered to be missing by a straight-shooting plod, the CCTV would be the first thing they would go through. There must be no trace of them on it. Not even their retreating backs.

Anna put down the paintbrush and arched her aching back, looking around. They had been in here for five days now trying to get the premises up to scratch before the furniture they had ordered was due to arrive. They had cleaned and scrubbed the place to within an inch of its life. And god, hadn't it needed it. The pair of them had waged war on layers of grime that must have been decades-old in places. Once they had finally beaten back the dirt, the pair had set about the place with rollers and brushes, getting the walls back to a neutral colour and sprucing up the woodwork. It wasn't good enough though, Anna was slowly realising. She bit the side of her bottom lip. If this place was going to look as professional as it needed to be, they would need to get proper decorators in. They couldn't half-arse anything. Not with everything they both had riding on this.

Anna's phone beeped in her pockets and wiping her paint covered fingers on her old dungarees, she opened her phone to read the text. It was from Freddie, asking if she was free to grab some lunch. A smile crept up her face. She messaged back telling him that she would meet him in an hour. She looked over to where Tanya was crouched down, painting the skirting boards.

"Tan, do you mind if I skip off for a couple of hours?"

"Sure, where you off to?" Tanya asked, swivelling around to look at her.

"Oh, just for lunch." Anna shifted her weight awkwardly from one foot to the other as Tanya gave a throaty giggle.

"I bet I know who that's with. Your mystery man, ey?"

"He isn't my 'man', he's just a friend."

"Mm-hm," Tanya raised her eyebrow sceptically, "sure he is. Because you don't blush or nothing whenever we bring him up, no?"

"Anyway, I'm going for lunch and I want to get out of these painting clothes."

"There! That, too." Tanya pointed her own brush at Anna accusingly. "You do that too, you brush me off like a bloody horse fly and change the subject, every time I ask. You sly old thing, I reckon you're keeping all the juicy bits from me really." She laughed as Anna threw an old rag at her.

"I do not," she laughed, "it's just that there really isn't anything else to tell." She shrugged and her smile faltered slightly. Tanya studied her face and gave her a sympathetic smile.

"That bothers you, don't it?" she asked gently.

"What? No, not at all." Anna frowned and moved about, agitatedly. "I don't care. Why would I? I don't want a man in my life anyway, not after the last one. What I need are friends and that is what I have." She took a deep breath and grinned, brightly. "So, I'm perfectly fine, thank you. And I am off to lunch with one of my friends. Whose company I enjoy without having to make it into anything else, thank you very much." She walked out the door purposefully, grabbing her purse on the way and lifting her hand in a brief wave.

Tanya shook her head with a wry smile. Anna might be fooling herself, but she certainly wasn't fooling anyone else. Or not Tanya at least. She could see the way Anna lit up every time she spoke to this guy, the way she seemed to bounce through the day when she knew she was about to see him. Sure, Anna had been knocked badly by her last relationship, Tanya knew that. But maybe it was time for her to begin opening herself up to new possibilities. She made a note to try and broach it again, next time they had a girls' night in. In the time they had known each other, Anna had become family. She loved the bones of the girl and wanted to help her find some well-deserved happiness again. She turned her attention back to the task at hand and attacked the offending piece of wood in front of her with the paintbrush.

"Sorry I'm late!" Anna sat down opposite Freddie and tried to catch her breath. He laughed at her, opening up his easy smile.

"That's alright, there was no need to rush. You look like you need a drink." He caught the attention of the waiter who rushed over immediately.

"I do, thank you," she grinned, unbuttoning her coat and placing it over the back of the chair.

"What do you fancy?"

"I'll have a white wine please, pinot if you have it."

"A bottle," Freddie instructed. "I'll join you," he said, turning back to Anna. "So, how's things?"

"They're good, thank you, very good." She smiled and looked around at the restaurant. She had met up with Freddie a few times since the party and every time, she felt herself relaxing a little bit more. Despite that though, she had still not told him the details of her venture with Tanya. He knew that he was starting up something new with her flatmate, but she hadn't elaborated. He hadn't pushed her on it either, which was one of the things she liked about Freddie. She didn't feel pressured to do or say anything she didn't want to. She flicked her eyes back to Freddie's face and asked him about his day. His face held the same calm, friendly expression it always did when they talked.

It was a habit of Anna's, to check people faces before processing their words, in case there was evidence of a threat there. Often Tony's mouth would tell her one thing, his silken words sounding innocent enough, but his eyes would tell her another. She couldn't quite shake the habit now, and doubted that she ever would.

She let her eyes roam subtly over Freddie as they ate. He looked just as good as ever today, in a beautifully fitted, black suit and open-necked shirt. Not a hair out of place and his aftershave romancing her senses just the right amount. Whoever he next dated, or maybe even was already dating, was a very lucky woman indeed, she thought wistfully. Anna never asked Freddie if he was dating anyone. It was not a question she wanted to hear the answer to. He almost certainly was. Why would he not be? He ticked every box. Well, women who wanted a partner that is, which -reasoning - she didn't. She pushed these thoughts out of her mind and focused back in on what he was saying.

"—so I took one home for Thea, she loved it. Not that it went down well there, of course.." Anna laughed with Freddie and covered her glass as he tried to refill it.

"No, I mustn't. I have to get back to Tanya, we've got so much to do still." She studied him over the table as he just nodded. "Talking of Thea, she texted me the other day actually. She invited me to go for a drink with her one night soon, which was kind of her. It'll be lovely to see her again. She's very nice, your sister."

"Yeah, yeah, she's a good sort." Freddie made a mental note to have a chat with Thea before she met up with Anna. He didn't want her spilling any details about his way of life. It wasn't time yet. He didn't know whether it ever would be time to tell someone like Anna who he really was, but if and when that time came, he wanted such information to come from himself.

Dodge tried to swallow the lump that seemed to be stuck in his throat, as he waited under the furious stare of his boss. Tony didn't blink or break eye contact, but just sat there, silently boiling with rage. Dodge didn't dare to move, though every muscle in his body was tense. When Tony was in one of these moods it didn't matter who you were or what you had done, there was every chance you would end up dead. Of course there was just as equal a chance that you would be given an extra wedge that day for your trouble and offered some of the good whisky. But that was what kept you on your toes with a boss like Tony. You never knew which way his mood would swing.

"You saw *nothing?*" he spat, "There was nothing there *at all* that made you suspect she could've been there?"

"No boss, like I said, she just met that woman on the bench and went for a walk past all the shops. They didn't appear to be going anywhere. I looked but it definitely wasn't her. Listened into as much as I could but it was all just small talk, nothing about Anna. We tailed them as far as we could but there was no one about, the girl kept looking at us funny and in the end she really started looking suspicious. We had to disappear, she was one look away from calling the local plod." Dodge fell silent and waited for Tony's response, his heart racing and his face smooth.

Tony bit his bottom lip as he processed everything he had been told. He had debriefed his men several times now. He'd worked out long ago that if he wasn't sure on something, he needed the person in question to retell the story several times under pressure. If there were any slip ups they were trying to cover up or any forgotten details, these usually came out in the end. This time though, it seemed pretty straight forward. This infuriated Tony beyond belief. He had been certain that it must have been her. He couldn't believe that she had managed to go all of this time without contacting her parents. He knew how much Anna loved them and how it must be eating away at her, to go without letting them know that she was ok. She must know how closely he was monitoring her parents, to have suffered without them for this long. This thought appeased him slightly. Even if he couldn't get to her yet, at least she was suffering.

He eyeballed Dodge hard, one last time. He enjoyed provoking fear in people. He watched Dodges Adam's apple bob up and down as he swallowed again. Leaning back casually, he picked up his glass of whisky again and fingered the large hunting knife he had out on the desk. Dodge's face immediately drained of colour, but still he did not flinch or move. Tony felt a small flicker of respect for the man.

"Go!" Tony waved him away and Dodge let out the breath he'd been holding in. "Take the night off. Go and have some fun. See me back here tomorrow afternoon. I have plans to discuss with you."

"Thank you, boss. See you then." He nodded curtly and swiftly retreated out of the room.

Tony stroked the hard, black handle of the knife and turned it slowly so that the light from the lamp glinted off the blade. This was the knife he was saving just for her. Whether he allowed her to live or not, he hadn't yet decided. It would be something he could only decide at the time. The rush and feeling of relief he would feel at torturing her was something he craved more than water, more than oxygen. It was a pull on his very soul that he couldn't ignore anymore. It grew and grew the harder she was to find. He dreamed of the day he finally had her in his reach. Closing his eyes, Tony rested his head back onto the headrest of the chair and ran his hand slowly through his thick, black hair. He pictured the terrorised tears that would fill her eyes and the way her soft skin would feel, as it popped under the slow ministrations of this knife. He could smell the sharp, metallic scent of her blood as it poured from the wounds he would inflict. Her agonised screams would fill the air and he would pause briefly, only to listen to her begging for him to stop. But he wouldn't stop. He was going to give her everything she deserved. And he would savour every single second of it.

Freddie sat upstairs in his bedroom, cleaning the gun he kept strapped under the mattress. It was a ritual of his to handle and clean all his various weapons every month, whether or not they had been used. Always alert, Freddie wanted to be sure that if he needed to suddenly go for his nearest gun, it would be in perfect working order. When you sat in a position such as Freddie's, there was always the distant threat of some competitor or hungry kid further down the food chain. If one of them got too big for their boots and decided in their vast stupidity to try and take him out, he needed to be prepared. It had happened before, it would happen again. Usually the idiot in question failed and suffered fatal consequences. But it did not stop young try-hards from giving it a go now and then. With Big Dom's demise still fresh and the culprit at large, Freddie was on even higher alert than usual. It was frustrating that there was still no word on the street about it. No one seemed to be taking ownership of the crime, which in itself was odd. Why make such an outrageous statement, then walk away totally anonymous? It made no sense. Freddie shook his head and frowned as he turned it over for the millionth time in his head.

Finally happy with the gleam on the cold, hard metal of his gun, Freddie carefully replaced it in its hiding place. He made his way downstairs to the kitchen, where he could hear his Mother and brother talking. The kitchen was full of the aroma of roasting lamb wafting from the Aga. Warm from the heat it was generating, it was a bright, cosy room and Freddie felt a pang of regret that he had to soon leave it. Paul sat at one end of the table, his hands wrapped around a steaming mug of coffee. Mollie was sat next to him with her own mug, but jumped up and bustled over to the kettle when she saw Freddie come in. She beamed at him, her face rosy.

"Ah, there you are. Here you go love, made enough for you." She poured the strong, dark liquid into a third mug and handed it to Freddie. He took it and smiled fondly at her.

"You're a diamond." He drank from the cup deeply, savouring the warmth travelling down his throat. It was a bitterly cold day.

"Fred, I heard something this morning on my way to the yard. Might be nothing, but it struck me as odd."

"Oh yeah? What's that?" Freddie said, turning his attention to his brother.

"Thought I would pop in on Damien as I was passing, see what the latest shipment was looking like. Nice stuff, by the way. You wouldn't be able to tell the difference. Anyways, so he's telling me about his weekend and mentioned that there's been a couple of Greeks hanging round The Black Bear."

"Oh?" Freddie raised an eyebrow. The Black Bear was one of their pubs, one that was fairly well hidden away from the general population and tourists. It was a hub of civilized criminal activity, all of which was under the management or watchful eye of Freddie. It was where his men spent a lot of their free time and locals that were not involved in his way of life avoided it. The only time that members of other London firms stepped foot inside that pub was if they had been invited for a meeting. It wasn't strictly off bounds to anyone - after all, it was technically a public place. But it was highly unusual for people in the know to ignore the unspoken boundaries.

"Did he say what they wanted?"

"That's the odd bit. They didn't speak to anyone. Apparently they sat there, had a couple of pints and left. Bill Hanlon told Damien that he'd seen them in there twice before. Did the same thing then too apparently, just had their drinks and pissed off."

"That *is* odd," Freddie agreed, "were they Cos' men?"

"No, apparently not. Bill said they were from one of the other Greek firms. They're all interconnected of course, but these guys don't work under Cos."

"Good." He was glad. The last thing he needed was for an ally to start acting shadily. He liked Cos.

"Bit of a statement, ain't it?" Paulie said, screwing his lips to the side, frowning.

"It is indeed," Freddie mused. "Find out whose crew they're on and get a tail on 'em. See if it's just that pair sniffing round, or if there are more. I want to know what they're doing. Cause that ain't a general visit. Especially if they aren't seeking out one of ours in there."

Freddie breathed out heavily. This could be nothing, but he doubted it. There was rarely smoke without fire. Downing his coffee, he grabbed his black, tailored coat from the back of the chair and shrugged it on over his suit. Mollie handed him his scarf which he put on and tucked into the front of his coat. Opening the back door, he shoved his hands deep into his pockets to protect them from the cold. He turned back towards them.

"Sort that out this morning then meet me at the docks for twelve thirty. I need to talk to Damien about upping the scale."

"I don't know if he can Fred, apparently this lot was a scrape to get through."

"Hmm. Ok. Well let's go over the operation then, see what we can improve on." He switched his attention to Mollie, "Laters Mum. Save me some of that, will you?" he motioned towards the Aga. Smiling, he gave her a wink and disappeared, shutting the door behind him.

Sipping his own coffee, Paulie went through the register of men he trusted in his mind. He needed the most discreet and efficient men for a tailing job. Heavy drinkers or gamblers were out of the question. Whilst they had their merits in other areas of the business, they would get distracted too easily on the hunt. Same with philanderers. The minute an attractive bird gave them the eye, that would be it. He needed the straight guys. Bill Hanlon was the first man who came to mind. Yes, he nodded to himself, he would definitely set Billie on it. Billie wouldn't so much as look at another bird with how loved up he was with his wife, nor would he be tempted to fuck up a job by drinking too much or hitting the cards. He knew Freddie was working on another job with him, but was sure that Bill would be able to handle both. Archie Tucker was the second man he thought of for the job. Archie lived for 'the life'. He occasionally had casual girlfriends but had no plans to settle down and no bad habits. He worked all hours and delivered well, whatever operation they had him on. Quiet and nondescript, he could blend into the background anywhere. Those two would do for now. If there turned out to be more of them nosing around, he would think of who else to set to the task. Paulie picked up his phone and scrolled down his contacts to Billie. He waited as it rang, knowing that Bill would pick up by the third ring.

"Billie, it's Paulie. I've got a job for you..."

The wind ruthlessly hammered against Freddie and Paulie's faces, the only part of them that was not covered up as they walked down the pathway to the dock. There was no protection against the weather down here by the river, no buildings blocking the worst of it. This was why Freddie preferred being surrounded by the busy, polluted hubbub of the centre. At least it was a little bit warmer. The river was swollen, brown with the muck and silt that was being churned up from the bottom. Freddie often wondered whether on days like this, the numerous bodies that lay at the bottom were at risk of dislodging and turning up on one of the banks. Not that he had ever disposed of anyone in the river, but he knew that Vince and Big Dom had used this option a few times back in the day. There had been many faces over the years who would have used the river as an anonymous graveyard. It would have been easy back then, before CCTV and a heightened number of tourists walking about at all hours of the night.

Paulie hunched his shoulders and blew into his hands, trying to warm them up.

"Fuck me, Fred. It's colder than a nun's snatch out here."

Freddie pushed his hands deeper into his pockets, attempting to draw out some sort of warmth. Their breath trailed away in white clouds as they walked briskly. The cobbles underneath their feet were still slightly icy, despite the clear sky and bright sunshine. They reached the small portakabin at the end of the dock and Freddie rapped on the door.

"Come in, it's open."

Paulie opened the door and shot inside, eager to get out of the biting wind. Freddie followed and quickly shut the door behind him, so as to not let any of the heat out. Damien was seated behind an old, chipped wooden desk, with a man Freddie hadn't seen before sitting opposite him. He raised an eyebrow at Damien, who quickly got up and walked round to the two brothers.

"Freddie, Paulie, good to see you. Let me get you a coffee, it's fucking 'orrible out there." His eyes darted from them to the newcomer and back again. "This is Ted. He runs one of the factories we order the whisky from." Damien poured two coffees from the ready-made pot on the side and handed them to Freddie and Paulie. "He was in town and I said about you coming in. Thought it might be good for him to join us, rather than us go back and forth. Save time and that."

Freddie nodded and sat down in one of the two empty chairs Damien had placed out ready for them. He didn't usually deal with suppliers once an operation was up and running. Damien had sourced this one, plus another couple, for the cheap spirits they smuggled into the country and sold through the clubs. It was a good earner and the product itself was good. Joe Public couldn't taste the difference and the profit through the clubs went up five fold. It also made it easier for Freddie to launder some of his illegal money through the clubs. Everybody was happy. Except the tax man, but Freddie didn't give a fuck about him.

Aside from being busy, Freddie steered clear of suppliers so that if they ever got a serious tug, they wouldn't know who to point a finger at. He trusted his own men implicitly, but he couldn't be sure of every single supplier on every single job. There were too many of them and they had their own interests. They were not devoutly loyal to him. Damien knew this though, and if he trusted this man enough to bring him in front of Freddie, then Freddie trusted that judgement. Damien was no fool. He wouldn't put Freddie at risk.

"You got some whisky to put in this, Damien?" Freddie motioned to his coffee. "Could do with a bit of an Irish one, on a day like this."

"Course," Damien smiled broadly and pulled a bottle out of a small filing cabinet next to the desk. "Here you go." Freddie accepted the whisky and then turned to face Ted.

Ted smiled politely and held his hand out to Freddie.

"Nice to meet you, Freddie. It's good to put a face to the name." Ted looked to be in his late twenties. He dressed smartly and subtly with neatly combed hair and a close shave. His tone was respectful and warm. Freddie wondered at his background.

Freddie shook his hand and looked him square in the eye.

"Indeed. So long as this face and name stays in your head and nowhere else." He said it jokingly, but everyone in the room noted the subtle warning. Ted nodded.

"Of course. Goes without saying."

"Good. Good. Ok," Freddie put his coffee down and got comfortable in his seat. "Let's get down to business. Damien, Paulie says the shipment is good quality, I trust his judgement. The demand is growing, so we need to up the order. I understand that you've had a bit of difficulty with this last lot. What happened?"

"Yeah," Damien sighed heavily and his face turned grave. "They've started doing spot checks on the ships. Luckily we always mask the product underneath legit stuff and in the middle containers just in case, but they got close Fred. Really close. Apparently these spot checks are going to keep happening regularly. They went through random containers with a real fine tooth comb. Didn't just take the contents on face value either, proper went through them. If they'd hit ours, they would have found the bottles underneath the other stuff in two minutes. John kept an eye on things whilst it was happening, said they did the container right next to ours." Damien paused to light a cigarette. "It's become way more risky. The odds are still on our side, just about. And I'm looking into ways to better hide the product. Might have to take up a bit more space, put more of the legit stuff in each crate and lower the secret bottoms. But we can't up the amount we're pulling through those shipments. If anything we may have to lower it. The more there is, the more chance we have of getting caught."

"I see." Freddie sat back and leant his head on his fingers, rubbing at his temples. "How long have these spot checks been happening?"

"Just this last shipment. I knew you'd be over, so I waited to talk to you now."

Freddie nodded his acceptance of this and mulled the situation over in his head. There was silence for a few moments. Paulie faced his brother, waiting to see what he wanted to do. Freddie frowned.

"I've got two supervisors at that customs' port on my payroll. These shipments are organised around their shifts so that this doesn't happen. Where were they while this was going on? What the fuck do I pay them for?" he asked Damien.

"Ben and Ralph," Damien confirmed. "They usually make sure there's no spotlight on our ships, but they weren't there. No one knows what happened to them, they just went on the missing list." He shook his head. "We already had the stuff on board, so they couldn't take it back off. There was too much. They would've drawn too much attention to themselves. So I told them to continue and sit tight. That's when the check happened. After we got the all-clear, I got one of the guys to ask around. Apparently they were both fired last week. Their head office got a whiff of foul play and saw them off the premises. One of them was seen fighting with security to get back in, kept saying he needed his notebook, made a right scene. They wouldn't let him back in though. My guess would be that the notebook held our contact details and that's why we didn't hear nothing."

Freddie nodded slowly, mulling this over.

"What number did they have?"

"A burner. I've chucked it, it's at the bottom of the river. They didn't have nothing else. There's no trail. We delivered their pay in cash each time, they knew no names."

"Right." Freddie was pissed off. They needed that port and now it seemed they had lost it. He had another, but they had a good set up at this one. It would take extra time and money to send it through the other available channels.

"What's waiting to be sent?"

"Ted has a shipment of vodka ready to move, but I've put it on hold until we have another route."

"Can you get your crates down to Calais?" Freddie asked Ted.

"It'll take another day, but yeah, I can get it down there. If you can give me the contact details for that ship..."

"Damien will sort out the details with you." He dismissed Ted with a flick of the hand and turned his attention to Damien. "I need you to contact the Calais guys, tell them there will be an extra load coming per month. Find out what ship you can get on and when. Find anyone that's going soon for this load, then arrange the regular shipment around their timetables. Tell them what's happened and remind them to be extra careful. As for Ben and Ralph..." He paused for a second. "Let that go now. No need to try to contact them."

There was a part of him that wanted to inflict punishment on them for allowing this to happen, when this is exactly what he had been paying them to avoid. But it seemed that it had been out of their control. There was only so much that men like them could do.

"Ok, I'll get on that today Freddie."

"Ok. And give the guys that were on that run a little extra in their pay this time. Paulie will sort out the cash for you." Paulie nodded his agreement. "Once we've done a couple of smooth runs on the new course, I want to discuss upping the amount we bring in each time." Freddie put his coffee down and sat forward. "Is there anything else you want to go over before I leave?"

"Yes, actually there is." Damien looked at Ted and then back to Freddie. "Ted's cousin is another supplier on the market. He wondered if we could do an introduction. Maybe use him for the overflow orders." Freddie turned towards Ted.

"And you don't want the extra business yourself?" he questioned, staring the young man down.

"Your orders already have me running at full capacity."

"And why should I use your cousin?" Freddie narrowed his eyes, "I have other established suppliers that would take on the demand."

"Well, yes, you do." Ted twisted his hands together in his lap. "But I'm guessing that you probably like to spread your business around so that if one of the factories go down, it isn't too much of a blow to you. So an extra supplier would be an asset to you. And on top of that, I'd like to bet that my vodka and whisky are some of the best you've had, every batch. My cousin uses the same methods. I can guarantee the quality." Ted finished his sales pitch and swallowed down the anxiety he was feeling under Freddie's steely, unwavering gaze. Freddie turned his attention to Damien and raised an eyebrow in question.

"I don't know him personally, Fred," Damien put his hands up. "I only take on suppliers I know, so you'd have to make the call on this one."

"Yes." Freddie agreed. Damien only trusted people that had already proved their worth to him. He wouldn't take on anyone that he wasn't 100% sure of personally. It was Freddie's business, so he wanted Freddie to make the decision. He stared at the hopeful, worried young man in front of him. He was bricking it that he'd asked too much - of Freddie Tyler of all people. That much was obvious. He didn't break eye contact though. He sat up straight and forced out a confidence he clearly didn't feel. A faint smile almost crept onto Freddie's face. He remembered what it was like, being a nobody, sitting in front of someone as respected and feared as he was.

"Ok. I'll give your cousin a meeting. I don't have time right now but I'll have someone contact you when I can do it."

"Thank you, thanks so much Mr Tyler. I really appreciate it." The gratefulness spilled out as he reached forward to shake Freddie's hand. Freddie gave him a tight smile, shook his hand and stood up. He needed to get on.

"Let me know when you've sorted everything, Damien. I'll catch you later."

"Will do, thanks Freddie."

Freddie sat down in Sammy's office without removing his coat. For once he felt like he was actually dressed appropriately for the arctic setting Sammy kept his air conditioning on.

"How you been?" He smiled warmly, a genuine smile he reserved for friends.

"Good mate, good." Sammy looked excited and animated. This was a good sign, Freddie thought. It meant he thought it would work. With how carefully Sammy made these decisions, Freddie trusted his instincts above almost anything else. "I've put together a list of people I think we would be best with. Let's go over them, see what you think."

"That sounds perfect Sammy," Freddie said with a wide grin, "absolutely perfect."

10

"It's here Anna. It's really, actually here! This is actually happening. Fuck!" Tanya was darting around the office at a hundred miles an hour, wringing her hands and biting her lip, looking like she might pass out from excitement and fright. Anna raised her eyebrows, her eyes wide. She had never seen her friend like this. If she hadn't been suffering from severely jangling nerves herself, she might have found it funny. But she was. Because this was the day they had been working so hard towards.

They had worked their fingers to the bone scrubbing and clearing the place out. They had organised re-decoration, furniture and floor plans. They had advertised for, interview and hired a small army of people to work the club, the door, the kitchens and of course, to perform in the shows. They had researched and even helped choreograph, to ensure that their acts would be the best. They had sweated and bled, shouted in frustration and cried with laughter to get this place perfect, shining and ready to go tonight. And now here they were. Here they were, hiding in the back room like absolute wimps. Anna took a deep breath and twirled the office chair she was sitting in to the side. Standing up, she straightened the simple, tailored black dress she was wearing and walked over to Tanya. She grasped her shoulders tightly, to stop her.

"We've got this." She said strongly, staring Tanya in the eye. "You and me, we have got this," she reiterated. "We did this," she motioned around her with one sweeping arm." Tanya's eyes scanned the small, cosy office. "We made this club from nothing. Just us. No one else. And you know what? It is absolutely amazing." Anna smiled broadly, excitement beginning to flow through her veins. "Tonight is going to be so much fun and everything's going to go just fine. More than fine. We've had loads of people check in on the website, so we already know we'll have a good crowd. And we are so central, the foot traffic will be queuing down the street."

Once they had earmarked the date for opening night, Anna had focused her energies into marketing it. They needed to have a successful first night in order for word to spread. A dead first night could kill them and that just couldn't happen. They had sunk everything they both had into this - failure was *not* an option.

Hitting the pavement, Anna and Tanya spent days handing out fliers to passers-by and through local offices, offering a free drink and free entry to anyone who registered their attendance on the website. They also promised canapés would be floating around inside. If there was one thing Anna knew people couldn't resist, it was free food and drink. Sure enough, the guest list began slowly filling up and now they were expecting over a hundred people just from that offer alone. If they could get a good buzz going outside and get the local traffic in, they would soon fill the place to capacity and might even have to turn people away. It would do them the world of good if that happened, Anna thought excitedly. To have people talking about the new club which was so popular that they couldn't get in would really boost bookings. People would be intrigued.

"Come on. Get yourself together," she laughed, nudging Tanya.

"Yes." Tanya shook herself slightly and stood up straight. "Yes, it'll be fine. It'll be brilliant. *We* are fucking brilliant."

"Exactly! Now, can you go and check that the girls out the back are ready and warming up?"

"Course." Tanya ran her hands through her thick, loosely curled hair one last time and re-checked her flawless makeup in the mirror. Rubbing her red, shiny lips together, she turned to give a dazzling smile to Anna and then walked out of the office with purpose. The chilled club music that was playing in the main bar came through loud and clear for a few seconds until the thick door clicked softly shut, leaving Anna in the quiet. She leaned back onto the front of her desk for a minute, her eyes glazing over. She had never been on the cusp of something so big and exciting before. It was something she had wanted for a long time, to do something big for herself. But before she ran away, it had been nothing but an impossible dream. Tony's cruel laughter bounced around in her head. She had asked him once if she could work again, if she could start something up herself. She had been so naïve back then.

"You what?" Tony sneered down at her. Anna lowered her eyes immediately, her cheeks burned but still she persevered. It was something she wanted so desperately, to have something of her own to work on and be proud of.

"I – I have some ideas. I'm actually pretty good with websites and brand developing. I, well I did do this before, you know...well, I did well, I think I could make it successful—"

"—did this before what?" Tony demanded, pushing his face down into hers. She flinched but forced herself not to move away. That would be a mistake. "Before you met me? Before I took your fucking ungrateful arse

in? Before I gave you a fucking palace and everything you could ever need? You ungrateful bitch."

"No, no I didn't mean it like that," she kicked herself and continued on hiding her hatred, "I'm grateful for everything. I just thought I could contribute, you know? I made good money..."

Tony snorted and paced around as if she had said something highly offensive.

"Your 'good money' is nothing but pennies next to what I make. And you think I'm going to sit by while you fuck off, pissing away your time playing around like lady muck at pathetic shit like 'brand building' which means fuck all in the real world? You think I am going to allow you time away from running the home I fucking gave you, which is your actual fucking job, to take the fucking piss out of me?" His voice rose with every sentence until he was screaming in her face, spittle flying out of his mouth and onto her fair skin. "Do you think I am that much of a mug, you piss taker? You don't deserve the shit on my shoe, you fucking bitch. Yet I give it to you, I give you fucking everything and this crap is what you come to me with?" He shook with rage, his black eyes glinting dangerously.

Anna felt the tears begin to sting the back of her eyes. Her hands trembled as she tried not to move. He was going to punish her anyway, she could already see that. She might as well have one more try.

"I know that you do a lot for us. I just wanted something to use my brain on, that's all. It wouldn't even have to be full time."

The punch to the face sent her flying across the room. It happened so swiftly that as she was heading backwards, she wondered for a moment how she was moving. The crack to the back of her head as it connected with the wall soon enlightened her. She slumped to the floor, the blinding pain resonating through her head so badly that she nearly passed out. Black spots danced in front of her eyes as she tried to hear through the ringing in her ears. The blow had been hard and the secondary bump to *the head hurt so much that she worried he'd cracked her skull.*

A hand gripped her face, squeezing her cheeks tightly and jerking her head to the side. She cried out at the stabbing sensation that this action sent through her brain. Tony's face came up to hers. His face shone clearly with the ugly, pure evil he usually kept hidden inside.

"You," he said in a shaking, deadly voice, "are a nobody. You are worth nothing outside of these four walls and never will be worth anything. You're too stupid, too weak and pathetically average. You already have two jobs, both of which you just about manage to do at an ok level. The first is to look after this house. The other is to fucking service me in the bedroom. That's it for you. This is what you amount to. You pass for an acceptable cleaner and an open pair of legs." Pressing his nose against hers he looked into her pained eyes for a moment before shoving her face away. "You're pretty, I'll give you that," he said, emotionlessly. "That's your saving grace. You look good when I need you to. It makes me look good. And I like to look good. But that's all you have going for you. Remember that next time you come to me with your misplaced airs and graces and your big fucking mouth." He spat in her face, before rocking back on his haunches and standing up. Anna didn't move, for fear of a continued attack. "Your own job indeed." He laughed, seeming to find it amusing now that his anger was spent. "Go and sort yourself out, you look a mess." He curled his lip in disgust and walked out.

Anna waited until she heard his office door shut at the other end of the house and then relaxed forward away from the wall. She cradled her head in her hands and let the moan of pain she had been holding in escape her lips. Her vision was still hazy and she felt like she was going to be sick. The pain was throbbing through her head violently. She touched her face, checking it for damage. Her nose wasn't broken, he had hit her slightly to the side of her face. Her cheek was already swelling, but with a gentle feel the cheekbone was still intact, from what she could tell. She tentatively reached her shaking fingers around to the back of her head. Pressing where the pain seemed to be coming from, she immediately retched. There was a huge lump and she could feel the sticky wetness of blood. She pulled her hand back to the floor in front of her, steadying her swaying body, trying to calm her stomach down. She needed to get some ice on her head.

Ignoring the blood on her fingers, slowly she pulled herself into a kneeling position and waited for the world to stop spinning before she gingerly stood up. Silently, she walked through to the kitchen and took a packet of frozen vegetables out of the freezer. She wrapped it in an old towel and winced as it touched the tender area. She closed her eyes and hunched over the kitchen table, leant her forehead on her free hand.

She closed her mind to what had just happened and focused on trying to fix the damage. There was no point thinking about it. If she thought about it too deeply she would begin to panic. Because there was no way out. There was no exit from this hell. And the more she allowed herself to think about it, the worse she felt. She closed her mind and curled up into a ball. She just had to survive right now.

Pulling herself back to the present, she shook off the memory. Her lips hardened into a thin line. She had come a long way since then. She had come a long way since that fateful night when she had finally escaped, nerves shot and expecting to be killed at every turn she took. He had damaged her, oh yes. That much was inescapable. But he hadn't defeated her and she grew more confident and stronger with every single day of her new life. She would always be looking over her shoulder, always hiding from her past, but she wouldn't wither away like some little lost soul. She would adapt and flourish. These days - though still wary - she jumped less. Her panic attacks came less frequently. The flashbacks and nightmares still haunted her, but they were weaker, not as crippling.

Walking to the mirror, Anna stared hard at the woman in front of her. This woman was so much more than that psycho had tried to make her believe. These days she was Anna Davis, independent woman, best friend, business partner. She was so much more than Tony's punch bag. And he couldn't take anything away from her anymore. She wouldn't let him. And she certainly wasn't about to let the shadow of him take tonight away from her. Not this night, nor any other. He couldn't hurt her anymore.

Tanya turned towards the group of people standing by the bar and grinned widely, her green eyes twinkling.

"This is it, guys. Let's give these bastards the best night of their lives!" There was a cheer and laughter as the staff became infected by Tanya's excitement. She raised her voice, passion shining through it. "When I open those doors, Club Anya will officially be open and within the following ten minutes, this club will be crowned the best gentleman's club in all of London!" She fist-pumped the air and more cheering ensued. She saw Anna enter the room from the back, out of the corner of her eye. "Well, it fucking best be, or I'm going home," she joked. They all laughed.

Anna smiled, shaking her head. Wherever they went, whoever they met, no one could help but be totally entranced by Tanya. She had all the staff hanging on her every word. If it wasn't for her thick, East End accent and the fact she couldn't get through a sentence without swearing at least once, she would have made a fantastic public speaker, Anna thought. She leaned against the wall, her arms folded comfortably. She didn't join Tanya. The front of house and all the staff were totally under Tanya's rule. It was the back office that Anna ran. It suited them both and made the most of their various talents.

"So," Tanya continued, quieting down but with a warm smile, "go to your posts and give it your all. Bar staff, I want speed, attention to detail and most of all, I want big smiles for the punters. They need best friends, that's you. Door men, keep it friendly but stick to the rules and I trust your judgements." The two burly men to the side nodded their agreement.

"Anything for you, Tan," one of them winked fondly at her.

"Girls." Tanya stopped and put her arms out wide. "You gorgeous, beautiful creatures. You know that I know what it's like. You are the front line troupers, the diamonds that they're here to see. Just you remember, that's what you are. Diamonds," she stressed. "This ain't like those shit-arse clubs back east, with back rooms where you're expected to do certain things. You're here to dance and put on a good show. Make them work for it, make them part with all of their money, you know the tricks. But anyone getting handsy, signal the boys to show them out. Ok?"

"Yes Tanya. Thanks Tan," the girls chorused. Most of them had worked in clubs such as the one Tanya had worked in herself. Some even knew her. All of them were excited to be working here, if a little wary of how good the job sounded. Anna had been unmovable on the fact that this was to be totally above board and not just that, but that the girls were to put on shows that outshone all of the other clubs of this type in the city. Between the two of them and a freelance choreographer, the girls were ready to perform a new mix of stripping and theatre. This way, the men got their fix of flesh, but there was something extra that made the experience a whole lot more interesting. Teaching the girls their moves had been challenging at times, but they had all buckled down and both Tanya and Anna were confident that they were going to shine tonight.

"Boys," Tanya turned to face the small cluster of kitchen staff. "Your food is pukka, let's make sure we stay up to standard and get as much out there as they can eat, yeah?"

"Yes boss," they grinned.

"Ok!" Tanya clapped her hands together. "Come on Anna, let's go and open this club."

Anna walked forward with Tanya, skipping along to the double front doors. She unlocked them and stepped aside for the two bouncers to take their places. Tanya walked out into the cold night air to greet her public, and swept up in the euphoric atmosphere Tanya had created, Anna almost stepped out after her.

Click. Click, click. Flashes accompanied the sounds and Anna froze, just inside the door. Her heart leapt up into her mouth and she quickly stepped back into the shadows. It was the local press. She had called them herself, offering them free drinks all night to promote the club. She kicked herself for forgetting. In her eagerness to promote the club, she almost forgot to keep herself hidden. Tanya, smiling for the cameras, turned to the side. Not finding her there, she looked back and gave Anna a quizzical look. Anna shook her head and motioned towards the camera. Confusion filled Tanya's face for a second and then understanding dawned. She tilted her head to one side, sadly. *It should've been them both out there.* But Anna ushered her forward, smiling encouragingly. Hesitating only a moment more, Tanya turned her attention back to the press and the waiting queue, and began her big introduction. Melting away, Anna turned back to the office. She had plenty to be doing back there. Tanya had this.

The night carried on as positively as it had begun and turned out to be a roaring success. To Anna's glee, they did indeed end up having to turn guests away and even ended the night with two future table reservations. There were a few minor creases that had to be ironed out throughout the night, but nothing bigger than the girls had expected to deal with.

As they said goodbye to the last merry, drunken guest, Tanya closed the front door and leaned her weight against it whilst she turned the lock. She was exhausted, but exhilarated at the same time. She still felt like she needed to pinch herself, just to check that all of this was real. Looking around at the end of night mess, a slow smile spread across her face and she hugged herself. It really was real. No more stripping for lecherous perverts, no more extra services in the back room in order to scrimp together the money for her dream. Her dream had finally become a reality.

Thanks to Anna. Her eyes wandered to the closed door of the back room.

Her life had been transformed since Anna had arrived. It wasn't that she'd had a bad life before, not at all. She had her independence, she called all the shots. Endless nights were filled with parties and clubs, her days were filled with shopping and laughs. Her job was soul-destroying, but at the end of the day it had been her choice and no one had made her do it. It was just that getting out of that way of life was a lot harder than it seemed, once you were in. Before Anna came along it had felt like she was wading through thick mud, in the dark. She had waded and waded, trying to find the exit. She could even see the door sometimes, but without the money she needed, it was as if the door was locked and bolted to her. Then Anna had come along and handed her the key. For this, more than anything else, she would always be more grateful than Anna would ever know.

The bar staff chatted away to each other, as they busied themselves with the clear up. They had a lot to do, they would be at it for at least another hour. Tanya looked around at the goings-on with a critical eye. The tables were being wiped down, the floors were being swept and the glasses were being polished. She nodded to herself and stepped behind the bar. Picking out a bottle of champagne from the fridge, she located two clean flutes and held them together in one hand by the stems. She flicked her hair back over her shoulder and, awarding one of her barmen with a wink and a smile, walked through to the back office.

The door opened and Anna looked up from the receipts she had been going through. Tanya appeared with the bottle and she smiled, ready for a drink after the long night.

"Oh yes, I think we have definitely earned this one." She cleared space for Tanya to put the bottle and glasses down and waited whilst she popped the cork.

"Whoop! Congratulations to us! Our first night as successful club owners. And we were a success, right?" Tanya paused and cocked her head to one side.

"Yes, we really were," Anna said excitedly and turned her laptop screen towards Tanya. "Look. I'm not through everything yet, but already we are showing to be in profit. That in itself is an achievement. Some businesses have to run at a loss for a while, before they turn even a penny in profit."

"Well, aside from the fact our club is obviously great, I think we have our location to thank for that. We couldn't have been more lucky with this place," Tanya commented, as she poured the champagne. She looked over the columns in the outgoings section of Anna's neat spreadsheet. "There is one more expense that needs to be accounted for though."

"Oh?" Anna leaned over and studied her list, frowning. She couldn't think of anything that she had missed. She'd gone over it a hundred times; her paperwork was airtight.

"It's not exactly something we can put through the books. We *will* need to pay out for protection. This sort of club," she gestured around her, "well, it's part of a different sort of world than a normal business. We're running a gentleman's entertainment club on turf that belongs to a particular firm. That's how it has *always* been," Tanya explained, "and how it always will be. We'll need to pay something out to a guy called Vince. In return, he will make it known to all of the other criminal firms around - and the little fuckers looking for places to scam - that this place is off limits. Anyone causes real trouble, they sort it out, anyone causes us financial damage, he pays out, that sort of thing."

Anna raised her eyebrows, not impressed by this bombshell.

"Why didn't you tell me this before? And why can't we just run independently?"

"Honestly, I just forgot that you weren't from this sort of life." She shrugged. "In our world, it goes without saying. And yes, technically we could run independently. We could say no thanks, politely, and Vince would let us be. He's actually a good guy, very fair. But within a week we would have three other firms in here trying to take over, trying to bully us into running scams and schemes. Because this would be known as the only club without a firm. Not only that, but a neutral club bang smack in the middle of the West End, which is a pie *everyone* wishes they had a finger in. We'd be a beacon for anyone trying to gain some ground here. Which is basically everybody who ain't above board."

Anna turned this over in her head. It annoyed the hell out of her, but she could see the truth and sense in Tanya's words. After years of living around Tony's firm and various criminal businesses, she had been elated to have escaped that world and thought she had washed it off completely. Now it seemed, she would have no choice but to accept that it would be a part of her life. She would have to be careful. People talked and the criminal underworld wasn't that big.

"I see," she said heavily. "Ok. Well, I guess we have no choice then."

Tanya studied her friend's weary, worried expression.

"Don't worry about it too much, mate. I'll deal with it, alright? I'll arrange a meeting in about a week and sort it out myself. You don't need to be involved at all. I'll just let you know how much it will be and you can work your magic with the figures."

Great, Anna thought sarcastically. Financial fraud, here we come.

"They will want to see the accounts for the first week before they decide what to charge us. They only charge what they know is affordable with a club's earnings."

"Ok, I'll leave it with you then. Just tell me what you need to take with you and I'll put it together for you. Tanya," she locked eyes with her friend, "please don't tell them my name. Please tell them it's just your club - with a silent partner. You know...well...You know. Ok?"

"Of course." Tanya leant forward and squeezed Anna's cold hand.

She bit her lip, but said no more. She knew now that Anna's ex was a violent man who had abused her terribly. She knew also that he had some sway, after seeing that he had men out searching for Anna. But that was pretty much all she did know. The finer details of exactly what he had done to her were still a mystery, as was what he did for a living. All she was sure of, was Annas deep terror and fear of being found.

"Right. Well, let's celebrate shall we?" Anna grasped the full glasses and handed one to Tanya. "Cheers! Here is to our new club, our ongoing friendship and many more happy years together."

Christmas passed quickly for everyone. Freddie invited Anna to his home for Christmas, on strict instruction from Mollie, but she had politely refused. Much as she'd been tempted, she and Tanya had already decided to spend the holidays together. They were as close as any two sisters could ever be and were family to each other. Anna spoke to her parents and shared holiday laughs with them over the phone whilst Leslie and Arthur huddled together by the secret mobile in the en-suite bathroom, door locked behind them. In the end they were on the phone for so long that Arthur went downstairs, dished up their Christmas dinner and bought their plates up on trays. They sat cross legged on the bathroom floor with their meals, keeping Anna on speaker phone, listening happily whilst she told them stories of her new life.

When Anna finally ended the call, Leslie wept in Arthur's arms for a few minutes. Then she looked up at her husband apologetically and gave him a watery smile.

"It's ok," he said gently. "I miss her too. But I'm just glad that she's safe and that we can talk to her." He looked around at the bathroom. "Might start thinking about redecorating in here though. Maybe add a couple of armchairs!"

Leslie laughed and wiped away her tears. She sniffed and hoisted herself up from the unforgiving tiled floor.

"Well, maybe at least a decently thick rug," she said. She sighed and hid the phone back under the sink where they kept it. Arthur stood up too and stretched. "I'm fine Art, I really am. I just miss her. It's Christmas day. She should be at home, lounging downstairs in her pyjamas, playing with her presents and picking at the stuffing."

"She hasn't done that for years, Leslie," Arthur said sadly, "but I know what you mean." He patted her on the back and followed her back out into the main house.

Over in East London, Anna put the turkey on the table and offered Tanya a cracker. Tanya pulled it with her and then handed Anna a sickly looking pink, sparkling drink.

"What on earth is that?" Anna laughed, already fairly tiddly from Tanya's other adventurous creations.

"Alright, don't judge it just yet, yeah?" Tanya said dramatically, also half-cut and giggling like a schoolgirl. "That, my friend…is a 'Double Bubble' and it's going to be our New Year signature drink for all the ladies that frequent our fine establishment." She hiccupped and cupped her hand over her mouth. Anna burst into peals of laughter.

"I do think you're a bit pissed Miss Tanya! Which is entirely your own fault, you red-headed, alcoholic drink forcer person. Oh God, I think I am a bit too. Anyway, what the hell is a 'Double Bubble'?"

"It's champagne, with bubblegum syrup. It's fucking immense, I've had two already in my little, you know—" she waved her hand over to the sideboard where she had been messily mixing up drinks, "—experiment area."

"Oh God. Ok, go on then." Anna took a big gulp of the new drink and grimaced. It was sickly sweet but also, as she swallowed it, very refreshing. "Wow. That is super-sugary."

"I know, right?"

"Not quite my thing, but it's a great one for the New Year ladies. Good shout."

Since their grand opening, the club had become popular with not only the men but a lot of women too. As the girls weren't just stripping, but performing acts with storylines and backdrops and dancing, it had become a novelty place for everyone to visit. These days, seeing naked women perform was not such a taboo. Not that Anna had mentioned this to her parents. As far as they were aware, her club was the kind you went for a bit of a boogie and a couple of drinks, nothing more.

Tanya was having the best Christmas Day that she had ever had. Christmas for her had always been a lonely affair, filled with crappy films, microwave meals and a shed load of booze. It was still filled with a fair amount of booze, but this year - for the first time she could ever remember - it was actually a real Christmas. It was being spent with someone she loved, there were actual presents and a real Christmas dinner with a whole roast turkey. Anna had gone the whole hog, making little stuffing balls and a mountain of vegetables and roast potatoes and there was even a homemade Christmas pudding. The flat was full of festive decorations and the tree was the most beautiful thing Tanya had ever seen. Sure, there were probably bigger and fancier trees out there than theirs. The tinsel was not perfectly placed and the baubles were every colour under the sun, to match the multi-coloured lights that twinkled away. But it was *their* tree. They had put it up and decorated it together. It filled Tanya with a warm happiness that she had never felt before, every time she looked at it. This must be what other people feel like every Christmas, she thought.

She thought back to her miserable Christmases as a child. If her father had been there he would sometimes fish out a toy or a treat for her. But those Christmases would be all about her mother trying to shove Tanya out of the way, to spend time with her haphazard husband. Tanya would always end up in her room whilst they spent the day either laughing drunk together, or fighting drunk together. If her father wasn't there that year, it would be much worse. Tanya would be punished for tying her mother down and being such a burden. There would be no dinner of any kind, let alone a proper Christmas one. There had never been a tree. As an adult with no family who cared for her, she'd carried on her mother's tradition of alcohol and miserable reflection. Until now, anyway.

Anna watched Tanya's face soften as she watched the lights twinkling on the tree. It had broken her heart when Tanya admitted that she'd never had a tree before. It was obvious that all of this was new and a hard lump formed in Anna's throat. What sort of childhood had her friend had? Tanya had actually cried when Anna gave her the silver locket she had bought her. Inside was a picture of Tanya and her hugging on a rare night out. She had put it straight on and cried into her hands for a good five minutes. Anna had laughed, both surprised and alarmed at the display.

"I'm sorry! I didn't realise my face was so upsetting!" she said, running over and hugging her friend tightly.

"No, it's just, I'm sorry, it's just...this is the nicest thing anyone's ever done for me. This is the nicest thing I have ever had," Tanya said, between heavy, heartfelt sobs. Anna had rocked her and jollied her out of it. Once she had a hold on herself again Tanya cracked some jokes too, clearly embarrassed of her reaction to the gift.

Tanya had bought Anna a beautifully soft pair of leather gloves that she had been admiring one day as they were walking through the shops. Anna was thrilled with her gift and couldn't wait to put them to good use.

As they sat down to dinner, with an array of cocktails surrounding the mountain of food, the two young women smiled at each other.

"Come on then, dig in!"

Over at Freddie's house the festivities were in full swing and the volume was deafening. Christmas songs were pumping out of the sound system Freddie had set up in the lounge, and the air was filled with wonderful smells from Mollie's kitchen.

"*Siiiimply, haaaaving, a wonderful Christmas tiiiime!*" Thea sang along as she danced around the living room with Paulie, each a little rosy-cheeked from the rather potent eggnog Thea had made. Paulie loved Christmas possibly more than anything else in the world. Freddie looked on at him in bemusement as his brother twirled Thea round and round, a huge smile plastered on his face. If their men could see Freddie's hard second-in-command now, they wouldn't believe their eyes. He rolled his eyes and turned his gaze subtly over to Michael. He was sat in one of the other armchairs, watching Thea and Paulie with a glazed expression on his face as though lost in thought. He wasn't smiling. He rarely did these days. It was worrying Freddie deeply. It was worrying everyone really. But he refused to open up and got angry when people tried to push him, so they had no choice but to back off. He wasn't happy though, that was a certainty. Freddie just wished he knew why.

"Hey, Mickey," Freddie called. "Michael?" Michael turned his head towards Freddie and blinked, coming back to the present.

"What?"

Freddie contained his annoyance at the rude tone his brother kept using towards him. If anyone else spoke to him like that they'd be skinned. But Michael was his brother and seemingly troubled, so he cut him more slack than he usually would. He saw Thea's eyes widen for a second though, before pretending she wasn't listening, obviously shocked that he would talk like that to Freddie. He breathed deeply.

"Your seventeenth birthday is coming up in the new year. What would you like us to get you? Anything you particularly want?"

"Driving lessons. I'm going to need those," he replied curtly, looking away.

"Right. Ok then, driving lessons it is. Then if you pass in time, I'll get you a motor for your eighteenth. You can come and pick one with me. That sound good?"

"Sure," he answered flatly.

Sure. Freddie let it echo in his head. No *'thank you'*, no smile, nothing. As if he were somehow just entitled to it, like it was owed to him. Had he spoilt him? Was it his fault? He didn't think so. He made sure Michael had what he needed and had sent him to a good school to help build a better future for him, but he didn't think he'd spoilt him.

Michael stood up and left the room, heading upstairs. Thea frowned and looked to Freddie.

"What was that about?" she asked, confusedly.

"I don't know," Freddie answered quietly, his eyes on the door Michael had just walked through.

Mollie bustled through, her face as red as the festive Christmas dress she wore underneath her snowman pinny. Her hair was wildly breaking loose of the bun she had put it in and there was flour on her cheek, but she was bursting with Christmas cheer and had a big smile on her face. Oblivious to the undercurrent of Michael's mood flowing through the room, she was excited and happy. She had all her children under one roof and they would stay with her, eating and laughing and celebrating with her, all day. There was nothing more that even God could give that would make her happier. Except perhaps the addition of her late husband, but she didn't dwell on that.

"Come through, come through, dinner is ready! Have you all got clean hands? Go and clean up and come through, all of you. Be a dear Thea and get Michael. I've made all his favourites! Come on now!" She disappeared back to the heavily laden and decorated table to make sure it was still as perfect as she'd left it thirty seconds before.

"I'll go get him," Thea said after a nod from Freddie. Freddie and Paulie shared a look. Somehow they needed to get to the bottom of this, before it began to hurt Mollie.

The last of Tony's chosen few men walked into the den, a larger office Tony kept in his house for large meetings such as these. He closed the door silently behind him and took his place around the large table, waiting to hear whatever Tony had called them there to discuss.

Angelo sat to one side of Tony, who was positioned at the head of the long, dark table. He was whispering urgently into Tony's ear about something, whilst the rest of the men chatted between themselves. Tony nodded and then sat back, looking at the faces around him. Immediately everyone fell silent and directed their attention onto their boss. Everyone had a drink in their hand, the well-stocked bar at the end of the room laid open and offered to them as they arrived. This meant it was a positive meeting, not a bollocking, which put many of their minds at ease. It was always a worry with Tony Christou, to be called to a meeting of which you did not know the cause. You could be walking away from it with a profitable job to do, or you could be carried away from it with a bullet in your head.

"Gentlemen," Tony spread his arms out wide and smiled. "Welcome. Have you all got a drink? Yeah? Dev, you got one?" Dev nodded and lifted his glass to show Tony. "Good. Good, good. Ok. Right. You lot are here because although I have a small army working for me, you few are the ones I actually fully trust. You are the few I know that no matter what the crack, you are 100% loyal. And I value that. Loyalty." He nodded to himself, gravely. "Mm. I value that a lot. And I want to reward that. So I have got a job for you. It's a fucking big'un. And it's dirty. Some of you've already been doing a bit of work on it, most of you are still in the dark, but I am going to enlighten you today." Tony reached into his pocket and brought out his cigarettes. He lit one and took a deep drag before continuing.

"As you know, our businesses are limited to the north of London. They're very lucrative, of course. But they *are* limited. And, why is that? Why are we so limited, when we're the best at what we do? We run bookies, dens, sharks, laundering," he ticked them off his hand, one by one. "And we run them well. We have the corner on the crack heroin market and the stuff we bring in is by far the best, so I hear. So why," he asked, narrowing his eyes, "are we being kept in our fucking box, up here on the side lines?" He eyed each of the men in the room, seeing who had worked out where he was going with this yet. No one seemed to be giving much away, so he continued.

"We're being kept up here, in our little patch, because the boys running around creaming all the money in central say so. Because they don't want anyone else coming over to their little gold mine and taking any of it. Now," he shrugged and pulled a nonchalant face, "I can understand that. I would want to keep other people off my honey pot too, if it were mine. But that's just the thing, ain't it?" He leaned forward suddenly. "It ain't mine." He flicked his cigarette ash carefully into the ashtray in front of him and took another large drag.

"The problem here, is that the more I think about it, the more unfair that seems. Why shouldn't it be mine? Why shouldn't it be ours." He encompassed the whole room with his arm. "Who decided that it belonged to those fuckers and not us? It certainly wasn't me. Now my cousin, Cos. He gets on with them and they've thrown him a few bones and a friendly smile and he's rolled over and agreed not to step on their toes. Apparently in return they won't step on his. But of course they won't!" his voice rose. "Why would they bother with the North, our little corner, when they've got the fucking heart! They're laughing at us." He banged his fist on the table. "Now Cos might be happy sitting there like a little puppy dog, never striving for more, but I'm not. And I don't think any of you are, either. I think, like me, you would like to taste a real piece of the pie for once. So this boys, is what we are going to do." He stood up and leaned his weight forward over the table. "We're going to take central London. West End, East End, all ours. We'll leave the south, those bastards can keep their shitty side of the river, but we're taking everything else. We're going to take it and make it ours and they won't know what's hit them." He stared around at the men in the room. Some of their faces looked shocked, but they quickly masked this. Some looked excited. A few looked concerned. All kept their counsel. He leaned back and eased down into his seat.

"You will all have heard about Big Dom's sudden demise a couple of months back. That was engineered by me. Angelo here took him out." He patted Angelo on the back and the baby-faced young man nodded confirmation to the rest of the men, smiling. "Big Dom was the first domino that needed to fall." He smiled at his own wit. "We toppled their old King. Now, I haven't been able to get anyone near Vince, but that's ok for now. We made our statement with Big Dom. Their people are uneasy and are losing faith in their boss' ability to keep them safe and deliver retribution. This much has been overheard already. I've had a few of you quietly watching the comings and goings of several of their higher ranking men. We've gained valuable intelligence on their routines. Their businesses have also been scouted and we think we've found a way into several of them, for a sudden overtake. The plan is to time this so that certain players of theirs are in certain places, out of the way. At the same time a diversion will be created to pull away the remaining few men that are in our way. At this point, there will be several of you with small teams in place to play out a takeover - all at once. Overthrow one place, they can oust us. Overthrow a number of places and they have a problem on their hands." He looked pleased with his plan. One of the men put their hand up to get Tony's attention. He looked over quizzically.

"What happens then? They'll still make an attempt to get control back, even if they go for one at a time, we'll be too thinly stretched."

"By this point there will be a secondary, much larger team of my men in place, ready to come in and heavily secure each location. There will be a number of armed men across the front of each site. When they come – and they will come – we will extend them an offer to join our firm, the winning firm. With their belief wavering in their own bosses, many will come to us. Many won't and that is their choice. At this stage at least. These days, the man they all follow is Freddie Tyler. Vince has retired. Freddie is who we're really up against. He is the one we need to take out. Now, as it stands," Tony filled his tumbler up with more of the whisky placed within his reach, "Freddie has no clue that we had anything to do with Big Dom's death. He has no clue that we're up to anything and as far as he believes, he has a good relationship with the Greeks in general. So before he hears that anything has even happened, I'll be sat having a friendly lunch with him. Introducing myself, offering a business-related hand of friendship. And before he even gets through his main course," a manic, excited glint shone brightly in Tony's eyes, "I will make an excuse to go to the bathroom. I'll walk up behind him and I'll slit his pathetic, weakling throat. That," he spat, "is the point at which *we* will win. That's the point where his men no longer have anyone to follow or give them instruction on how to take back their businesses. They will flock to me, and London," he smiled wryly, "will be ours."

11

The two nondescript black SUVs pulled up down the abandoned side street and stopped, their engines turning silent. There were no CCTV cameras down here, or in fact on any of the last mile of road they had been driving down. They'd had to travel the long way round in order to avoid these cameras, but it was important that they were not picked up in any searches around the vicinity afterwards.

Freddie looked at his watch and then pulled his sleeve back over his wrist. He was dressed from head to toe in black, as was Sammy, who sat next to him in the driver seat. They both wore plain black, long-sleeved, high-necked, skin-tight jumpers and black jeans. They each had a pair of new, black leather gloves on and balaclavas sat on the dashboard awaiting use. In the second car, Paulie sat waiting in the same get up, along with Bill Hanlon and John Daley, another man of Freddie's, who usually worked on collections. After some conversation, Sammy and Freddie had decided that five men were more than enough. John would guard the front gate and alert them if anything unexpected went down. Bill would stay out by the car, grabbing the bags from them and loading them in. Freddie, Sammy and Paulie would be on the run, grabbing the bags and getting them out as quickly as possible. They had all been briefed down to the last tiny detail. They had planned the entire operation to be completed in eight minutes, to be sure that they were out and well on their way by the end of the ten minute window that they had open to them.

Freddie breathed in and out, deeply. He was wired and completely on edge. But this was good, he reasoned. It would keep him alert. Sammy looked sideways at him, appearing decidedly more relaxed in his seat, leaning his arm on the side of the car.

"You ok? You seem tense."

"I *am* tense," Freddie admitted. "It's a risky one, you said that yourself." He glanced back at Sammy. "You look like we're just popping for a quick pint before a quiet night in."

Sammy laughed, a deep, rumbling laugh that seemed to come from his stomach.

"Hopefully we will be, later. Yeah, I'm alright. It's a solid plan, it's simple enough. If anything goes wrong it won't be from the plan or one of us, it will come from a direction we have no control over. I have every faith in what we are doing. And if something I can't control happens," he shrugged, "well, no point worrying over it yet, ey?"

Freddie pulled a face and nodded. He couldn't argue with that. Still, he was too wired to relax and that suited him just fine. His watch beeped and Sammy restarted the car. The CCTV was now down throughout the police station, for the next ten minutes until the automatic reboot would override the manual action. As they pulled out of the narrow side street, Freddie watched Paulie through his wing mirror, following in the second car. They turned the corner and came to a stop outside a pair of wire gates. Barbed wire was curled across the top in aggressive loops all the way up to the tall walls either side, topped with cemented-in spikes of broken glass. They were at the back entrance of the police station. Freddie and Sammy reached for their balaclavas and put them on.

As they reached the gates, they began to open. The guard in the small portakabin inside the gate lifted his hand in greeting and then disappeared for his tea break, as planned. John jumped out of the car behind, gun in hand, and took his place inside the gate. Checking around just in case, he waved them through the second the gate was wide enough. The two cars slipped through and headed straight for the small door to the right of the large, brick building in front of them. It was eerily devoid of movement in the large loading area. Police cars and vans littered the space around them, left there until their drivers would collect them on the next shift. A sliver of light appeared from the door they were aiming for, as they backed the vehicles up against it as close as possible. The light grew stronger as it was opened fully by one of their paid plods waiting on the other side. Freddie and Sammy jumped out and were joined by Paulie. Bill swung the boot open on both vehicles as the three of them walked in with purpose.

The outer door was closed, the plod standing by ready to open it again when they came back through. It had to be opened using a code and triggered an alarm if left open for more than a minute. Freddie nodded a greeting to the man. They quickly made their way through the next sealed door where another of their payrollers, Gavin, was awaiting them. He smiled as they entered and began walking with them through the hallway to the room they needed to get to. They reached the door and he slid a card through the reader to unlock it. Freddie looked at the card.

"It's the visitor card. Can't be traced to me. Don't worry."

"If it was traceable, it wouldn't be me that has to worry mate," Freddie replied. He patted Gavin on the shoulder and they entered the hold.

Freddie looked around and whistled under his breath. There was a small armoury in there of confiscated weapons, alongside enough drugs to satisfy the whole country for a month. It was a criminal gold mine. He shut away these thoughts and concentrated on the job at hand.

"Where is it?"

"Here," Gavin skipped forward and dragged out a large evidence box from a wall of boxes. "It starts here and goes about six boxes that way." He pointed along the wall.

"Right - Paulie start that end, Sammy go for the middle. We have five minutes to get this done. I reckon two runs. Go!" he ordered.

The three of them began hoisting the sealed bags of money over their shoulders. Freddie had asked for everything to be bagged up ready to go beforehand and it seemed that the men here had delivered. Laden with as many of the heavy bags they could carry, they jogged through the doorway and down the hall. They burst through the next door, breathing heavily, and Freddie looked up to check the outer door was being opened so that they didn't have to stop. It was opened and swiftly held back as the three shot through with their first load. Lurching forward, they all dumped their bags on the ground outside the building. Bill jumped forward and started loading them into the boot spaces.

Freddie caught his breath on the run back through to the room. They loaded up again and started the journey back to the car. Freddie's back muscles strained under the weight of the heavy bags. His breathing became more ragged and a few beads of sweat began forming on his brow, as he made it through to the outside a second time. *Christ*, he thought, half smiling at himself, *I need to make it to the gym more.* Bill was ready to grab for the bags again but his face was tight.

"You need to make this run quicker boys, we're pushing it," he said with urgency.

They redoubled their efforts and flew down the corridor to get the last few bags. Freddie had been right - three runs with three people would just about do it.

The static sounded on the walkie-talkie attached to Freddie's belt as someone got ready to talk. He froze for a millisecond, then carried on keeping his ears trained on the voice coming through. Time was of the essence.

"Gate to runner, there's a car approaching. It's stopped up the road, lights on facing the gate."

Freddie swore, loudly. He wound another bag over his back. Paulie stared at him, eyes wide.

"Can't see if it's wrapped in bacon, lights too bright and it ain't moving."

Freddie squeezed his eyes shut for a second. He went to grab his last bag, but Sammy took it off him, gesturing to the walkie-talkie.

"I'll take this, you do that," he said. He began the third run back and Freddie and Paulie joined him. As they ran, Freddie opened up the line and began to speak into the small device.

"Runner to gate, has it moved yet?" They ran quicker than ever back through to the outer door. Freddie's heart was pounding from a mixture of the physical exertion and the threat that had just presented itself. Worst case scenario, he reasoned, would be a copper who smelled a rat, calling in to check things out. This could potentially cut their time down and leave one or more witnesses. They should still be able to get out though, but it would still have to be dealt with.

"Wait," John's voice came through the radio. "Oh for pete's sake, false alarm. It's just some couple having a barney. She's stropped off and he's driving away. He'll be paying for that in the morning," he added, humorously. Paulie and Sammy laughed quietly in agreement. Freddie just breathed out the huge breath he had been holding in. Bill carried on shovelling the bags in, his face betraying nothing. Freddie threw the last of his load in the back and checked that nothing was missing.

"Right," he glimpsed at his watch. "We have to go now. Right now. Quickly."

His men did not need telling twice. They jumped in. Both engines roared to life and started moving with their cargo. The door shut for the final time behind them.

"Runner to gate, open up and get ready."

"Gotcha."

Ahead of them, the slow gates began to open up. As they neared them, they were just wide enough to head straight through. Freddie opened the back door of the car from the inside and running alongside the vehicle, John leaped in and slammed it shut behind him. The car didn't stop. John pulled his balaclava off and straightened up in his seat. He peered his head through the middle.

"We fucking did it," he grinned.

"Not yet," Freddie said curtly. They made it through the gates and Freddie watched in the mirror as the second car did the same. He glanced quickly at his watch and breathed an audible sigh of relief.

They had done it. They had pulled off the heist. Turning to Sammy and John, he allowed a slow smile to cross his face.

"*Now* we've done it." Opening the radio line to the other car, he continued. "Let's get this to the yard, burn these clothes and get down to the 10, to celebrate. Get your wives and girlfriends out. But just tell them it's a jolly. Our work here tonight is between us."

A cheer came down the line from Paulie and Bill murmured his acceptance. Freddie lifted his phone out of his pocket and sent a text to Anna. Anna wasn't his girlfriend of course, he didn't know what she was. But whatever she was, he wanted her here with him tonight. He wanted to celebrate with her. Even if she didn't have a clue what it was about, he just felt the need to be around her. He waited for the ping that told him his message had been delivered, then put his phone away back in his pocket. He hoped she accepted his invite.

Anna looked at the long queue in front of the club she was meeting Freddie at. She ignored it and walked past it, straight to the bouncers at the front. A few disgruntled comments flew out at her but she ignored them. She knew that this was Freddie's club and he had instructed her to come straight in. Stating her name at the door, the bouncer smiled and let her through, pointing her towards the VIP area. She stopped to hand her coat in on the way, not wanting to carry it.

She had been excited to receive the message from Freddie. No matter how hard she tried not to think of him, he still filled her thoughts whenever she wasn't busy. It was dangerous, because she knew without doubt that he only cared for her as a friend, but she couldn't seem to help her excitement whenever she had a chance to see him. She was supposed to be working at the club that night, but as soon as Tanya heard that she'd received a rare invitation to go out, she immediately took over Anna's shift.

"Oh no, I can't, that's not fair on you," Anna had protested.

"Oh shut up. I'm not asking you, I'm telling you," Tanya had replied forcefully. "You never do anything and this Prince Charming—" as was Tanya's nickname for him, "—has asked you out to go and have some fun for once. Go and have a dance and a drink and you know, whatever else you fancy." She winked.

"It's not like that," Anna automatically replied.

"Yeah, but you wish it was, don't you. Go and get tarted up and go out. Have some fun. All work and no play, you," Tanya grumbled, pushing her friend back into the bedroom. "And wear something sexy, yeah?" she shouted after her. Anna had rolled her eyes. *As if.*

Now here she was. She wished Tanya had been able to come with her, but this was how it was these days. Unless they were at their own club, they rarely had any time to do anything together anymore. But that was the curse of running your own business, she thought. No time of your own anymore.

She walked through the throng of people dancing away on the dance floor to the latest hits, laughing and relaxing as the booze went to their heads. She wondered how many people were with Freddie tonight, whether or not she would get much chance to speak to him. He had told her that it was a get-together with a bunch of friends. What had he told them about her? she wondered. She shook her head. He probably hadn't said *anything* about her. Why would he? She was just another friend joining this social gathering, like they all were. Maybe he would even have another girl there with him, one he was seeing. She paused in her step, ice grasping her heart with its cold fingers.

Would he do that? Would he parade another woman in front of her? Would this be a perfect opportunity to introduce some casual fling to his friends, making it less casual and more like a full-on relationship? It isn't like he would have any clue as to her feelings for him, so he wouldn't have any cause to act delicately in front of her. She breathed deeply and reined in her dramatic train of thought. This was ridiculous. Freddie was a great friend and someone she cared for, that was all. She was just lonely and worried that a girlfriend would get in the way of their friendship. That was all this was. That was all she could allow these silly feelings to be. Anything else was too complicated and dangerous.

Holding her head up and straightening her shoulders, Anna walked into the VIP area. There was a group of about twenty people, milling around the two large tables. The chairs looked luxuriously comfortable and a number of women sat chatting together, cocktails in hand. Was one of them with Freddie?

"You made it!" Freddie's voice was warm and jovial and he wore a relaxed smile on his face. She couldn't help but smile back. His was so infectious.

"I did. Well, my business partner insisted. She took my shift tonight so that I could come."

"Good of her to do so," Freddie commented, handing her a glass of champagne. "Cheers to her then."

"Cheers to her," Anna agreed and chinked her glass to his. Bill Hanlon stepped over and nodded hello to Anna.

"Nice to see you again," he said. "This is my wife Amy, Amy this is Anna." Like her husband had noted when he met her at the Tyler's party, Amy picked up that there was no explanation as to who she was. Assuming that she was Freddie's latest bit of stuff, she smiled at the younger woman and shook her hand.

"Nice to meet you, love. Not often Freddie brings a girl along these days. He's always too busy running things. Good to see he's met someone though. How'd you two meet?" She waited, expectantly.

"Well, er," Anna laughed awkwardly, "We're just friends. I met Freddie when I moved to the area a few months back. He helped me pick my spilt oranges off of the road." She glanced up at him but he was totally engrossed in a conversation with Bill.

"Oh!" Amy said, her eyebrows shooting upwards. "Well. That's a new one and all!"

"Sorry?" Anna asked, confused. Surely she couldn't be the only female friend Freddie had ever had.

"Well, um...anyway, how you doing with that drink? Fancy a cocktail? We've got some jugs over here." Amy began leading her away over to the table full of chattering women. Some smiled at her as they approached, others looked her up and down critically. One woman in particular gave her a hard, mean look. Anna blinked. *What was her problem?* The woman in question sat with her long, bronzed legs crossed to one side, showing off a pair of very high stilettos. Her flimsy, gauzy dress hung off of her shoulders, showing her plump cleavage off to perfection. Immaculate makeup enhanced her features and her blonde locks were styled as though she had just come from a photo shoot. Anna took this all in and immediately felt incredibly average. She wished she had made a little more effort with her appearance. She had come in a plain black wrap dress and plain, not-too-high heels, and although she had taken some time with her make-up, she had done little more than run her fingers through the ends of her hair. She probably looked a sight. She turned her attention away from the golden goddess in the corner and realised that Amy was introducing her to a couple of the more friendly looking women.

"Darcy, Lola, this is Anna. She's here with Freddie." Anna sat down on the seat offered to her and smiled at the two women. Amy sat next to her and handed her a shot of something.

"Oooh, you dark horse, how did you snag him?" Darcy shrieked. "Well done gal. Good to meet you."

"Oh, er, no, it's not like that," Anna protested, "really, it's not."

"Of course it isn't like that," a voice behind Anna said, laughing venomously. "Look at her. She's hardly his type, is she? Looks like she's just stepped out of a library." Anna turned to find it was the woman who had been giving her the evils. She had left her space to come and circle the newcomer, like a snake watching its prey. "He's got some business-related use for you, hasn't he? He must do. It certainly ain't 'like that'," she mocked, snorting as though this idea was preposterous. "This is Freddie Tyler we're talking about girls. He can have the cream of the crop, he don't have to put up with sad rags like 'er."

"What, cream like you?" Amy butted in, bitingly. "You already tried that love, didn't you? He didn't want ya, did he? Off you trot you old scat bag. You're only here because you got in with John, ain't you? Go shower him with your cream then and fuck off."

Anna was surprised at how loud a person as petite as Amy could be. The other girls all jeered at the bronzed woman, backing Amy up. Scowling, she tottered off without a further word and sat back in her corner, averting her eyes away from their general direction. Amy turned to Anna, who was red-faced and feeling more inadequate than ever.

"Don't pay no mind to that strumpet love, honestly," she said kindly, squeezing Anna's knee. "No one likes her. She's a nobody, just some 'orrible little creature from the estates trying to sleep herself up the ladder to someone with a bit of cash and status. She's a right piece of work. Got two kids at home by different dads, treats them like shit. I've seen the poor little mites. Always in clothes too small for them, never enough layers, always dirty." She shook her head. "Skinny little things too. She don't feed them. Leaves them to it. Minute she gets a bit of attention, she can leave them for days. Think the neighbour takes them in sometimes. It's a miracle social services haven't taken them off her yet." She huffed. "Anyone that can treat their own kids like that, they ain't worth the shit on my shoe."

"Smacks them about something rotten too," added Lola. "My aunt lives near her, says she's seen her going for them in the street loads of times."

"Well anyway," Darcy changed the subject, "fuck her, let's get drinking , ey girls? Here's to Anna and Freddie."

"Anna and Freddie," the others chorused.

"No, I—" Anna started, but then gave up and laughing, downed the shot along with them. She'd tried to correct them. It wasn't her doing that they were getting the wrong end of the stick. She looked over to where Freddie was still talking to Bill. The top two buttons of his impeccably white shirt were open, showing off the taut lines of the top of his chest. Her breath caught in her throat as she imagined touching it. He laughed at something and his face lit up. He was beautiful. He looked hard and masculine, but somehow beautiful at the same time, she thought.

She was going to have to admit it to herself at some point, she realised. She was going to have to accept that somehow, despite everything she had been warning herself against, she really was falling for Freddie.

Across the room, Freddie welcomed Vince to the celebrations.

"Hello mate, I'm glad you could come. Here, have a whisky."

"Thank you Freddie, I think I will. So," he took the drink and looked his protégé in the eyes, searchingly. "How'd it go today? Well, I take it, by the looks of things."

"Everything went to plan. The money is back at the yard, so once I've paid the men I'll run it through the laundry and get your half over to you, soon as I can."

"Good man." Vince looked around. "Which one is this bird of yours then? I'd like to meet the woman that caught Freddie Tyler's attention."

Freddie tensed and grimaced internally.

"Actually Vince, I'm still flying solo. I do however, have an interesting stallion to talk to you about. There's a fixed race coming up at Newmarket, so we need our bookies in on it and there won't be any harm making a little cash ourselves, either." He subtly turned Vince away from Anna and switched back to business.

It was too hard to explain Anna to Vince and he didn't want to try. Aside from the obvious embarrassment that it would bring him after asking Vince for advice, it was a sore subject. Every time he saw Anna, he felt more and more drawn to her. It was like she was a magnet, or a drug. He couldn't pull himself away, even though he knew that she held no romantic feelings towards him. And even if she did one day hold a candle for him, if she discovered the sort of person he really was and the world that he lived in, a nice woman like that would soon turn away. His way of life wasn't for the likes of her. She was gentle and good. She had been bought up by hard working, gentle parents who valued honesty and education and the law. Not that his Mother didn't, but it was different. Anna would never have known the slim options and hard choices that they had faced. Even if she did hold some feelings for him, he could never let her quite near enough to know who he really was. Because he wouldn't be able to bear seeing the disappointment and disgust in her eyes when she found out.

12

Tanya sat down in the chair opposite Anna in the back office and took off her hat, shaking out her long hair from where it had been tucked underneath it. It had been snowing all day. The snow was too wet to settle, so the streets of London were filled with grey, icy sludge and the air was even colder than before. She was glad to be in from the harsh conditions and on her way through had ordered one of the bar staff to bring them both some hot chocolate to the office. That would soon warm her hands up, she hoped.

"How did it go?" Anna asked, wiping the droplets of water from melted snowflakes off of her desk, where they had fallen from Tanya's coat.

"Yeah, it went well I think. He started off a bit high, but I managed to negotiate it down a bit to what I think is pretty reasonable from my experience."

"Ok, so what sort of figure are we looking at?" Anna asked nervously, pulling up her expenses spreadsheet.

"Two hundred and fifty a week."

"What?! That's a lot of money Tanya, to basically just not be done over. Especially when surely that's the job of the police anyway."

"The police?" Tanya raised one eyebrow. "They don't touch these clubs, they steer well clear. I think this is pretty fair. Our profits are high, this won't hurt us. Other people will though. And at least it's only that much. He started out wanting five hundred a week."

"Jesus." Anna sighed, heavily. "Ok then. Two fifty it is. I'll have to put it through as an extra member of staff and pay it out that way. Let me know what I have to do with the money."

"Don't put it through that way, have it down as petty cash. With the amount of traffic coming through here we can claim needing all sorts of extras for the kitchen and cleaning products, things like that. I'll get the cash over to them. If you could create a petty cash list to use against it each week, that would be perfect. Or I could do it, if you like."

"No, that's fine, I'll do it. Better to have all the finances under one person or we could get muddled. I'll get you the cash out each month, just tell me when."

"Perfect. So, on another matter, when are you bringing this Prince Charming of yours over to see the club. And by club I mean me." She smirked and winked at Anna. Anna laughed.

"He is not my Prince Charming, ok? He's just a friend. He's made it super clear that he doesn't think of me that way. And...you know what, ok, yeah," Anna leaned back and opened her arms up as she finally admitted it out loud, "maybe if he was interested then that would be nice."

"I knew it!" Tanya said, pointing a finger at Anna. "You can fool yourself, lady, but not your best friend. I've seen your puppy eyes all these months."

"Yes, well," Anna held up her hands to push back the onslaught. "It doesn't matter anyway, so there's no point talking about it. Ok?" Anna gave her a tight smile and straightened her jacket. Tanya cocked her head to one side and looked at her fondly.

"Do you really think that he would do all these things with you if he didn't have feelings for you? Do you really think you would have met his family, gone off to the beach, shared nights out with him and his friends - if you were just some mate? Nah." She shook her head. "No way." She walked back towards the door. There was a lot to do before the club was ready to open tonight. "Who is he anyway, this little heart throb of yours? What's he do?"

"Nice try," Anna said and raised her eyebrow at her. Tanya scowled, annoyed. She had never given Tanya any details about Freddie. It wasn't that she didn't trust her, it was for the same reason that she hadn't told Freddie about the club. It was just another way of keeping safe, compartmentalising her life. It was a habit she had formed out of fear. Perhaps it was time that she stopped living like this to such an extreme. She would always be hiding, always looking over her shoulder, but if you couldn't at least act normally around your closest friends, what did that make you? She made a decision.

"Ok. Alright, I'll bring him to the club one night. I'll introduce you." Tanya's face lit up, excited to have finally been let in. "But," she warned, "just remember that we are nothing more than friends, yeah? That's all there is to it. Don't go running away trying to orchestrate anything."

"I won't, I promise. I will behave perfectly," Tanya replied. "Just let me know when and where and I'll be there."

"Ok." Anna watched the door slowly close and stared at the dark wood. Her stomach turned in knots. She pushed the feeling away, irritated. This was the right thing to do. She had to stop living in fear. It was time to truly embrace all the aspects of her life and accept them as a whole.

Bill knocked on Freddie's door. It was barely past the crack of dawn, but this couldn't wait until he got into one of his offices. Thea opened the door still in her thick dressing gown and slippers, holding a large mug of tea.

"Alright Bill, what you doing here so early?" she asked, opening the door wider and giving him a friendly smile. He walked in and stamped the frost off of his shoes on the welcome mat. Thea closed the door against the cold. It was toasty and warm inside which Bill was glad of, having been out all night following one of the Greeks.

"Sorry Thea, didn't mean to interrupt your breakfast but this couldn't wait. Is he about?"

"Sure, yeah. Come through to the kitchen. Mum will get you some breakfast while I go get him down." Thea took Bill's coat from him and pushed him gently towards the kitchen. He looked knackered.

"Thanks love," Bill smiled tiredly at her. He had known Thea since she was a tot. He had known the whole family pretty much all his life actually. He ambled through to the kitchen where Mollie was piling up a mountain of food on the table. A plate sat piled high with thick slices of bacon, next to a large serving bowl of fluffy scrambled eggs. The toast rack was full and still slightly steaming, indicating that the slices were still hot. Grilled tomatoes, fried mushrooms, the lot. His mouth started watering. He hadn't eaten anything since the sandwich his Amy had packed for him last night. Mollie beamed up at him as he entered.

"Billy Hanlon, I ain't seen you in ages. Where have you been hiding? Come for breakfast have you? Go on, take a seat. The others will be down in a minute. Get it while it's still hot." She ushered him into a seat and gave him a plate. She immediately began piling eggs onto it for him. "There you go love, get some of that bacon too. Dig in. You look like you need it. Let me get you a coffee."

"Thanks Mollie, you're a star." He tucked in as instructed and wolfed down his breakfast as fast as good manners would allow. Mollie placed a mug of black coffee down in front of him as he ate.

"Milk and sugar there if you want some, love." Bill nodded his thanks as his mouth was full.

He was mopping up the juices left on the plate with a slice of toast as Freddie entered.

"Alright mate, how's things?" he sat next to Bill and began to fill his own plate.

"They're ok, ok. Just need to talk to you about something." His eyes flickered to Mollie. He knew Freddie preferred not to discuss the details of his work in front of his mother. It wasn't that she didn't know, she did. But it worried her and Freddie didn't like to add to her worry. Putting Freddie's coffee in front of him she smiled at the two and removed her pinny. She could take the hint.

"Right, well. I'll leave you boys to it then. I need to go and get ready for the day myself." She patted Freddie on the shoulder as she walked out of the room. "Make sure you eat enough. Breakfast is the most important meal of the day you know. See you later Bill," she called over her shoulder.

"See you later Mollie, thanks for the breakfast," he shouted back. They waited until they heard her begin to climb the stairs then began.

"What's going on then? You alright?" Freddie asked, his first concern for his friend.

"I'm fine, but you might not be." Bill twisted so that he was face on to Freddie. "Dev, that Greek that Paulie put me on the tail. I've been watching him these last few weeks. He's been all over our turf, specifically going to places that we have prominent, but not documented, hands in. At first he was just moving around, spending time there. Then he started coming back at night, checking the joints over for access points." Freddie frowned at this information. "Then I followed him to a guy called Tony's house. Tony is Cos' cousin. He has an interlinked firm up there. Cos doesn't work closely with him, says he's too much of a loose cannon, but has to keep him on side as it's all family. You know what the Greeks are like with family. I've had a touch with Tony before, he's paid for my services on a couple of bank jobs." Freddie nodded. This wasn't unusual. Bill's area of expertise was much sought-after in their world, he tended to freelance when he wasn't busy with Freddie. "There was a big meeting, loads of them there. I couldn't get anywhere to hear what was going on but I figured it was big. I've been following him since, closer than ever. I finally heard what I needed last night." Bill took a deep breath. "Dev met up with his brother for a drink at a club up north last night. I got the table behind them. He said that Tony has told them that he's taking over central London. And get this, apparently it was Angel Face that took out Big Dom on Tony's order and now, well now he's said he's going to take you out. Apparently thinks that you are all that is standing between him and the East and West End. His plan is that he's going to invite you for a friendly meet, and do it then."

"That jumped up cunt," Freddie spat, furious. "He orders a hit on Big Dom, face fucking royalty, and then thinks he can roll in here and take our fucking turf? He thinks he can get away with this?" Freddie's blood boiled. Not only was this the ultimate piss take, but the fact that this joker thought he was big enough and clever enough to take what was theirs was just unacceptable. "Right. Right." He nodded hard, his eyes staring through the table. His lips formed a thin line as he thought over how to handle this.

He would love to go over there now, burst in all guns a-blazing, and take the fucker out. But this wasn't a sensible plan. Aside from the fact that it would start up World War III, Freddie would need to be sensitive to Cos in all of this. If this was handled correctly, the good business relationship they had would not be affected. Cos was as well versed in the laws of this life as he was. If Freddie gave him a courtesy visit to explain what his cousin Tony had done, Cos would understand and support the repercussions. It may hurt him personally but this was the life, this was how things were. If you did something like Tony had done, the offended firm had the right to dole out the punishment.

Bill sat back and drank his coffee whilst Freddie thought it all over. He had stayed in the club until the early hours of the morning whilst Dev and his brother discussed the merits of Tony's plan. He had hoped to find out if there was a date in mind. But if there was, Dev hadn't disclose as much. He could have beaten it out of him of course, but that would have alerted Tony to their knowing. That wouldn't help anyone. After they had finally gone home, he drove back to Freddie's and waited outside until it was just about an acceptable time to call in. There had been no point going home for a brief hour in between.

"Ok." Freddie sat up, his hard face sober. "We need to set up a meeting with Cos. We have too many dealings with him to do things the wrong way here. Aside from that he's a decent bloke who I want to do right by. Soon as we have shown him that respect, I want Tony brought to me at the warehouse by the docks. I need you to prepare it, make sure we have enough plastic sheeting to cover the area and stock up on bleach for the clean down. He's signed his own death warrant. Do we know when they mean to move?"

"No, they didn't let on any more information than that. I waited around, but that was it."

"Ok. Can you keep a twenty-four hour detail on Tony and his closest men going forward, and keep me up to date. I'll be fine for now, at least until I receive an invitation for this meet. I've got a meeting already arranged with Cos at the beginning of next week. I'll leave it until then. In the meantime, let's prepare properly and find out as much about Tony's routine as possible."

"Yep, I'll get on that straight away."

"Great." Freddie stood up and Bill followed suit. The conversation was over. Bill was ready to get home and fall into bed for a few hours. He looked at Freddie's hard expression.

"Fred, you good?" he asked, gruffly. He wasn't a man who particularly showed sentiment, even to old friends.

"Me?" Freddie smirked, "I'm fine. It takes more than a badly planned death threat to get to me, mate. Come on. Let's go."

It was a bright, brisk day. The only clouds about were the ones coming from Freddie and Paulie's breath as they walked together down the busy London street. They were off to see Estelle, a tough old bird who ran one of their massage parlours. They were thinking of moving her to larger premises, as, since she had been running the place, it was always full. There was now room for expansion.

Freddie's phone rang shrilly in his pocket. He picked it up and listened for a minute.

"On our way." He ended the call and halted in his tracks, grabbing Paul's arm to stop him too. "Forget this, we need to get home."

"Why? What's happened?"

"Not quite sure but Thea said it's urgent. Something to do with Michael. Come on."

"Shit," Paulie exclaimed worriedly, turning around and keeping up with Freddie's fast pace.

Half an hour later Freddie's car screeched to a halt outside the house and the pair rushed inside. Thea opened the door the second the car came into view. She had been waiting for them. She bit her nails anxiously, her face serious for once.

"What happened?" Freddie demanded.

"He's in there." She pointed to the living room and stepped back, crossed her arms across her chest, and said nothing more. Freddie entered the lounge and looked around. Mollie was stood in the doorway leading through to the kitchen, crying softly into her hands. Michael was sat nonchalantly sprawled in one of the armchairs. His expression was relaxed, unaffected by his Mother's tears and he stared off into the distance. Freddie blinked. What the fuck was this? Paulie went straight to his Mother and enveloped her in his big arms, letting her cry into his chest.

"What's going on?" Freddie demanded. "Michael? What are you doing here? And why is Mum crying? And why," he asked incredulously, "do you not seem fucking bothered by that?"

"I'm back," Michael replied in a lazy tone.

"You're back? What do you mean you're back? Why aren't you at school?"

"I don't go there anymore."

"What do you mean you don't go there?" Freddie was beginning to lose his temper at the rude and careless attitude his youngest brother was displaying. "What happened?"

"They chucked me out. Didn't you get a call? Oh, you must have given them one of your burner numbers by mistake. You have lots of them, right?" Michael said mockingly, turning to look at Freddie for the first time. Freddie took a step back, shocked by the naked hatred he saw in Michael's eyes.

"What?" he asked, not quite believing that his brother could have been expelled. Michael had always been a nice kid, a clever kid. What could he have done there to provoke such a reaction? Michael shrugged, theatrically.

"Apparently they didn't like how well my business was going."

"Your business?" Paulie asked, confused. He frowned and looked towards Freddie.

"Yeah, my business. I was doing pretty well up there with all those stupid, rich bastards around me. I was cleaning up." He puffed his chest out proudly, but the bitterness still marred his young face. "Made loads of money. My setup would have made you proud," he said to Freddie sarcastically.

Freddie went cold. He was beginning to understand what Michael was dancing around. Surely not. This was why he had sent him away to that school in the first place. It had been seriously expensive but from his research it was academically one of the best private schools in the country. It had the best facilities, it was in a nice town with lots to do. It was far enough out of London that Michael would have nothing to do with this kind of life, but close enough that he could visit whenever he wanted on the train. Michael was so bright, he had so much potential. Freddie had sent him there and paid the extortionate fees so that he would have the best start possible in life. So that he could sleep, safe in the knowledge that he had managed to get at least one of them out of this game.

"You were dealing drugs," he said flatly.

"Bingo!" Michael said and stood up clapping. "You got it in one."

"But why? I bought everything you needed and gave you a decent allowance each month. If you needed more all you had to do was ask." Freddie was devastated. There wasn't much in life that could hurt Freddie Tyler. His one weakness was his family. They were everything to him. And right now he felt like he'd failed them and let every single one of them down.

"Not everything's about money," Michael shouted. Freddie's eyebrows shot up at the unexpected outburst. Michael shook with pent up emotion. "That's all you care about isn't it? Money," he spat.

"That is not true—"

"Shut up!" Michael shouted. Paulie stepped forward defensively but Freddie held his hand out. His eyes were dangerously bright but he spoke quietly.

"No, let him speak."

Michael looked around the room at them all resentfully, then back to Freddie. "You sent me to that stupid school to show off your money, to show that you could. You didn't stop to think about me though, did you? You didn't stop to think about what I might want, or whether I could be happy there, did you?" he yelled. "You sent a fucking east-ender into a school full of toffs! At what point did you really think that was going to work out? At first I put up with it. I kept my head down and told myself that the comments and the jokes and the alienation would stop eventually. I figured they would get tired of it, start to just put up with me, if nothing else. I tried to distance myself from my life here. I would stay up late at night, trying to change the way I spoke and learn their ways. Thought if I could start sounding and looking more like them, that it would help." He laughed, bitterly. "I kept my nose clean, did my work well. But nothing changed. And then one day while they were all around me, taking it in turns to shove me to the floor, they asked me if I was related to the big London criminal, Freddie Tyler. Apparently one of their Dad's works for the Department of Justice and he had overheard a few stories about you one night." He paused and narrowed his eyes at Freddie. Freddie closed his eyes and groaned internally. "Once they knew you were my brother, it just got worse. I couldn't even go and hide like I used to, to escape it. They sought me out. The kid brother of the big bad criminal," he cried. "So eventually I thought, fuck it. If I couldn't escape you, then I might as well be like you. So I started fighting back. And I fought dirty. Just like I learnt growing up here."

"I never let you fight as a child," Mollie cried.

"No, you didn't," he snapped back, "but that don't mean I didn't pick it up from watching those who did. So I fought back and blacked a few eyes and though there were a lot of them, they were pansies at heart. But then you see," he paced back and forth in front of them all, "I was then the feared one. No one would come near me. I had no friends, no one would talk to me or even look my way. No one." His face darkened. "So I made myself useful. I got some new contacts in town and began supplying those toff-nosed little weasels with things to help pass the time. Mainly cocaine, some ecstasy or whatever they were after. They had more money than sense and no one else in the school had the balls to deal, so I took advantage of that gap in the market. Things got a bit better. People needed me. I gave a few perks to a couple of guys, to help me with distribution. That was my business. That is, until that bitch of a headmistress ordered a spot locker check. And mine was on the list." He stepped back and opened his arms wide. "So, there you go."

A heavy silence fell over the room. Freddie's mind was whirling with horror at all this new information. All this time his baby brother had been in pain, unhappy and bullied, made to feel like an outsider. And it was his fault. Michael's life had become hell and he had been too busy to notice. He groaned.

"I'm so sorry," he said, helplessly. "Michael, I had no idea you were struggling with all of this."

"Of course you didn't. You were too tied up in your sordid little empire to notice anything about those closest to you. You know, I used to look up to you. I used to think so much of you. But I don't now. Not anymore. And I've learnt a good lesson. Don't put your faith into anyone else. Lean only on yourself and what you know. And I know a fair amount now. So watch this space, big brother." He leaned towards Freddie, venom in his voice. "I'm going to do what I know how to do. And one day I'm going to overtake you. And the day that happens, I want you to remember one thing." He came right up to Freddie and finished in a deadly calm voice. "You made me who I am."

Staring Freddie in the eye for a moment more, he walked out of the room and disappeared upstairs. The only sounds in the room were the ticking of the clock and Mollie's subdued sobs. Eventually Freddie seemed to break out of his trance and turned to her.

"Mum? Mum, it's going to be ok. I'll sort it, alright? He's sixteen years old, he's just an unhappy kid acting out. He doesn't mean anything he might have said to you. He's just venting. We won't press it with the school, sending him there was obviously a mistake. My mistake." The guilt settled heavily onto Freddie's chest. "From now on he stays here, around his own. We'll give him some space to calm down and try and help him get back to the boy we all know and love." He turned to Thea. "Go and make Mum a strong cup of tea." He rubbed his temples. "I'll stay out of his way for a while as it's clearly me he's angry at." He watched as Thea took Mollie through to the kitchen and waited for the door to be closed.

"What are we going to do?" Paulie asked.

"I don't know. I wanted him out of all this and it turns out I've just pushed him right into it." He sighed. "I'll have to think on it. First things first, we'll need to talk the local school into accepting him with an expulsion on his record. That won't be easy. We'll probably have to buy them a new science lab or something."

Paulie walked over to his brother, who looked as though he had just aged about ten years in the space of ten minutes. He grasped his shoulder and squeezed it.

"It ain't your fault you know. You did the best you could. He was always too clever for his own good, even when he was a tyke. He could have handled it a hundred different ways. He could have just told you he was unhappy in the first place and we could have avoided all of this. That's what I would have done."

Freddie looked at Paulie and smiled, sadly.

"Thanks mate. Guess you just can't win 'em all, ey? I'll work something out. Come on, we need to get back out. Don't think there's much we can do here for now."

13

Anna picked up her phone and read the text message that had just beeped through. She smiled. It was Freddie. He was outside. She had invited him here to meet her, but all she had given him was an address. He still didn't know that the club was hers. She glanced over to Tanya who was busy arguing with one of their suppliers. He kept trying to charge them for crates of drink that arrived broken.

"It's not our fault if you're too cheap to use a reliable delivery company. I'm only paying you for the orders that have turned up in usable condition. Mhm.. mhm.. Well, take this one, the invoice for week commencing the seventeenth. Oh, hang on a minute will ya?" She put her hand over the speaking end of the phone and turned her attention to Anna. "Is he here? Ok. I'll just deal with this joker and I'll be out yeah? Get some drinks going." She turned her attention back to the phone. "Right.. what? No I'm not talking to you, why would I be having a drink with you? Anyway, as I was saying…"

Anna grabbed her jacket and swung it around herself, quietly leaving Tanya to it. Skipping through the club, she slipped out of the side door at the front of the building. She glanced up and down the street, spotting Freddie standing a few feet away, his back to her. She stifled a giggle and crept up on him.

"Got you." She pinched his sides and he jumped, startled.

"Jesus, didn't no one ever tell you not to sneak up on people like that?" he laughed.

"Nope," she answered, merrily. "How are you? It's really good to see you."

Freddie looked down at her soft face and into her deep blue eyes. If only she knew how good it felt to see her too. He resisted the urge to stroke her cheek. God, he was going soft. He cleared his throat.

"Yeah I'm good, how's tricks with you? You going to tell me what we're doing here then?"

"Well… I was thinking that we could check out this new club. This one here. What do you think?" Anna hid her smile.

"What, in the middle of the day?" he answered, bemused. He looked up at the front and frowned, cocking his head to one side. "Um, I don't think this is the sort of club you would enjoy, even if it were open." He shifted his weight from one foot to the other. "It's er, well it's not like, a dance club..." his voice was stilted as he awkwardly tried to avoid explaining the nature of her club. Anna couldn't help herself, she giggled a deep rumbling giggle from her stomach. "What's so funny?" Freddie narrowed his smiling eyes.

"Just - come with me. I want to show you something." She grabbed his arm and pulled him to the side door which she had just come out of.

"Hang on, wait, what are you doing?" he protested as she dragged him through to the inside of the main club. She turned around and stretched both arms out to the sides.

"Ta-da! This er, non-dance club, is actually mine." She clasped her hands behind her back and waited nervously to see Freddie's reaction. This was an exciting moment for her. She hadn't been able to show off her great achievement to anyone so far. Her parents thought this was a nice little dance club and she couldn't be within a mile of them anyway, for her own safety. And so far, given how guarded she was, she had gained a total of two friends. One of which was her business partner and the other who was standing in front of her, right now.

Freddie looked around, putting the pieces together. This was her club? He'd heard about this club, knew that the new owner had a deal with Vince. But he had told him that the woman in question was an old hand in this game, a flirty little minx. There was no way he could have been talking about Anna.

"This is yours? All yours?" he questioned.

"Yes! Well, half mine. I'm actually more on the paperwork and finances side of running things. My business partner Tanya runs the front of house. My office is back there." She pointed over towards a dark doorway past the end of the long bar. "I tend to stay in there mainly. Tanya is more the face of our brand, so to speak."

Ah. That made more sense, Freddie thought.

"Well, wow. I did not see that one coming. You're just full of surprises aren't you," he laughed. "Well, congratulations. This place has turned into a real hit, from what I hear. I had heard about the opening, just didn't realise that it was anything to do with you." He shook his head in admiration. "Right, well," he clapped his hands together, "this is cause for celebration. Again. I'm sure you have already celebrated, but this time it's my turn to toast to your good fortune. How can I buy a drink?"

"No need, it's on me. I have some bubbles in the fridge, if you fancy popping the cork, we can have a toast that way." Anna nipped around to the back of the bar and pulled a bottle from the champagne fridge. She handed it to Freddie and fiddled around on the shelves until she had hold of three flutes. Freddie unwrapped the cork and popped it.

"Who's the third one for?"

"My business partner, she's just on the phone but she'll be through in a minute. She's actually my best friend and flatmate too. I've probably mentioned her a few times to you already. Now, can I get you anything else?"

"No, no, this is more than enough. Thank you."

Tanya finally ended her phone call, having got the result she wanted. Feeling smug, she flicked her hair back and tousled it to add some more volume. She checked her face in the mirror and opened the door to the club. Stepping forward she put a big, welcoming smile on her face, ready to meet Anna's secret crush. She looked over to where the voices were coming from and focused in on the scene in front of her. In that split second, time seemed to slow down and she somehow forgot how to breathe. The sound around her seemed to move further away, like a strange echo ringing in her ears.

She heard the laughter, saw the full champagne glasses and the bubbles creeping up the sides. She saw the happiness radiating through her friend's face as if in slow motion. She saw the way the dim uplighters around the bar did their job. But the part of the picture that almost stopped her heart dead in her chest was the man seated on the bar stool, looking at Anna as if she were the only girl in the world.

It was the sight of none other than Freddie Tyler. The only man that she'd ever loved. The one man who had totally, and utterly, broken her heart.

Anna sat staring at the television in her dressing gown, not really watching it. She fiddled with her pocket and went over the events of the afternoon in her head. Something was not quite right, but she couldn't put her finger on why. Freddie had come in and seemed excited and happy for her, which was exactly what she had been hoping for. Tanya had been eager to meet Freddie for ages and had been upbeat most of the morning. Then when Tanya had come out, the atmosphere seemed to go downhill. Tanya had been cold and distracted and seemed to be in a terrible mood. She had politely greeted Freddie, but trying to draw her into further conversation was like trying to drag a cat into water. Freddie had closed down and become quieter too. Not that she was surprised after he received such a frosty reception. He had stayed long enough to be polite and drink his glass of champagne, then made his excuses and left. It had been a disaster. Before she had a chance to even properly question Tanya on what was wrong, she had disappeared again claiming she had a mountain of work. She'd told Anna to go on home. It was her day off, after all.

So, bemused and more than a little disappointed, Anna went home, poured herself a glass of wine and treated herself to a long bubble bath. Even that didn't shake off this feeling though. What was going on with Tanya? Pouring another glass of white wine, Anna stared out of the lounge window, over the bright lights of the busy East End. She sipped from the glass nonchalantly and looked over at the clock hanging in the kitchen. Nearly ten o'clock. Maybe she should just have an early night. She was fairly tired. Her phone rang over on the kitchen table where she'd left it. Putting her wine down on the coffee table, she tutted and left her cosy end of the sofa to get it. She looked at the screen. It was the number for the main club line. She picked it up quickly.

"Hello? Yes, it's me. What's up?" It was Carl, one of the barmen on this evening.

"It's Tanya. She's, well.. she needs picking up."

"Picking up? I've had a couple of drinks, tell her to get a taxi," Anna replied frowning. Why was she getting Carl to phone her for a lift?

"Er, I don't think she's in any state to get a taxi Anna, she's pretty much passed out blind drunk on the bar."

"What?" Anna's eyebrows shot up in disbelief. It was Tanya's turn to manage the club tonight, what on earth was she doing?

"I tried to cut her off a while back, but she kept threatening me with the sack if I didn't serve her. She doesn't know I'm calling you," there was a pause, "she er, well she threatened me with the sack if I called you too, but I didn't know what else to do. She's starting to get a bit lairy. I know you wouldn't want the customers to see that..."

"Don't worry Carl, you've done the right thing. And I promise you that no one will be getting the sack." She rolled her eyes, pissed off at Tanya. "Give me an hour, it's going to take me a bit to get ready and get over there. Just try to manage her as best you can. Oh, and don't let her leave in that state, ok?" she added. As annoyed as she was, she wasn't about to let her best friend wander the streets in that condition, if the fancy took her.

"Yeah, don't worry, I'm pretty sure she ain't moving anywhere."

"Right, I'm on my way." Anna closed the call off and swore loudly. What the hell was Tanya thinking? It was one thing being moody and rude to her, but it was another to be so reckless when in charge of the club. If she hadn't wanted to work tonight all she had to do was say, Anna would have happily taken her shift for her. She stormed into her bedroom and pulled on a pair of jeans and a jumper. She tied her hair into a quick ponytail and stalked back through to the living room. She shoved her feet into her boots and grabbing her coat and keys, left the flat.

Tanya stared at the empty glass in front of her. It was kind of blurry and kept splitting into two glasses if she didn't concentrate hard enough. She couldn't stop her mind playing the image of Freddie, standing there in her club, over and over again. The way he looked at Anna, so adoringly...

"Carl, get me another one. And a shot of tequila."

Carl pursed his lips but he did as she asked. Good, Tanya thought. She was his boss, the owner of this place. He should know his place.

"Damn right," she muttered to herself.

The fresh double vodka, soda and lime was put in front of her along with the shot. She downed the tequila immediately, not bothering with the salt and lime. She felt the burn as is slipped down her throat and relished it. She knew at some point that if she kept drinking she would reach oblivion. That was what she was aiming for. There were people all around her, laughing, talking, having a good time. She ignored them all and nursed the vodka in front of her.

How could this be happening? Of all the people in the world that Anna could have met, how could it be Freddie? She rested her head in her hands for a second. Of course she would fall for him, who wouldn't? He was Freddie Tyler. Smart, handsome, fun, charismatic. When he looked at you that way, you felt like you were the only girl in the world. She squeezed her eyes shut at the memories.

It had been a long time ago, a good couple of years. They'd met in a club and hooked up that night. He saw her casually over the next few months and she would live for those moments, when he would give her his time and attention. She started falling in love with him, tried to move their relationship onto more serious ground. The more she tried to do that, the more he pulled away. In a desperate attempt to make him see how perfect they were together, she had opened up to him one night and told him of her feelings and her vision of how they could be a proper couple. He had gently but firmly told her that this was not what he wanted. He told her that he enjoyed her company, but only for a bit of fun. That he thought she understood that. Scared of losing him completely she had backed down, put a fake smile on and told him this was ok with her. But from that point on, Freddie had distanced himself from her, made excuses not to see her and eventually stopped talking to her altogether. She had been crushed.

She knew why he didn't see her as worthy girlfriend material. It didn't take a rocket scientist to work out that a decent man would never have any real respect for a stripper and prostitute. Other than her body, which he had already enjoyed, she had nothing to offer him. It was then that she had realised what she needed to do. She'd picked herself up, brushed herself off and set about making plans to do something worthy with her life. She focused all of her energies on doing what she had to, to move up in the world. She swore to herself that one day she would be worthy of Freddie Tyler and even if nothing ever happened between them again, she would show him what a mistake he had made. She would show him that she was a force to be reckoned with and that she was worthy of respect and love. Then, maybe one day, she could even love and respect herself.

Now though, here he was pining for Anna. The lovely, beautiful, perfect Anna. Her best friend. It wasn't like she didn't know that he'd been with other women, of course he had. She had even seen them out together sometimes. But they were all like her, just bits of fun. He had never had a serious one. This though...this was different. Freddie Tyler never bothered with a woman he actually had to work for. He just accepted the best of those who threw themselves at him. Anna hadn't even slept with him and yet here he was, going out of his way to make plans with her, inviting her to meet his family, even taking a genuine interest in her life. This wasn't just a phase for Freddie, it would have been far too much effort. He was in love with her. And Anna was in love with him.

"Carl, another shot." She waved her hand at him and closed her eyes again, trying to squeeze the image out of her head. She felt a tap on her shoulder and looked around, bleary eyed. It was a middle-aged man she hadn't seen before.

"Do I know you?" she asked.

"How much for a private dance?" he asked, pulling out his wallet.

"What?" she shook her head slightly, trying to understand what he was asking through her drunken haze.

"A dance. How much?" he asked again, smiling at her.

Tanya finally caught onto what he was asking. She sat up straight in her seat and rounded on him angrily.

"How dare you? Who the fuck do you think you are? I'm not one of the girls, I fucking own this place," she slurred, loudly. He man backed off, his cheeks reddening as people turned to look at what was going on.

"S-sorry, I didn't realise, you looked...well..."

"I looked what?" Tanya screeched at him, the alcohol making her louder than she had meant to be. "I looked like a stripper?" She looked down at herself. She was wearing a knee length pencil dress, but it had ridden halfway up her thigh whilst she had been sat drowning her sorrows and her cleavage was on show. Even so, she was sure she didn't resemble one of the girls. "Really?" she demanded sarcastically, pulling her skirt back down into place. She narrowed her eyes and swayed in her chair.

"I'm sorry, my mistake." The guy put his hands up in surrender and hurried back to his table, across the room. Tanya glared around her at the people still looking at her.

"And what are you lot looking at? Can a girl not just have a fucking drink in peace?" she yelled. The people around her quickly looked away, though some continued to laugh at her under their breath. She laughed quietly to herself, without humour. Maybe that guy was right. Maybe underneath these nice clothes and behind this big successful club, at the heart of it all maybe she would always be just a low-life tom. Maybe somehow, despite her best efforts to hide it, she did shine out as who she really was. Who was she kidding? Even now, she would always be the club owner who used to be a prostitute. That would never change. Not in this town. Not now. She lowered her head and rested her forehead on the bar. At last the tears came, silently falling as she finally passed out.

Anna jumped out of the taxi and her doormen cleared a path for her to go inside.

"Glad you're here," one of them remarked. "She's been causing right hag in there. She ain't herself at all."

"Sorry Mick, I'll get her out of your hair," Anna replied tiredly. She rushed over to the bar and looked around. She couldn't see her. Carl came over to her.

"I've just put her in the back room. She's out cold."

"Fuck sake...Ok. Can you ask Mick to get me a taxi and can you get Ron to come and carry her out for me?"

"Sure thing." Carl disappeared and came back with Ron a minute later. "There's a taxi outside ready for you."

"Brilliant, thanks. Ron, could you put her in and tell them to wait for me?"

"Yep, she in the back?"

"Yes, thanks. Ok, Carl," she turned her attention to the club. "Do you think you could make sure that clean down is done properly, mark down everyone's leaving times and lock up? I need someone to manage things with us both gone."

"Sure, no problem Anna. What do you want me to do about the tills?" Usually they brought the tills and receipts through to whichever one of them was managing the club that night and they cashed up themselves. Anna bit her lip.

"I'll give you my key to the safe," she rummaged through the keys on her keyring and pulled one off. "Can you bag up each till and put the respective receipts with each bag, then just place them inside the safe. I'll come back early and cash up. When you've locked the safe, put the key at the back of my bottom drawer. That should be ok for tonight. Take the spare front door key from my desk and post it pack through the letterbox once you have locked up. That ok with you?" She looked at him expectantly. He nodded.

"That's fine."

"Great. I appreciate that Carl. I'll pop a little something extra in your pay this week. Thanks for calling me."

"Of course. Anyone would have done the same."

Anna squeezed his arm and headed out towards the waiting taxi. She knew she could trust Carl. He was a solid, dependable man who often helped them out with things. It was probably about time that she promoted him to supervisor. It would be a good idea to have someone on hand to look after the club in case there were times that neither of them could be there.

Closing the door as she got in, the taxi began to move. A comatose Tanya flopped against her. She sighed irritatedly, but put her arm around her to hold her steady. She still was no closer to knowing what had made Tanya act like this tonight.

After what seemed like the longest journey in the world, the taxi driver parked up and helped her get Tanya upstairs.

"Thank you so much, I can't tell you how much I appreciate this," she said in a heartfelt voice. She had no idea how she was going to get Tanya up the stairs, and her attempts at waking her up after she'd paid the cabby totally failed. In the end, the cabby had offered to carry her in. He was a big, burly man in his fifties, with a kind face and a jovial nature. She had been beyond grateful at his offer. He climbed the stairs slowly now, with Tanya flopped over his shoulder in a fireman's lift.

"That's alright love. Your mate here seems to have lived life to the full tonight. She'll be feeling that tomorrow." He laughed. "I'm just glad she's so skinny. Wouldn't have been able to carry her up all these stairs if she were a salad dodger." Anna laughed out loud at the reference. Tanya moaned, starting to come to. They reached the front door and the cabby set her gently on her feet. Anna took her weight as Tanya draped both arms around her shoulders.

"I should be alright from here. Thank you so much again. You've been a real life saver."

"No worries love. I've got daughters meself. I like to make sure you young ladies get home safely. Hopefully the cabbies that pick up my girls do the same." He smiled, tipped his hat at her and left.

Anna shuffled into the flat and shut the door behind her, awkwardly. Lurching forward one big step at a time, she finally managed - after some struggle - to get Tanya into her bedroom. She shoved her none too gently onto the bed and stepped back to catch her breath, hands on hips.

"Jesus Christ, Tanya," she complained loudly. "You could at least bloody wake up."

"I am awake," came a barely audible slur. Anna opened her eyes wide in disbelief.

"Are you serious?" she demanded. "And you let us carry you up the bloody stairs and all through here?"

"What?" Tanya moaned, "What are you talking about?"

"Oh you are just ridiculous," Anna snapped. She set about undressing her, trying to get her ready for bed. "What were you thinking tonight? You were supposed to be working!"

"Working, ha!" came the slow reply. "Yeah thassss it...just a working gal, me. All the work never goes away. Bring on the cocks, thasss all I am..."

"What?" Anna frowned at Tanya's reference to her old job. "You've had more than I thought." She pulled Tanya into a sitting position so that she could unzip her dress.

"Yeah haven't I just...more cocks, more and more and more. Thasss all I am...thasss all you sees me as isnn – isn't it..."

"What the hell are you talking about, you daft mare?" Anna frowned. "You run the club, with me. That's your job. Or at least it's fucking supposed to be, except you didn't bother with that tonight, did you!" she snapped, angrily. "I've had to come all the way across London to get you, because you were so incapable, and I've had to leave Carl in charge. All because you decided to get bloody wasted."

"You're so pretty," Tanya said sadly, looking at Anna through her glazed eyes for the first time. "You don't look like – hic – like a tom. No...you, you're perfect. Prrrrrrroper. Thasss why he wants you. Thass why..." She swayed and Anna steadied her. Tanya began to laugh, a long, deeply sad, heart wrenching laugh.

"Tanya?" The laughing went on. "Tanya?" Anna shook her by the shoulders and she quieted down to a strange, drunken smile.

"He never loved me you know. Never..."

"Who never loved you? What are you talking about?" Anna was beginning to feel concerned. Tanya sounded like she had lost the plot. Tanya lurched forward and brought her face close to Anna's. Anna squinted at the potent stench of alcohol on Tanya's breath.

"Freddie. Myyyyyy Freddie. Yourrr Freddie..."

"What?" Anna's blood ran cold as she started to piece together Tanya's ramblings.

"He broke my heart. He di-nt want me. I'm not good enough, jussss a tom." She shook her head sadly. "Never good enough. Not even now. Now he hasss...he has you. He found a diamond. You," she stabbed Anna's chest with her finger, "you're a real diamond. Rare. The – hic – best. I'm just...a bit of...of broken pretty glass. Cheap. Not worth nothing...Never will be." She fell back on the bed as Anna let go of her. "Never ever..." she trailed off and began to snore, quietly.

Anna stood there, stunned. It couldn't be. It couldn't be him. Except, it was. Her heart painfully skipped a beat as she realised the implications of this. Oh God. Her hand flew to her mouth. No wonder Tanya had gone off the rails tonight. Seeing Freddie, realising that this was the man Anna had spent all this time with, the man she was falling for, it must have hit her like a brick to the face.

"Oh my God.. Freddie is the one who hurt you," she whispered to the sleeping form in front of her. "And I've bought it all back. I've hurt you."

Tears formed in her eyes as she realised what she'd done to her friend. Those tears began to swell and fall as she realised that after this, she could never see Freddie again.

Tanya gingerly opened one eye the next morning and immediately regretted it.

"Oh God," she groaned. She pulled the duvet over her eyes and held her aching head between her hands. She felt as though there were a hundred midgets inside her head, hacking away at the sides with pickaxes. She gingerly looked out of one eye again, checking where she was. She was in bed in her own room. Well, that was a small relief. But how did she get there? She fought through the fuzz enveloping her brain and thought back to the night before.

She had decided to take the edge off of the shock she had received, seeing Freddie there with Anna. She'd sat down at the bar and let herself have a couple of drinks. Except those couple of drinks had turned into a lot of drinks. She had been rude and aggressive to her staff. She groaned as she remembered battering Carl verbally. Then there was that punter...she'd made such a spectacle of herself. She curled into a ball and wished the ground would swallow her up. How was she going to show her face there today? She needed to go and apologise, and hope and pray that the people watching last night were just tourists passing through.

She ran her tongue around her teeth. Her mouth was so dry. She desperately needed water but she wasn't sure yet whether she could stand up without being sick. She slowly pushed herself up onto her elbow and was about to swing her legs around when she saw the pint of water and two pills on her bedside table. Oh thank God for Anna, she thought, downing the pills and taking a deep drink from the glass. She fell back into the pillows, closing her eyes once more against the offensive sunlight. She ran her hands down her torso. She was in her nightie. Anna must have got her undressed too.

Suddenly she remembered Anna dragging her through the flat. She replayed it in her head and groaned loudly when she remembered their conversation. She couldn't remember exactly what she had said, but she knew that she'd told her about Freddie. She could remember Anna's face draining of colour and filling with horror. Shit.

Shit, shit, shit. She kicked herself mentally. This was exactly what she had decided she wasn't going to do. She had made the decision to go and deal with her feelings on her own, lick her wounds privately and then just get on with it. She had even decided to seek Freddie out and tell him to keep schtum. It was water under the bridge. It was years ago and as much as it had hurt her and left its scars on her heart, it was something that meant nothing to anyone else. It shouldn't be the thing that stood in the way of Anna finding happiness. Much as she had fallen for Freddie, she loved Anna more. And Anna was the one person that actually deserved her love.

"Fuck sake Tanya..." she berated herself. "What have you done?" She rubbed her hands up and down her face, trying to wake herself up properly. "Right. Ok." She hoisted herself up and swung her legs over the side of the bed. "Wow. Oh God..." she held back the bile that was threatening to come up from her stomach. Gingerly, she stepped up out of the bed. She swayed slightly and the banging in her head grew worse, but she carried on walking slowly forwards. Each step was more painful than the last. She took a few deep, slow breaths. She was never drinking again.

"Anna?" she called out in a cracked, throaty voice. She listened but there was no reply. She made her way down the hallway to the open lounge and kitchen. She peered around the corner but there was no one there. There was a note on the kitchen table. Padding softly over, she picked it up and scanned the brief few lines.

Gone to cash up and sort out the club. There's a sandwich in the fridge for you and more painkillers in the cupboard. Don't worry about anything. Love Anna x

Tanya sat down and began to cry. How could Anna be so sweet to her after everything she had done? She had ruined the moment her friend had been so looking forward to, the moment Anna finally got to show off her hard work to her only other friend. She had neglected the club and created multiple embarrassing scenes. She had forced Anna to babysit her and God only knows how she had managed to get her up the stairs. Then to top it off, she had drunkenly crushed Anna's dreams of being with Freddie and for all she knew, probably mouthed off offensively in the process.

She sighed, angry at herself. She needed to put things right. Standing up, she glanced over to the mirror on the wall. Her hair was a mess, tangled in all directions and her make-up was smudged all over her face. She looked like a fully-fledged member of Kiss. Well, first she needed to shower, she thought determinedly, then it was off to the club to fix all the messes she had made.

Anna finished logging the last receipt and pressed 'save' at the top of her spreadsheet. She closed the laptop and filed the receipts together in the correct file, before placing it back onto the shelf above her head. Her phone went off. She stared at the screen. It was Freddie, asking if she was still on for meeting up for a drink later that day. She breathed out heavily. Picking up the phone she typed out her response.

I've got to work tonight. Things are getting busier here these days. No rest for the wicked. Sorry.

She hovered her thumb over the send button for a few seconds, then with a sad expression on her face, pressed down. She couldn't quite bring herself to tell Freddie outright that she couldn't see him anymore. She would just keep herself busy with work and use that as an excuse to not make plans. It was easier that way. He would eventually tail off, and anyway, he would be fine. It wasn't as if he harboured any feelings for her deeper than friendship. Really, this was a good thing for her too. Without Freddie around, maybe she could fall out of love with him again. It was the sensible thing to do for her own heart, as well as for Tanya's. Unrequited love was a dangerous thing to spend time with. For both of them.

There was a soft knock on the door.

"Come in."

Tanya walked in with a sheepish expression on her face. For once she was wearing casual clothes and only had the most basic amount of makeup on. Anna raised her eyebrows. Tanya really must be hungover to have left the house like this. She wouldn't usually even open the door unless she was sporting a full face and a show stopping outfit.

"How are you feeling?" Anna asked with a half-smile. The guilt she felt at seeing the state Tanya had got herself in because of her was still raw.

"Oh, I've felt better," Tanya chuckled wanly. She sat down in the chair opposite Anna. "Anna," she started, "I'm so sorry. For everything. For the way I acted yesterday, for—"

"No, stop. Please. Tanya, you have nothing to apologise for. I had no idea and you know what, that is totally my own fault. If I hadn't been so secretive with different parts of my life then I would have known from the beginning and I would have never started spending time with Freddie."

"It's not your fault at all, it's just one of those things, don't be so daft!" Tanya replied. "And as far as Freddie goes," she took a deep breath, "I acted awfully yesterday. It was a shock, yes, but that is no excuse for going off the rails like that, or even for telling you."

"For telling me? Of course you had to tell me, Tan. Freddie is the man you love and I'm your best friend. There was never an option not to tell me."

"Loved," Tanya corrected. "Did love. Not love now. Anna, all that was a very long time ago and it's old news these days. I reacted badly yesterday. Unfairly, actually. And I am really sorry for that."

"Well, we will just agree to disagree then. Ok? You don't owe me an apology, I understand. And it doesn't matter now anyway, because I'm not going to see Freddie again." Anna nodded her head down to cement her statement and busied herself with tidying her desk. It hurt saying it, but it had hurt more seeing Tanya in such distress the night before. She never wanted to be the cause of that again. Tanya stared at her, frowning.

"What? No! You need to see Freddie again. This is what I have come down here to tell you. Oh God, I've messed things right up now..." she tutted, angry at herself. "Listen, I saw the way he looked at you yesterday. He is *so* in love with you, Anna, it's unreal. I've known Freddie Tyler for years and I can tell you now, he has never looked at a woman the way he does you. Never. You must tell him how you feel," she beseeched. "I won't get in the way and I will be absolutely fine. More than fine - I'll be happy to see you happy. It was just the shock, it brought it all back. But it really *is* in the past and I don't have any feelings for him anymore. I promise you. Please Anna," she begged, "don't give up a chance of real

236

love and happiness because of me and my stupidity."

Anna looked at her friend's strained, open face. Of course Tanya would say that to her. Because Tanya was a real friend who always put Anna's feelings before her own. Maybe there was some truth in her words. She seemed genuine enough. But if Tanya's past with Freddie had taught her anything, it was that loving Freddie Tyler only bought you heartache. She didn't want to end up like Tanya, devastated, suffering in the prison of unrequited love. And that was where she was heading. Because no matter what Tanya said, she knew Freddie didn't love her back. He couldn't. There had been a million chances for him to have let her know that he thought of her that way. But he'd never even so much as hinted towards it. No. She needed to close the door on Freddie Tyler for her own good. This had just cemented her decision. She smiled sadly at Tanya.

"You're wrong. The only thing Freddie feels towards me is friendship. That's it. And that's just not healthy to be around when you feel something more. So, thank you, but I'm still not going to see him again. For my own sake. I just want to move on and focus on the club and you and me. And that's the end of it." She smiled brightly and shoved the pile of papers she had been collecting up into the wire tray to her left. "Now, how about we go for lunch. Because you look like you need it. In fact, I don't think I have ever seen you look like such a tramp!"

They both laughed.

"Yeah, I've never felt so awful in my entire life. I was convinced I was going to hurl in
the taxi on the way here. Couldn't face the tube. Eugh..." She groaned and slipped down further into her seat.

"You should have stayed in bed," Anna said.

"Well, I can't say it wasn't tempting, but I needed to get over here and try to put things right. Which reminds me, I need to get Carl's number out of his file. I may have been slightly offensive towards him last night."

Anna raised one eyebrow at her.

"Ok. *Very* offensive."

Anna laughed.

"Ok, come on, let's go get some lunch." She grabbed her coat and ushered Tanya back out of the door. Closing it behind her, she shut away her painful thoughts of Freddie. There was no point dwelling on him now. She needed to move on. They all did.

14

Freddie stared out of the window of the car. Paulie was driving. They were on their way to meet the potential new supplier that had been discussed in their last meeting with Damien. Freddie took his phone out of his pocket and read Anna's last text again.

Sorry I can't. I'm busy.

It had been nearly two weeks since the last time he had seen Anna. Since that game-changing meeting in her club. He had never pushed Anna into giving him more detail about her life than she wanted to give. She'd always been so guarded that he didn't want to scare her off. When she had talked about her housemate she never used her name and only referred to her occasionally. He wished now that he had asked a few more questions. He could have perhaps managed the situation. Instead, he had been taken by surprise. Sod's law that her best friend in the world, and her business partner, happened to be one of the women he used to see.

The second he saw Tanya his heart dropped. He saw the recognition, then confusion, then pain flit across her face before she'd masked it behind cold indifference. He had groaned internally. It would have to be her, wouldn't it. Years before, he had been distracted by her obvious charms. She was a good laugh and very attractive. He'd enjoyed some good times with her, had a bit of fun whenever he found himself at a loose end. But then one day she started getting ideas, getting a bit above herself. He'd had to stop seeing her then. She was a tom for Christ sake. Surely she had to know that he was after the same as her other punters. The only difference was that they paid her cold hard cash and he paid her by taking her out and showing her a good time. She had desperately tried to get close to him, even told him that she loved him. He felt bad for her, but at the end of the day she wasn't the sort of woman he would consider tying himself to. So he stayed out of her way from then on. Gave her the space to move on and forget him. Clearly though, seeing her reaction as she spotted him in her club, she hadn't quite moved on completely.

She hadn't said anything there and then, but he knew it would come out between them eventually. They were too close for it not to. And from the following day, Anna had made excuses not to see him. She hadn't outright told him she didn't want to meet up anymore, but her texts became shorter and she no longer suggested alternative times when she might be available. He knew what this meant. Friends stuck together, no matter what. Tanya would always come first. And why shouldn't she? It wasn't even like they were an item. Anna had never shown any interest in him, in that way. She had no clue how he really felt about her. So cutting him off to save her best friend heart ache would be an easy option. If only it didn't feel so damn painful for him, he thought angrily.

He wasn't angry at Anna, or even Tanya. He was angry at himself. He was angry because he'd let someone mess with his head. He was Freddie Tyler. He was one of the heads of the largest and most prominent firm in London. He had responsibilities and heavy-duty issues that needed to be dealt with, which couldn't wait. He didn't have time to be distracted by emotion. Especially when he had no control over it. But no matter how much he tried to put it to the back of his mind, he was still in a dark mood.

"You alright Fred?" Paulie asked, glancing sideways at his brother. Freddie had been unusually quiet for the last few days, snapping at anyone who so much as looked at him the wrong way. Paulie had just put it down to the growing tension in the household now that Michael was home, but he didn't seem able to shake it off whilst they were out either.

"I'm fine. Come on." Freddie said, curtly. They were there.

The brothers stepped out of the car and walked down to the

portakabin on the dock. Freddie entered without knocking, the freezing wind too cold to mess about in.

"Freddie, Paulie, good to see you," Damien greeted them warmly. "Here you go. Saw you coming so poured you a coffee." He handed them each a mug. They sat down in two of the vacant chairs laid out ready for the meeting.

"Thanks Damien. Don't know how you stand the freeze down here on the river," Freddie said. Damien chuckled, going back round the desk to sit down.

"Oh, I got used to it years ago. It's been that long."

"Freddie, hi. I'm Tom." The lanky youth leaning against the wall interrupted and stepped forward, holding his hand out, a confident smirk on his face. Freddie turned towards him and stared at him steadily, with a cold gaze. Tom's hand hovered in the air for a few seconds before he pulled it back.

"Alright then," he said sarcastically. "Friendly chap, aren't you?" He laughed, amused. Freddie lifted an eyebrow, his eyes glinting dangerously. Paulie caught the look on his face and took a deep breath in, getting ready for whatever happened next. No one mugged off Freddie Tyler and got away with it. Especially some new kid, fresh off the boat. Tom looked around at the three sober faces in front of him. Damien tried to warn him by shaking his head slightly, but Tom didn't pick up on the subtle hint. Tom frowned and huffed.

"Ok, well if you don't want to talk to me there are plenty of other people who will," he said, indignantly. Freddie tilted his head to the side and frowned.

"You come in here asking for an audience with me," he said, his voice dangerously quiet, "you make the effort to lug your wares across the border," he pointed at the box sat on the sideboard next to Tom, "and then you stand there with the attitude and body language of someone meeting the local fucking grocer. Do you actually know who I am?" he questioned.

"Of course I know who you are," the boy answered, snorting as though this was a ridiculous question.

"Right then." Freddie nodded at this confirmation and stood up. He marched over to Tom, grabbed a handful over his thick, wavy hair and slammed his face down onto his knee with force. Tom's nose split open upon impact and blood spurted everywhere. Freddie released him and waited with his hands back in his pockets for Tom to regain his balance.

"Arggh, my nose, my nose, oh my God! Look at what he's done," he beseeched, looking helplessly from Damien to Paulie and back to Damien. They didn't react. "Look!" he yelled. He held his hands out. They were shaking and red from holding his nose. Damien tutted quietly as blood dripped over the floor. Freddie came forward again, this time grasping his neck and slamming the man back against the wall of the portakabin. He lifted him a few inches, so that Tom's feet were barely able to reach the floor. Tom grasped at Freddie's wrist, trying and failing to fend the much stronger man off. Gone was his earlier swagger and bravado. He was now genuinely scared.

A lazy bum of a young man, he had come from money but never liked to do anything that cost him actual effort. He had flitted from job to job until his father had given him the money to invest in his own venture. Not knowing anything much himself, he had followed his cousin into the illegal spirits business. He copied his business model, used his methods and let him set up some small contracts on his behalf. This was the first time that he'd actually come out to meet a potential new client himself. Never having had to deal with the real world, let alone the criminal world that he'd entered into, he had far too high an opinion of himself and gave no real thought or respect to anyone else. That had been a very big mistake in this particular instance.

"Right, you jumped up little shit," Freddie yelled in his face, "now if you hadn't known who I am, I might have let you off with a warning. Might. But you know who I am and you still came in here, mugging me off like I'm some fucking nobody, when you're in here asking for *me* to do *you* a fucking favour. Well...that isn't sitting too well with me, you see. You understand me boy?" Tom choked and made gagging sounds where Freddie's vice like grip was still crushing his windpipe. "You ain't selling your shit to the local fucking barmaid. I'm Freddie Tyler," he spat. "I run this city. In more ways than your tiny little brain could possibly comprehend. I've done things that would have you running in the night back to your Mummy's arms," he snarled. "The hardest men in this city wouldn't have the balls to come into a meeting with me and talk to me the way you just have. The only reason you haven't just signed your own death warrant is because I think you are genuinely just that stupid to have done it without thinking. Am I right?" Tom made more gargling sounds, the veins in his temples sticking out and his face turning purple. Freddie relaxed his grip just a little.

"Yes," he choked with difficulty. "Yes, I am. I'm stupid."

"Yes, you are fucking stupid," Freddie said, releasing him and curling his lip in disgust. He shook his head. Tom fell to the floor, grabbing his neck and gulping deep breaths in. Freddie wiped the blood from Tom's nose off of his hand with the old rag Damien handed him, before turning back to face him again. He looked him up and down. "Now. You are going to take your box and go back to your little factory. You won't be supplying me, or any other of the larger firms here in London, ever. I don't want to hear your name again. If I so much as hear a whisper of it, your cousin can kiss goodbye to his contracts too. Understood?"

"Yes," Tom said shakily, still sat in a pile on the floor.

"Good. Now fuck off."

The young man got to his feet and ran out of the door immediately, leaving his box of booze behind. Freddie reached into his pocket and pulled out a thick pile of notes. Counting nearly half of them out, he put them onto Damien's desk.

"Sorry about your carpet. Get yourself a new one."

"Thanks Freddie," Damien said in a normal tone as if nothing untoward had just occurred. "We still ok dealing with his cousin? There's another shipment due to arrive this week."

"Yeah, that's fine. He's a good supplier, no need to rock the boat there."

"Literally, in this case, ey?" Damien joked. Freddie smiled and Paulie laughed.

"I'm off. Catch you later."

"Bye mate." The door closed behind the two brothers and Damien sat down in his chair, looking over to the blood stain on the carpet thoughtfully. Freddie had seemed very tense today. The outcome of their conversation hadn't shocked Damien, the boy was an idiot. He had asked for it. But Freddie wasn't himself. He shrugged. Oh well, wasn't any of his business, he thought.

Anna stared at the computer screen in front of her, not really taking in the bright lines of figures. She had been sitting here trying to log all the invoices for the last month, but so far she had only input about three. And she had been there for over an hour. She rubbed her eyes drowsily. She hadn't been sleeping well at all lately. Not since she had found out who Freddie was to Tanya. His invites to meet up were getting further and further apart. It tore her apart inside, every time she had to bluntly decline. But she knew it was the right thing to do.

Tanya kept on at her, trying to get her to reconsider. After numerous heart to hearts, she genuinely believed Tanya when she said that this had forced her to realise that her life had moved on. She even believed her now when she said she wanted Anna to reach back out to Freddie, because she wanted her to be happy. That was no longer what was causing her to walk away. It was seeing what it had done to Tanya after all this time. It was seeing the outcome of someone who had allowed themselves to dwell in the unrequited love they held for Freddie. It had been a hard realisation that this could easily be her, if she didn't curb this addiction to Freddie now. He didn't feel the same way for her. It was time to move on and let her heart re-heal. It wasn't Freddie's fault, not this time at least. He'd done nothing wrong. He had offered her true friendship at a time where she'd needed it most, which she treasured and would miss greatly. But it wasn't wise to try and stay friends given how strongly her feelings had grown. She was too embarrassed to explain to him the reason that she was backing off. He would just have to put it down to one of life's great mysteries.

She picked up her coffee and took a sip. She grimaced. It was stone cold. She'd been sitting here self-indulgently thinking about Freddie for far too long. She tutted, annoyed at herself. Picking up the next invoice, she began typing in the details, violently. If she was here all night, she would get this finished, she vowed.

Tanya's head popped around the door.

"Are you ok then, if I head off? Leave it to Carl to lock up, if you fancy coming home early. You've been here all day again," she said, scolding her. "We could watch a girly film, crack open a bottle? I'll cook us something nice," she added. Then she screwed up her face. "Actually maybe you should cook. We both know all I'm good for is an oven pizza."

Anna laughed.

"As much as I do love your oven pizza, I really do need to get these on the spreadsheet. I need to send them over to the accountant by Monday and I have the whole month backlogged." She pulled a face. "I'll probably be here late anyway, so I might as well stay until lock up tonight."

"Ok," Tanya said. "Well, if you change your mind, that's what I'll be doing. And Carl's on until finish anyway."

"Thanks babe." Anna scrunched her nose up and smiled warmly at her. Tanya waved and disappeared.

Since that fateful night when Anna had dragged Tanya's comatosed figure home, Anna had officially promoted Carl. He was a well-liked figure with the rest of the staff and proved himself to be reliable time and time again. He was hugely proud of the new responsibility that had been placed on his shoulders and grateful for the rise in his pay. He made himself available whenever they needed him and they knew they could count on him to treat the place as they would themselves.

Tanya had apologised profusely, red-faced and with her head hung in shame the first time she'd seen him after her drunken escapades. He had laughed, deep from his belly and told her that he'd grown up in a house with three older sisters. Nothing she threw at him was anything more than he'd grown up dealing with there. The pair had gotten on like a house on fire ever since. Tanya had even confided in Anna that it felt like having one of her own long lost brothers around again. Anna had hidden her smile, amused that Tanya couldn't see how completely Carl had lost his heart to her, like so many before him. It certainly wasn't a sibling-like relationship from his side of things. But she wouldn't be the one to bring that issue to light, she thought. That one can play out on its own.

Finishing that invoice she paused before picking up the next. She glanced up at the clock. It was seven. The new act they'd hired would be debuting right about now. Sure enough, she heard the dull drone of the music go quiet and a deep voice introducing the next act. These two had trained with a touring circus and were looking for a home in London where they didn't have to keep moving around. Tanya had given them a week-long trial, starting tonight. If they did well and the punters seemed to like them, they would be given a regular slot two evenings a week. They were too expensive to use every night. Anna had promised Tanya she would watch them and feed back to her. They would be on for half an hour now, then twice more for half an hour throughout the evening. By rotating the acts like this, more people would get to see them.

Picking up her mug of cold coffee, Anna headed out of the office into the bar. She stood at the end, out of the way of the paying customers and waited for one of her staff to become free. The new act was in position and the spotlights suddenly turned on to them. In perfect synchronicity then began whirling and dancing around the stage, then jumped high up into the air and landed together in a perfect split. Anna winced. There was no way on earth she could do that with her body. The audience cheered. They picked up batons and began twirling them in their hands whilst they danced, faster and faster, until they burst into flames at each end. The audience gasped in awe as they put on an edgy, exciting fire show. Anna nodded, impressed. She would check out their later performances too, but from what she could see it would be worth keeping this duo around. She would text Tanya and say just that, when she got back into her office.

She smiled at the young barmaid who hurried over after dealing with her last customer.

"Hey Jessie, could you get me a fresh coffee? Just a flat white, thanks love." Jessie smiled and scurried off to get her boss's coffee. Anna turned her back to the bar and leant against it, crossing her arms to watch the rest of the latest act. Soon enough Jessie tapped her on the shoulder and she turned to receive the hot cup of coffee. She smiled her thanks and disappeared back into her office to carry on with the paperwork.

She didn't pick up on the man across the room at one of the smaller tables, watching her through the narrowed slits of his eyes. He reached into his pocket and pulled out his phone.

Tony looked up from his card game to the screen of his phone. Cursing in annoyance at being interrupted, he answered it irritatedly.

"Stavros. What?"

"I've found her, boss. Anna, I've just seen her."

"What?" Tony jumped up from the table. Remembering where he was he turned back for a second and threw his cards in. "All yours, I fold." He grabbed his jacket and jogged outside the small backroom before he continued. "Where?"

"In a club on Greek Street, central. Looks like she works here. She's in an office through the back. Just came out to the bar, got herself a drink and went back in."

Tony wet his lips with his tongue excitedly. His heart began to race. He had found the bitch.

"Who's with you?" he demanded.

"No-one. I'm only here by chance," Stavros admitted.

"Are you pieced up?"

"I've got a knife."

"Good. Do you have your car?"

"Yes, just down the street." He had been on his way through from another job, when he decided to stop and take in some entertainment on the way home. He'd heard of this club, and wanted to see it for himself. He hadn't realised at the time, of course, that he would strike gold in finding Anna.

"Do you think you can get her into your car on your own?"

Stavros paused, thinking about where he had left his vehicle. It was down a dark side street where there were no cameras. Something he always automatically checked.

"Should be fine."

"Ok, I'm going to text you an address. It's a small warehouse of my cousin's, just outside of London, down the river. Get her there and tie her up. I'm on my way."

"Got it." Stavros put the phone down.

Tony let the small smile creep over his face until he was beaming. He began to laugh, a deep, sadistic laugh. Oh, the things he was going to do to her. After she dared leave him, after she had dared to disappear this way for so long, after trying to bring such shame down over his head, she was going to pay. Oh yes, by the time he had even gone through a fraction of the punishments he had in store for her, she was going to wish she'd never been born. He would kill her, eventually. He had already realised that it wouldn't be sensible to let her live, nor could he be bothered with her afterwards. She was tainted now, he no longer wanted to keep her. But he wouldn't kill her until the time had come that her body had been through so much she could barely even feel his ministrations anymore. By the time that moment came around, her body would be a bloody mess and she would be unrecognisable.

He let his psychotic intentions play out in his head. He would strip her naked, watch her shiver and freeze in the cold. Every inch of her skin would be cut, slit and sliced into criss-crosses. He would remove her ears then her fingers, slowly, one by one. He would beat her face until it was nothing but a swollen pulp. His excitement rose as he thought of her bloodied body tied up in the chair. Maybe he would relieve himself in her halfway through, roughly and hard, just because he could. Maybe he would let the others rape her too. She was, after all, nothing but a defiant whore. She had probably slept with a hundred men since leaving his house. Tony's nostrils flared with anger. He punched the wall and roared. Yes, that's *exactly* what she would have done. Just to shame him. She would have opened her legs and let anyone in, laughing whilst she did it. Laughing at him. Showing him up to everyone. He punched the wall again, three times, cutting his knuckles open in the process. He suddenly backed away from the wall, holding his hands in the air and muttering to himself.

"No, no. No, no now." He shook his head. He must control his temper. He musn't get too angry, or he would end up killing her far too soon. That could not be allowed to happen. No, not after all the plans he had made. He couldn't miss out on them. Taking a deep breath to gain control of himself, he dialled another number.

"Angelo, meet me on the corner of Hunter Street in ten minutes. We've got somewhere to be."

Stavros stood at the bar, pretending to watch the show in front of him. He was no longer interested in it, not with his new task for the evening. It was a golden opportunity. Being the one to find and take Anna to Tony would boost him right up the ladder. He would be greatly rewarded and be in Tony's good books for months to come.

He swirled his drink around in his hand. It had been an hour and a half since he'd seen her come out of that office. There was no back door, he had checked. She must still be in there. The music changed and the limber, fire-swinging girls from earlier came back on. He liked them, they were something a bit different. He saw the door open out of the corner of his eye.

Anna walked out, her attention trained on the two girls on stage. She wandered over near to where he was standing, still not paying any attention to her surroundings. Her arms were folded over the thin, cream jumper she was wearing. Stavros looked her up and down. She wore beige trousers and knee-length brown leather boots. Hardly the right sort of outfit for a club, he thought. She wandered nearer, like a mouse unaware that it was walking into the jaws of a snake. Stavros stepped sideways so that he was right behind her. He moved forwards and pressed the tip of the knife he was holding against her back, grasping her arm at the same time so that she couldn't move.

"Make a sound and I'll stab this knife right through you."

Anna froze, her body tensing into a rigid line. Feeling the sharp blade pushing against her skin, she didn't try to pull away. Her eyes filled up and her body started to shake. No...this couldn't be happening. He couldn't have found her, not now, not after all this time. She squeezed the tears out of her eyes so that she could see again. Twisting her neck slowly to the side, she glanced at the man holding her. It was Stavros. Oh God. Shit. She kicked herself for not seeing him before he had seen her. She tried to think quickly, thoughts racing through her head and falling over each other as she desperately searched for a good idea. There wasn't one. If she didn't do exactly as she was told, she knew that the knife in her back would slip through her ribs faster than she could blink.

"Ok. Now you and me are going to go for a little walk. You are not going to look at any of your staff on the way out, or anyone else for that matter. You got that?" She nodded, tears dripping off the bottom of her face. "Don't even think about trying to make a run for it. Now come on." He shoved her forward, hiding the knife with his own body and holding her close. He moved quickly, pushing her ahead.

They were out of the club in seconds, slipping out of the side door to the main entrance. Anna had hoped against hope that the bouncers would notice how she was being held, but the queue outside was long and they were busy trying to count people in and out. They didn't even notice her as they exited. She swallowed back a desperate sob. That had been her only half-hope.

"Where are we going?" she asked shakily, through terrified tears.

"You'll see," Stavros answered gruffly. He didn't particularly care what happened to Anna. He found women to be a general annoyance, especially when they cried. He was uncomfortable however, with being in such close proximity to Anna. When she had been back at home with Tony, they weren't allowed to speak to her unless there was a specific reason. She was Tony's property and Tony did not like anyone so much as looking at his possessions. It was putting Stavros on edge, now that he had to talk to and touch her. It was probably safer to put her in the boot, he thought. In case Tony saw it as him getting too cosy with her in the car. It would save him from any escape attempts too.

He hurried her across the busy London street and down into the small, dead-end side road. It was dark and dank with only the reflective light from the main street. Anna's breathing spiked into fast, panicky breaths when she saw his car. If she got in that car, that would be the end of it. There would be no escaping from wherever they were going.

"Please, Stavros please, I'm begging you, let me go," she pleaded, half turning towards him. "Let me go, say I got away. Say my bouncers saw you and saved me, anything. I'll make it worth your while. I have money, lots of money. You saw my club. I'll give you anything you want."

"Stop it," he growled, pushing her against the car with the knife whilst he fumbled for his keys.

"Stavros please," she sobbed. "He'll kill me, you know he will." Stavros hesitated, something that resembled guilt flashing across his features just for a millisecond. Anna saw it and pushed forward. "He'll kill me Stavros. And that's after whatever punishments he has in store for me." Her voice cracked and she shivered. "He'll torture me, badly. He won't kill me quickly. Not after searching for me for this long."

This seemed to remind Stavros of the lengths his boss had gone to to get this girl. He snarled and opening the boot, grabbed a pair of handcuffs.

"Put your hands behind your back. Now," he barked.

"No, oh please Stavros no. You have to help me. Just let me go, please," her panicked cries became whispers as he pushed the blade harder into her back. "Ok, ok, I'm sorry. I'll be quiet, I'll be quiet" she pleaded quietly, wincing as the blade pierced her skin. Fat, hot tears streamed unchecked now down her face.

Stavros cuffed her wrists behind her back, roughly. Grabbing her hair, he shoved her head into the boot. Her face scuffed along the rough carpet on the floor of the open boot, as he lifted the bottom half of her body and dumped it unceremoniously inside. She bit her lip to stop herself crying out in pain as her face took the brunt of her weight and her neck twisted awkwardly. She tasted blood and realised she'd bitten through the skin. The boot slammed on top of her and she was enveloped in total darkness. Awkwardly lying on her side, she tried to wiggle into a better position. It was impossible with her hands behind her back.

The muffled sound of the driver's door slamming shut came through the back wall of the boot, then the engine started up with a rumble. The car began to move, jolting her around. It backed out of the side street slowly, then jerked forward as Stavros began his journey. The action sent Anna flying back against the back of the boot. The back of her head connected with the metal door of the boot and she cried out in pain. Closing her eyes against the white dots dancing in front of her eyes, Anna tried to control her breathing. As the throbbing subsided she moved her head forward. It was a hard hit but she had survived worse.

She narrowed her eyes, trying to make out anything at all in the dark. There must be something she could do to get out of this. She had read somewhere once that a woman had been saved from a kidnapping when she'd kicked out a tail light and waved out of the hole. The person in the car following her had called the police, alarmed. She clearly hadn't been restrained in handcuffs though, Anna thought. Perhaps she could still kick out a tail light and hope that Stavros got pulled over by the police for that. It was a long shot, but it was all she had. She had to do something. It was either fight or die at this point. And she wasn't ready to die today. Not like this.

She wriggled, trying to turn herself over so that she could face the back of the boot, but after several attempts she gave up. She couldn't turn over her twisted arms and the boot wasn't high enough for her cramped legs to move properly anyway. She caught her breath and felt the edges of the cramped space with her foot. She gauged where she thought the tail lights would be and kicked out as hard as she could. As her foot connected, her body rocked forward and she struggled not to end up on her face. Pulling the left knee up and forward to spread out her balance, she tried again. That was better. She pushed her right leg forward then kicked and kicked and kicked with all her strength and energy, not stopping until she physically couldn't keep kicking anymore. Nothing happened. Nothing gave way. Each time her foot connected, it didn't even sound like she was hitting tail lights. The thumps were muffled, like all she was hitting was the hard, carpeted lining. She probably was. This was a new model BMW. They probably covered up eyesores like tail lights in the boot. It wouldn't be attractive.

She laid her now aching leg down and sighed, squeezing her eyes shut. The tears began to fall again, scalding the graze on her cheek from the rough carpet. There was nothing she could do. There was no escape. She'd tried everything that she could think of. There was no chance of Stavros showing pity on her, he wasn't that stupid. If he let her go, *he* would be the one to suffer the fate that Tony had in store for her. He knew that as well as she did. There was no way out of this car now and she could feel the speed picking up. Wherever they were going, they were now on a main road headed straight for it. It was just a matter of time. She began to shake in terror at what lay ahead. Tony would have no mercy on her. If she begged, he would be elated and make it worse, to make her beg more. If she said nothing, he would be angry and make it worse anyway, in order to break her. The only thing that she could think of to do now, was taunt him to the point of uncontrollable rage. Maybe that way he would get so angry that he accidentally killed her quickly. Sobbing uncontrollably, she nodded slightly to herself. That was what she would have to do. This was the end for her. And if she could do nothing else for herself now, she would at least do that.

She thought about the people she loved - her parents, Tanya, Freddie; their faces all popped up in her head. Her heart ached as she wished that she could have at least seen them all one last time. She knew that Tanya would look after her parents. She had asked that of her once, when they had soberly discussed what would happen if either of them died. But she would have given anything to see them all again, to hold them. Freddie too. She loved all four of them vehemently. But it was too late now. Her time was up. These would be her last few hours on this earth. It was time to finally face her demon.

15

Freddie leaned against the tiled wall of the shower, letting the water cascade over the back of his neck and down his broad, muscular back. He had his eyes closed. It had been a long day. He had been standing there trying to soothe the tension in his body with the hot water for nearly half an hour, but it hadn't really helped. Standing up straight he picked up the shampoo and washed his hair with vigour. He ran his hands up and down his face, trying to shake off the heavy mood that seemed to follow him around lately, and turned off the water. He stepped out and wrapped a thick, soft towel around his waist. He rubbed his hair with a smaller one until it was no longer dripping, then stepped out of the bathroom and padded back into his bedroom.

His phone was ringing where he'ad left it on the bed. It rang off just as he picked it up. He looked at the screen. There were eighteen missed calls from Bill Hanlon. Freddie frowned, concerned. What was going on?

Before he had a chance to dial back, the phone rang again. He picked it up on the first ring.

"Bill, what's happening?"

"Freddie!" Freddie had never heard Bill sound so urgently relieved. "It's Anna. The Greeks have taken her."

"What?" Freddie exclaimed in disbelief.

"I'm following them now, I'm on the A13 heading east. Just get in your car and call me from there. I'll direct you and tell you the rest when you're on route. Bring guns."

Freddie didn't bother wasting time answering. He put the phone down and grabbed his clothes.

"Paul, Paulie," he yelled at the top of his voice as he shoved his legs into his trousers. Paulie appeared in the hallway almost immediately, concerned at the urgency in Freddie's voice.

"What?"

"Tool up - now!" Freddie demanded. "Get the keys and be in the car in two minutes." Paulie disappeared and Freddie heard the clunks as Paulie grabbed the gun from under his mattress. Freddie lifted his mattress to collect his own. Shrugging on a jumper and coat, he shoved the gun into the inside pocket. He ran downstairs, Paulie already ahead of him with the front door open.

"Freddie?" Thea questioned as she saw her brothers running past. He didn't answer. He was already in the car. He revved the engine as Paul slammed the passenger door shut and screeched his wheels on the tarmac as he raced down the street. He dialled a number from the car phone. It rang three times before Sammy picked up.

"Sammy, can you be outside the front of your place with two guns, in exactly five minutes?"

"Yes," came the immediate answer. No questions, as Freddie had known there wouldn't be.

"Good. Be ready." He clicked the red phone button to end the call and dialled Bill's number. Bill answered straight away.

"What happened?"

"Right," he started. "I had one of my boys on Tony tonight. I was following another one of his guys, Stavros. He's been getting a little too close to your whereabouts the last few days, I wanted to be sure there wasn't a change of plan. He stopped off this evening at Club Anya on Greek Street. He saw Anna come out of the back office and his whole body language changed. He made a call. Nothing happened for a bit, then she came back out and he took her. Got a knife in her back, forced her to walk out quietly. She was terrified, poor thing." Bill shook his head sadly. He still didn't know whether or not Freddie was aware of her connection to Tony. "I didn't even know she worked there." If he had known, he would've tried to warn her. He liked Anna. She was a good sort, a kind girl.

"She owns it," Freddie said, sighing heavily. "Fuck!" he shouted, hitting the steering wheel. He breathed deeply, trying to calm down. "What then, Bill?" he said, back to business. He indicated to turn left towards Sammy's place.

"He took her outside. I followed them but couldn't grab her, he had the knife right up on her ribs. He cuffed her and put her in the boot. I jumped in my car and I'm following them now. Just gone past Dagenham, still going East. Not sure where he's taking her yet. Where are you?"

Freddie gauged it in his head.

"Maybe fifteen minutes behind you. I'm just grabbing Sammy now." As he said this, he pulled over to the side of the road and Sammy jumped in the back. Freddie sped off again.

"Put your foot down Fred, because I have genuinely got no idea what to expect. I haven't seen any of them out this way before."

"On it." He put the phone down. Paulie had quietly updated Sammy. Sammy looked at Freddie through the rear view mirror.

"What the fuck is he doing?" Sammy asked, unable to comprehend this.

"I have no idea, but he won't be breathing for long after this." Freddie's lips formed a thin line and he focused on the road. He couldn't understand this latest move. It wasn't in keeping with the rest of Tony's game play. Going after big players was one thing, going after civilians or family members of your enemy was another thing entirely. No matter what the case, no matter how dirty or vengeful things got in their dealings, people in these categories were totally off limits.

Clearly the reason they had taken Anna was to get to him, Freddie surmised. Their intel must have shown her as his bird. An easy mistake to make perhaps, but even so, what were they doing taking her? This was a totally unacceptable move. When he finally had Tony in front of him he was going to give him the kicking of his life before he sent him back to his maker. He had better find Anna totally unharmed or not only would he beat and kill Tony, but he would rain hell down on North London for years to come. He put his foot down on the accelerator. He hoped and prayed that he wouldn't get there too late.

The car came to a stop and Anna's ears pricked up, trying to make out what was going on around her by the muffled sounds. The door opened and shut and then there was silence again until the boot suddenly swung open. Anna looked up, fearfully, expecting to see Tony's face. She almost felt relief when she saw that it was still only Stavros. Not that it would be for long, she thought. Stavros grabbed her awkwardly by her upper arms and yanked her up over the lip of the boot. She teetered there for a moment whilst he tried to shift her weight, then she fell onto the floor, face down in the dirt. She spat out some grit that had made its way into her mouth. Stavros picked her back up and left her on her feet. She stretched out, her muscles complaining from the cramped up position that they had been forced to stay in for the last hour.

"Can you take these off of me, please?" she asked, shaking her wrists behind her back.

"No," Stavros grunted. "Move. That way." He shoved her in the direction of a small warehouse. Anna looked around as she walked, slowly. She couldn't see any other cars at the moment. It was just them. But then again, there was a wire fence surrounding the immediate area and the warehouse, with large grass-covered verges surrounding most of that. There could be vehicles on the other side that she couldn't see. The ground was not tarmacked, just hard earth beaten down by years of use. They appeared to be somewhere remote, but that was all she could tell about her location. She wished she'd put her phone in her back pocket, but unfortunately it was sitting on her desk where she'd left it.

The stars were bright in the clear night sky. It would have been beautiful, Anna thought, if she weren't walking towards the scene of her own murder. Her breath hung white in the air. She was too terrified to feel cold right now.

They entered the metal sheet-covered building. It was dark in there. Stavros fiddled around until he found a light switch and flicked it on. One solitary light bulb hung low from the tall ceiling, in the middle of the room. It swayed slightly with the breeze that was coming in from the open door. Stavros picked up a wooden chair from the side of the room and put it down under the light, dragging Anna by the arm as he did so. He pushed her down onto it.

"Stay there or I'll cut you. Got it?" She nodded. He didn't go far, only to the corner to grab some rope and a hessian sack. He kept one eye on her the whole time. There was no opportunity open to run, much to her disappointment. Hurrying back over, Stavros tied the rope around her middle, securing her to the chair. He tied her legs to the thin wooden feet of the chair and then without warning, shoved the large hessian sack over her head and shoulders.

"Wait, what? No! Get this off me!" She struggled but immediately stopped when a large hand grabbed her throat through the sack. She nearly passed out with terror. Was it Tony? Was he here? She couldn't see. Stavros' voice came from near her ear.

"Shut up or it'll be worse for you. Be silent." Anna trembled in her seat as he backed away.

Oh God, please let me die now, God please give me a heart attack, she prayed silently. *Please let me die, please let me die.*

Freddie parked where Bill had instructed, around the back of the building, off of the track. No one would be able to see the vehicles there.

The three men ran over to where Bill was waiting for them in some bushes.

"Bill," Freddie nodded in greeting.

"Freddie. Paulie, Sam," Bill greeted them grimly. "They're in there. It's just the two at the moment but I caught a phone call. Tony's on his way. I don't know how many will be with him.

"Ok, good. That's good," Freddie replied, nodding. His eyes were bright and hard. "Sammy brought you a gun. I figured you wouldn't be carrying."

Sammy handed the gun over and Bill thanked him. He hadn't been carrying anything. None of them did unless there was a reason. It was a stupid bastard indeed that could pull off a big job, to then get nicked on something as small as carrying a weapon. Wasn't worth the risk.

"Can we get in?"

"Yes - the door's open and from what I can tell, all he has is a knife."

"Ok, then that's what we do. We go in there now, get her out and knock that fucker out. Then we wait for Tony." His eyes glinted coldly in the moonlight. "He ain't leaving this place alive."

"Lead the way," said Sammy. Freddie looked at Bill.

"You ok to come in with us? I wouldn't blame you if you want to leave now. You've done more than your share if that's the case." Freddie patted Bill's shoulder to let him know he meant it. But Bill shook his head.

"No, I'm all in. I wouldn't forgive myself if something went wrong and I'd clocked off like a wanker. And anyway, I like Anna. She gets on well with my Amy too. Amy would have my balls for earrings if I could have helped her and didn't," he joked. They all laughed. Paulie looked back at the road.

"We should hurry if we want to be a step ahead," he said.

"Yeah, let's go." Freddie ran ahead silently, the others following.

Freddie stared through the crack of the partly open door. Anna was tied up in the middle of the room with her back to him. She wasn't making any noise. Freddie began to worry, then noticed her clenching and unclenching her bound hands, nervously. He closed his eyes in relief. She was ok. For now at least.

They barged in and marched over to Stavros, Freddie in the lead. He gasped in shock at the sight of the four men coming towards him with their guns pointed in his direction. He blinked and his head darted back and forth between the four very angry looking faces as they approached. They didn't look friendly. He held his knife out in front of him, but he already knew this was pointless. He was outmanned and outgunned. He shifted his weight, trying to think of a way to buy time. The men reached him and Freddie immediately took the knife off of him.

"Get on the floor," he yelled in Stavros' paling face. "Get – on the fucking – floor, I said!" His face turned red with rage as he spat this in the other man's face. Stavros swore and got on his knees. Freddie took a step back and kicked Stavros in the face with all his might. Stavros fell back on the floor, out cold. Freddie wiped the spit off of his chin with the back of his hand. He put his gun back in his pocket and straightened his hair. He breathed in deeply, trying to dispel the worst of his rage before Anna saw his face. "Tie him up. Quickly," he ordered. Paulie went in search of some rope in the general debris and junk that was spread around the edges of the warehouse. Bill and Sammy began to drag Stavros from the floor to one of the metal support beams. Freddie walked over to Anna's shaking form. He made to lift the hessian sack, but as his shadow fell across it she began to scream.

"No, no! Get off me, no!" her screams began to turn hysterical and she struggled against her restraints, nearly toppling her chair over.

"Anna, Anna stop. It's ok, it's ok," Freddie stopped her chair from going over and pulled the hessian sack off. She was still screaming uncontrollably, convinced that it was Tony. As her face came into view he could see her eyes were squeezed shut. She was still sobbing and screaming, not having taken in his words. "Anna," he tried again. "Anna!" he yelled, grabbing her face between his hands. "It's me, it's Freddie." Anna stopped struggling. Slowly, not quite believing it, she opened her eyes, still shaking like a leaf. When she saw him she blinked and frowned, confused.

"Freddie? What...what are you doing here?"

He knelt down in front of her, grasping her head between his hands and turning it gently from side to side.

"What has he done to you?" he said, his voice full of emotional anger. He took in the grazes down her cheek, the cut on her swollen lip and the mud smeared across her face. Her eyes were swollen and her face blotchy where she had been crying for so long.

"Nothing, I'm fine," she croaked. Her voice was hoarse from all the screaming. She cleared her throat as he set about untying her. "Freddie, what are you doing here?" she repeated.

Although she was more relieved than she had ever been to be set free, fear for Freddie was now setting in. She had no idea how he had known that she was here, but he'd put himself in grave danger by saving her. He had no idea what he was really dealing with. Tony would arrive at any minute, she had heard his phone call to Stavros.

Freddie still hadn't answered. He was still trying to work out what to tell her and how to break it to her that it was his fault that she had been kidnapped. Not something he was looking forward to. He finished untying her and pulled her up from the chair.

"That can wait. Are you ok? Nothing broken?"

"No, I'm fine, but Freddie - we need to go," she urged, her eyes darting towards the door. "Please, we have to leave right now." She grabbed his arm and tried to pull him towards the door but he stopped her.

"Not quite yet. There's something I've got to do. But you're going to be ok, I promise. I'll explain everything later."

"*You'll* explain everything?" Anna questioned, frowning. "Don't you need me to explain things?"

"What?" Freddie stepped back and looked her in the eye as though she was mad. They both paused, unsure what was going on.

Bill stepped forward and cleared his throat.

"Um, I don't mean to interrupt, but Tony's going to be here any second. If we're going to take him, we need to get in position. Preferably outside, so if there's too many we can disappear."

Anna shook her head, trying to understand. What was Bill talking about?

"Wait, how do you know about Tony?"

"What do you know about Tony?" Freddie answered, warily. How could she possibly know about Tony?

Bill groaned internally. He hadn't wanted to get involved, it was not his business. This was about to get really awkward and it was the worst possible time for it. He stepped forward.

"Ok, look...Freddie, she's Tony's ex. She ran away and has been hiding from him ever since she arrived over this way. He's had a small army out looking for her, on the quiet like, that's why she's been taken." Anna's eyebrows shot up and she felt her cheeks grow hot. How had Bill known all of this? She studied his face. He looked away towards Freddie. He shrugged apologetically. "It wasn't my business, Fred. I kept out of it." Paulie sighed heavily and walked over to the door to keep watch. Clearly they were not moving as quickly as had been hoped now.

Freddie studied the other man's face, his brain working ten to the dozen. He didn't blame Bill for not bringing this to light sooner. You kept your mouth shut in this game as far as other people's business was concerned. Still, it pissed him off that he was only finding this out now. What had she been doing with a cunt like Tony? He turned towards Anna, grimly.

"You were with Tony?" he asked. She nodded.

"Yes. Or rather I was kept by Tony. For most of that relationship I wasn't there by choice." She held her head up and felt a stab of anger at the disappointment she saw on Freddie's face. "Don't you dare judge me," she said heatedly. "You don't know anything of my life back then. I was young, an idiot, and I fell into his trap. He then beat me and threatened me for years, in order to keep me there. Told me if I ever left that he would hunt me and kill me." She sniffed and blinked away the tears, not wishing to break down in front of Freddie. It was bad enough the way he was looking at her now, she wasn't about to embarrass herself further. "I had my duties and was expected to do exactly as I was told. I was a prisoner. Our local hospital became my second home," she laughed bitterly. "Broken bones, cuts, bruises, concussions, internal haemorrhaging, you name it, it's on my file." There was silence around her as everyone took in this new information. She looked around at them. Bill looked at her sadly. "How did you know, Bill?" she asked.

"I met you a couple of years ago, Anna. At Tony's house." Anna frowned and thought back. She didn't remember Bill's face. If she had of recognised him she would have run, months ago. "You don't remember because you never looked in my direction. We were in the office. You bought a tea tray through. I believe this was a mistake, from Tony's reaction."

"Well, that sounds about right," Anna said flatly. "You should have said something to me when we met," she continued accusingly.

"Perhaps. But you seemed to be happier thinking no one knew you. So I didn't."

Freddie seemed to snap out of his silent daze.

"That fucking bastard. That absolute fucking bastard." His anger and horror was mounting as it hit him what Anna had been through. No wonder she had always been so secretive and reserved. She was on the run from an absolute monster. "So that's why you were taken tonight? Not because of me?"

"You? Why would I have been taken because of you?" Anna turned back to Freddie. "What are you not telling me?"

Freddie narrowed his eyes and bit his lip. This was the last scenario in the world that he could have imagined being in with Anna, when he told her who he really was. Perhaps this was the worst one too, because once she knew that he was in the same background as the man who had tortured her for years, she would probably run away as fast as her legs could carry her.

"Do you know what Tony did for a living?" he asked carefully, studying her face.

"Of course I knew," she replied. "How could I not, living with him for so long. Like Bill said, they had meetings in the house..." she stopped and frowned. Bill had been in one of the meetings. Which means that Bill was involved in that sort of work. She suddenly looked down to the guns that Bill and Sammy still had out in their hands. Freddie moved to catch her attention again. She looked back at him.

"We're in a similar line of business," he said gently. "The life is...well, I'm in that life. It is who I am. The clubs are mainly above board, but everything else I do isn't," he admitted, simply.

Anna nodded slightly, turning away and pacing the floor slowly. This was a lot to take in. For everyone today, it would seem. Freddie's words echoed in her head. He was a face. Freddie was a face, like Tony. Her heart began to beat too fast again. Was Freddie like Tony? Had she really been that stupid all over again? Surely she couldn't have been that wrong about someone twice. Freddie seemed to pick up her line of thought.

"I'm not like Tony, Anna. I don't treat people I care about the way that Tony treated you. I may be in the same line of work, but that's it."

She looked at him from where she was pacing and studied his face. Was he the person that she thought he was? Did this information really change anything, or was she judging him on her experience with someone else? His greeny-blue eyes pierced into her and she thought back to that day on the beach. Her heart softened at the memory of his face close to hers, both of them in a heap on the floor, laughing. Freddie wasn't Tony. He wasn't anything like Tony.

"I know," she answered softly. "I know you aren't." She smiled a tight smile, grimacing at the pain that shot through her cut, swollen lip as she did so.

"Freddie, I see lights." Paulie raised the alarm. He jogged back over. "We don't have time to get outside, get either side of the door in the shadows. Cut him off at least, once he's in."

Freddie shot a look at Anna. She had paled to a ghost-like colour.

"It's ok. I won't let him hurt you again." He grabbed her by the tops of her arms and levelled his face with hers. "He will never, *ever* touch you again. I won't let it happen. I'm going to finish this once and for all. For both of us," he stated vehemently, his eyes boring seriously into hers. He searched her face. He needed her to be on board with this. Anna nodded, believing in him. She still wasn't quite sure what Tony had done to Freddie, but she figured she was about to find out. Suddenly she felt invigorated. Tony was here, expecting to find her tied up and scared and instead, he was going to find Freddie. She straightened up.

"I'll sit in the chair, as if I am still tied. Draw him into the middle of the room. Go." She pushed Freddie towards the shadows where the others were already in place. She could hear the car doors closing now. One, she counted, then two. Two people. Ok.

"Are you sure?" Freddie looked concerned.

"Yes, now go," she ordered.

Freddie crept off to the side and Anna sat down again, her back to the door. Her nerves jangled now that she could no longer see what was going on behind her. She didn't like not being able to see. She squeezed her eyes shut. It was going to be ok. She wasn't alone this time.

Soon enough she heard the sound of the door being banged open and fast, heavy footsteps coming towards her. Once she gauged them to be a few feet in, she stood up and turned around. Tony stopped, surprised to see her stand. Anna's new found strength seemed to sap out of her the moment she laid eyes on Tony. There he was, the demon she had been running from all this time.

She looked at him properly as they stood there, facing each other. He wasn't a particularly tall man, nor muscular. His strength had always come from packing his weight into each punch. A few stone overweight and broad, he had plenty to throw at her. His black hair was beginning to speckle with grey and his swarthy face was starting to puff out. His large brown eyes which she had once thought looked warm and passionate were glinting dangerously. His madness shone through them as he grinned wickedly at her. It reminded her of a hyena playing with its prey. She shuddered as the sight of him brought back a flood of horrific memories.

"There you are, you slippery little bitch. Happy to see me?" he laughed at the disgust on her face. "Oh, you look at me that way now, I'll wipe that off of your smug, ugly fucking face soon enough. I'm going to fuck you up in every way you can think of," Tony looked her up and down slowly, his words became more and more excited as he stepped forward. Anna stepped back, her eyes shooting to the men who were now creeping up behind Tony and Angelo.

"I don't fucking think so, mate," Sammy said. Tony turned just in time to see the gun handle being smashed down on his temple. Angelo turned to see what was happening, but he too was knocked out before he could get any further.

Tony came round, his head pounding. He groaned and tried to put his hands to his head. He couldn't. He pulled his arms again but the wrists were bound tight. What had happened? He blinked his eyes open and as his focus cleared, he looked around confused. He was tied to a chair. Stavros was tied similarly on one side and Angelo on the other. Angelo was cursing and sending eye daggers to the people in front of them. Stavros was just hanging his head, looking worried. Tony honed in on Anna. She was perched sideways on the edge of a fold-down table that had been dragged over, one foot on the floor. She was studying her nails, seemingly unfazed. Tony's blood boiled. *How dare she look so comfortable.* To one side of her leaned a well-built man wearing a dark suit and a dark expression. He had a gun in one of the hands he was leaning back onto the table with. Three more men lurked around them. He recognised one of them as Bill Hanlon. Licking his dry lips, he honed in on this one piece of information that he had. He had no clue as to what was happening here, or why. His business with Anna had nothing to do with anyone.

"Billy Banker...Or should I say Billy Wanker, seeing as I'm currently tied to a fucking chair for some reason." Bill didn't rise to the comment, staying silent as they all stared hard at him. Tony narrowed his eyes and picking another one of them, tried a different approach.

"She's alright in bed, I'll give you that. But a bird ain't worth causing hag with the likes of me over. Especially one that's been mine for so long. She tell you how many years she's been leeching off me, did she?" He aimed this at Freddie, seeing as he looked like the main man, but not a flicker crossed his cold face. His rage began to bubble over. How dare these fucking try-hards ignore him after this diabolical move.

"Do you know who I fucking am?" he raged. "You might think you're some knight-in-fucking-armour crew here, saving some bird from getting the hiding she deserves, but you haven't got a fucking clue who you're dealing with. Except you," he aimed at Bill, "you should fucking know better. If you lot don't let me and my men out, right now, you're gonna wish you'd never been born, you jumped up little cunts." He seethed with anger and strained hard against his restraints. Freddie stepped forward and stopped in front of him.

"Do *you* know who *I* am?" he questioned, curiously.

"No I fucking don't, you no-mark," Tony spat back sarcastically. Why on earth would he know him? Freddie nodded soberly.

"In that case, your plan was doomed from the start really. It's never a good idea to plan to take someone out, when you don't even have a clue what they look like." Tony didn't answer. Freddie could see the cogs turning slowly in his head. "I believe that you were planning to take me out over a friendly meet up. Was that how it went down with Big Dom?"

"Freddie Tyler," Tony hissed, the penny finally dropping.

"Ahh, you've caught up. Good." Freddie scratched his chin, pacing up and down in front of the three men. "So how *did* it go down with Big Dom then? I'm curious how you managed to pull that off without leaving any clues. Which no-brained lackey did you get to pull the trigger then? And they really must be fucking stupid to follow you into taking one of the most revered old faces in the country."

"I'm the one who put that bullet in his head, you asshole," Angelo spat. "And I'm no fucking lackey. When we get out of here we're taking you down and that's just the start of it. I made the big move to get the ball rolling, it will be me whose name they tell in the stories of how we took over central London in years to come," he spewed, puffing out his small chest. Freddie half smiled and shook his head, dismissing this ridiculous statement from the passionate young man. He turned to Tony and, raising his eyebrows, gave a short laugh.

"He really is stupid, isn't he? I can see why you picked him. He even thinks he still has a chance of walking out of here." He stopped and leaned in nearer to Angelo's face. "The minute you walked through that door your chances of leaving here alive were zero. Now that I know you were the silly little cunt who pulled the trigger on my friend, the chances of your death being quick have also gone to zero. Is that clear enough for your little brain?" He left the young man with his mouth flapping open, unsure what to say. Tony tutted in annoyance of how much Angelo was showing him up. He shot him a glare.

Freddie looked at Tony and felt the urge to rip him apart. He pulled his fist back and smashed it into his face without warning.

"You took out Big Dom," he hit him again. "You planned to take me out and steal my businesses," he punched his face twice more. "And now I find out that you repeatedly and consistently hurt someone I care about." He grabbed Tony's bloodied face and shoved the end of his gun into his mouth.

"No, wait!" Anna cried out. She stepped forward. Freddie pulled back, shooting her a questioning look.

"Anna?"

Tony started laughing - a deep, mocking laugh.

"She won't let you kill me. She would never forgive you, she's too fucking soft. You're screwed mate." His laugh grew louder. Anna took Paulie's gun from him and cocking it, pointed it at him. He stopped laughing.

"You're wrong, Tony," she said, her voice unsteady. "You were wrong about a lot of things." She stepped forward in front of him and her voice grew stronger. "You know nothing about the person I really am, because you never allowed me to be a person. I was your servant. I was a punch bag. I was a toy. But I was never allowed to be a person. I will let Freddie kill you today. I might even watch. And you know something?" she cocked one eyebrow, coldly. "I'll be glad."

Anna stared down at the man who had ruined her life for so long, the man who had haunted her dreams and who had nearly managed to kill her. His nose was bleeding where Freddie had hit him. He was staring at her with unbridled hatred. Little did she know, this was mirrored in her own expression.

"You beat me. You used me. You tried to destroy me in every way possible. But I escaped you, didn't I? And the real me was still in there, deep down. You never truly broke me completely. I've flourished out here in this world. *My* world. I have friends and I have a good business that I built with my own two hands. Mine," she yelled. "I'm not stupid. I am *not* worthless." Angry tears began to spill down her face. Tony sneered at her and laughed. She saw red. Stepping forward, she smacked the handle of the gun around his face. She put all of her force into the blow and his head shot to the side, silencing him. "Yeah, I'd be quiet too if I were you. It's not so much fun on the other side of things, is it?" she spat. He didn't laugh again but he looked up at her with a smirk on his face.

She stared at him bitterly and began to tremble under the weight of all the emotions finally coming out. She handed the gun back to Paulie.

"You took so much from me for so long. Well, you can't do that anymore. You will never take anything from me again." She began to walk away from him, her energy spent.

"No matter what you do, you'll always be a worthless slag," Tony called after her. She turned and a half smile crept up on her face.

"You can say whatever you want. It means nothing now. And at the end of the day Tony, I've won." She paused, looking him up and down, her face hard. "I'm off to live my life, exactly how I want to." She gave Freddie the nod and walked out of the warehouse.

"Anna. Anna! You fucking slag, get back here!" Tony yelled. How dare she leave him to die like this, how dare she! He turned back to face the barrel of Freddie's gun.

"You're lucky," Freddie said quietly. "If she hadn't been here I'd have beaten you until you begged me for death. It's funny the form that small mercies take." He pressed the gun against the other man's forehead and pulled the trigger.

Outside Anna heard the sharp crack of the gunshot through the air. Looking up at the stars she ran her hands through her long, dark hair and breathed a heavy sigh of relief. Her body relaxed for the first time in as long as she could remember, as she finally let go of all the fear and anger that had been weighing her down for so long. Her deep blue eyes shone in the moonlight, the haunted shadow disappearing from them completely. She was free. She was finally, truly, completely free. She wondered absentmindedly if she should feel sorrow or guilt at Tony's death. But she didn't. He hadn't won, but he had succeeded in killing some parts of her. Perhaps if he hadn't, she would still be soft. Perhaps she would have asked Freddie to spare him. Maybe she would have seen his murder as wrong. Now, he was dead. He was finally gone and she would never have to hide again. She smiled, a slow, elated smile. She felt so weightless. She could live her life now. And she could finally go home to see her parents.

Freddie wiped the end of his gun with his top and put it back into his pocket. The other two men started begging for their lives. Sammy approached Freddie.

"What do you want done with these two?"

"That one signed Anna's death warrant," he pointed to Stavros. "And that one put the bullet in Big Dom," he moved his finger to point at Angelo. "They both need disposing of. And that," he addressed the two tied up, snivelling men, "is me being fucking kind. Be thankful I don't have time to teach you a lesson first."

Paulie tapped him on the shoulder.

"You take her back to London, we can finish this and sort the clean up here." Sammy and Bill nodded their agreement to this.

"Ok. Come by the club tomorrow evening all of you, when you get a chance. And thanks. For everything." He patted all of them on the shoulder as he passed. Nothing more needed to be said. They were his men. They would always have his back and he would always compensate them for the grit they had to deal with. He appreciated them and they were loyal to him. It was the way things were. It was what made them his first-hand men.

He stepped outside into the cold and made his way over to Anna's slight figure. She was standing a few feet ahead of him, staring up at the sky, her arms crossed over the thin jumper that she was wearing. His heart leapt when he saw her. He had never felt such rage and so sick to the heart as when he saw that she'd been hurt tonight. And that feeling had doubled again when he heard all the things that Tony had put her through. He had come close to losing her tonight, forever. It had scared him and there was very little in this world that could scare a man like Freddie. He stepped forward slowly, approaching her. It had put everything in stark perspective. They would go back to London and she would thank him, before going back to distancing herself. He was going to lose her anyway. Now was the time to tell her how he felt. At least that way, when she disappeared from his life, he knew he'd done everything he could. He gently touched her shoulder and she turned around.

"Freddie, I—"

"No Anna, listen to me, please. I'm sorry you had to find out who I am this way. I shouldn't have hidden it from you. But it is what it is. I know that you've always seen me as just a friend and that now, considering my past with Tanya, you don't want to see me anymore. I get that. I do. But—" he lifted his hand to her face, pushing back a loose strand of hair from her forehead. He stared into her eyes, intensely, "—I need you to know something. I don't care about many people. My family, my close men, them and no-one else. But I've grown to care more about you than anyone I have ever cared about before. I love you, Anna. And if you never talk to me again, that's fine. At least now I know you're safe. But I had to do this, just once."

Freddie grasped Anna's head with both hands and pulled her lips to his. He kissed her deeply, with a passion he had never felt before. To his surprise, after initially tensing Anna pulled him close and held him tightly, kissing him back with just as much fervour. They kissed for a long time, neither wanting to pull away from this perfect moment. Eventually Freddie pulled back and looked into Anna's face.

It shone with happiness.

"I..." she laughed, disbelievingly. "I didn't think you thought of me that way. I thought that it was just me. I haven't been around lately because I couldn't bear to feel all these feelings for you, knowing you didn't feel the same way."

Freddie shook his head.

"What have we been doing, for fuck's sake," he bent his head and put his forehead to hers. "We've wasted so much time."

"No, we haven't," Anna said, touching his cheek. "This - in a very strange way - has happened just as it should have. The door to, well, that—" she glanced back towards the warehouse, "—is finally closed. I can move on. With you."

Freddie looked at her soberly. She was forgetting one thing.

"Anna..." he stepped back slightly, giving her room. "You know who I am now. That's never going to change. This is me. Can you accept me for who I am?" He waited for her answer, not sure what it would be. She had suffered badly over the years with Tony. He wouldn't blame her for wanting to start afresh, out of that world completely. She stepped forward and grabbed his hand, squeezing it and pulling him back to her.

"I accept you, Freddie Tyler. Not in spite of who you are, but because of it. I know who you are. And...well, I love you too. That's all that matters." She pulled his face back down to hers and kissed him again as though it was their last minute on earth. Happier than he had ever thought he could be, Freddie wrapped his arms around her and picked her up, never losing contact with her lips. Then he carried her off in the direction of his car.

Freddie felt invincible as he made his way to the car with Anna. It was as though he was walking on air. Tonight, he had neutralised their biggest threat, saved the woman he loved and was finally holding her in his arms for the first time. Their world would go on. There would always be another fight and another problem. He still had to deal with people who were getting out of line. He still had to keep one step ahead of the law. He still had to try and fix things with his angry, lost little brother. But right now, he had he woman the loved in his arms. And that, as she herself had said, was all that mattered.

Note from the Author

Thank you for reading my first novel, Life Game. I hope you enjoyed getting to know the characters as much as I enjoyed creating them!

For more information on the upcoming sequel please follow my facebook page, or sign up to receive the news and events email on my website.

All the best,
Emma

www.facebook.com/emmatallonofficial

www.emmatallon.com